SISSIE

SISSIE

A NOVEL BY

John A. Williams

THUNDER'S MOUTH PRESS
NEW YORK

Copyright © 1963, 1988 by John A. Williams

All rights reserved

Published in the United States by

THUNDER'S MOUTH PRESS,

93–99 Greene Street, New York, N.Y. 10012

Cover design by Loretta Li

Grateful acknowledgment is made to the
New York State Council on the Arts and
the National Endowment for the Arts
for financial assistance with
the publication of this work.

Library of Congress Cataloging-in-Publication Data

Williams, John Alfred, 1925-

Sissie : a novel / by John A. Williams.

p.   cm.—(Classic reprint series)

First published in 1963.

ISBN 0-938410-66-0 (pbk.) : $9.95

I. Title.   II. Series.

PS3573.I4495S5   1988

813'.54—dc19   88-9732

CIP

Manufactured in the United States of America

Distributed by Consortium Book Sales

213 E. 4th Street

St. Paul, Minnesota 55101

612-221-9035

For all my family

"The family is destroyed today and speech is destroyed today; and speech and the family, being the creations of the tribes, we will find again at their fountainhead, where they were most intensified, because it is there they were first created."

Eugen Rosenstock-Huessy

"Some day history may record with amazement that a man's whole life was once determined by the color of his skin."

John Andrew Rice

1

AT LAST AND FINALLY! Iris thought when the plane sped away from Boston, where they had been forced to land because of fog in New York. Once more they were on their way, and Iris assumed that her brother Ralph, who was meeting her at the airport, must have been waiting for hours. Just my luck that we had to run into bad weather, Iris thought.

Beside her sat the woman she had met in the airport in Barcelona. For the moment Iris was too busy with her own thoughts to speak, and Helen Kessler respected her silence. Both of the women smoked cigarettes. "Damn, it's cold in here," Iris said half aloud, when they were once more over New York. The plane seemed to slow, gradually losing momentum in the gray, and banked above the cottony storm clouds racing endlessly by. Iris took a deep breath and glanced at Helen. "Here we go again." Breasting the currents of air like a huge, stiff bird, the craft circled lower and lower. There was a sharp, high whine and Iris heard the massive wheels thud into place. The plane hung motionless for one frightening instant, and then hissed downward through the clouds.

"Landings always make me nervous," Helen whispered hurriedly, glancing at Iris' taut, unlined brown neck.

"I noticed that at London and at Boston," Iris said. "Relax. If it happens you'll never know what hit you."

Unsure whether Iris was joking or not—she sometimes seemed a little strange—Helen glanced at her before replying. "God, you're cheerful," she said.

Iris smiled briefly and turned back to the window, watched the plane right itself—slowly, majestically. Suddenly, much too suddenly, they were out of the gray, floating over a bay which seemed perilously near. Iris shut her eyes; when she opened them she saw gray asphalt hurtling by. Another slight jar and the plane had landed. Both women gasped with relief. Helen grinned sheepishly, Iris grimly. "Damn," Iris said, trying to restrain the fluttering within her. "We're here." She took out her compact, snapped it open and leaned her face toward the mirror.

"You look all right," Helen said, "damn you."

Iris, laughing softly, closed the compact, and Helen recognized that this laughter—unlike Iris' merriment on the long flight—was genuine. "Thanks," she said. "I'm sure glad I met you—"

It was Helen's turn to laugh.

"—no," Iris said, suddenly realizing that she might have been too withdrawn during the trip. "I mean it." Their eyes

4

met and Helen turned away shyly. At first sight Helen Kessler didn't look more than twenty-two, but a second glance revealed the pouch of a double chin and thin, seared lines radiating from the corners of her eyes. She was a small woman, with dull brown hair. When she smiled, her cheeks dimpled. Iris figured she was in her middle thirties—Iris was thirty-two. Helen had a nice figure, Iris had observed at dinner the evening before in the London airport restaurant. She looked as if she might be French, but was really an American returning to New York. Her presence had helped quiet Iris' apprehensions; Iris hadn't been in America for thirteen years. Helen (and Iris was grateful for this) was only superficially like many American women Iris had met and known in Europe. Perhaps it was Helen's size that saved her; she could never be loud nor brash nor vulgar. Only fiery, scintillating, risqué, or cute. She had seen Iris' show only the week before at the Emporium, she had shyly explained at the Barcelona airport. People were always saying something like that, but it had been a surprise to discover that Helen was so nice.

Iris climbed down the ramp on wobbly legs. She and Helen followed the other passengers into the multicolored glass-and-chrome terminal. The building reminded her of those structures which had risen like full-blown giants while she and Harry were in Germany.

The line shuffled forward over the speckled black marble floor. Now there were more Americans visible, those who worked in the banklike building. "They look so angry," Helen said. "Don't you think so?"

Iris was searching for her brother, but said, "I guess they ought to." And this made her recall the fact that Helen didn't consider herself an American. The sound of the taxiing jets was muffled now; only the single-pitched scream of the blowing engines penetrated the area where she and the others waited, behind a white horizontal marker. Ten feet beyond, uniformed customs officers stood checking papers. Iris looked about her at the lines of people, and was reminded of the storefront of the disbursing office where every other Tuesday she and Ralph had gone to pick up their ration of government-issued surplus food during the Depression: tinned beef, dried prunes, grapefruit, wheat, oatmeal, apples, and everything marked with the telltale stamp. They had moved with the line smelling the rich aroma of the apples until they came to a halt at the white marker. There they had waited until the joking men behind the makeshift orange- and apple-crate counter had laughed and smoked their fill. An imperious, stiff-fingered summons, just like the one the officer at the small booth was now making, had started them shuttling forward again.

When they entered the customs room, Iris looked up and saw Ralph standing in the glass-enclosed terrace. He waved and she waved back, anxiously watching for a sign.

"Is that your brother?" Helen asked.

"That's him," Iris said with a sober smile. "That's my big brother." Then Iris wondered who was meeting Helen. She almost asked but changed her mind, thinking Helen might be embarrassed.

"Entertainer?" the customs officer asked with a polite smile. He held Iris' passport in his hand which stated her profession quite plainly. Iris answered, "Yes, I am." The officer excused himself, passed beyond a series of slowly moving belts and entered a small office.

"What's that for?" Helen asked.

"I think," Iris said slowly, recalling what the musicians and entertainers had told her about America, "narcotics." She smiled bitterly. "If you're an entertainer and you're colored you get the works—"

Helen nodded. "I thought so," she said, compressing her lips. "It's too bad you had to come back. The bastards." Iris turned and glanced up at her brother again. She held out her hands in an impulsive, supplicatory gesture and he signaled back, urging restraint. Iris nodded and looked at Helen. Since Barcelona she had had the feeling that Helen understood. "Yes," Iris said. "It's too bad."

After the officer had been gone twenty minutes, he returned smiling broadly. "Sorry to keep you waiting." Neither woman answered and he looked at them, puzzled. Helen Kessler went through customs without difficulty.

The two women walked through the turnstiles past the colored guards, Iris trying hard not to stare at them. Ralph came down the stairs. The look in his eyes told Iris that the laughter which came from her lips was not inappropriate. She threw herself into his arms. "Ralph!" she said.

He grinned at her, "Goddamn, baby, you sure look *good!*" They kissed, broke apart, and smiled at each other. He kissed her again and grunted, "You look *good!*"

"Man, you lookin' pretty fine your*self!*"

They laughed, and then, their laughter dying, looked into each other's eyes. Iris asked, "How's mother?"

His head sagged slightly.

"Oliver said she was holding her own. Fighting her way back."

Iris heaved a great sigh. Funny that he should have said

7

"fighting" because that was the way she had always pictured Sissie—never giving up, making small of whatever happened to her. The time she had had the tumor operation, they had gone to see her, and found her sitting up in bed examining the growth which she had preserved in a jar of formaldehyde.

"Thank God, thank God," Iris said.

"It's not over," Ralph answered.

"I know, but at least she's fighting."

Arm in arm they walked together to where Helen was waiting.

"This is Helen. My brother, Ralph Joplin."

Ralph held out his hand and Helen's reached out tentatively. Then they seemed to recognize something sympathetic in each other, and both smiled.

"You wrote that play!" Helen said, surprised, turning from Iris and back to Ralph. Iris was laughing. "Why didn't you tell me? Here I was ranting about how you *had* to see it, and it turns out your brother wrote it—"

"God, it's cold here," Iris said, pulling the mink tighter around her.

"So you wrote *Shadows on the Sun*," Helen said to Ralph. "What an illustrious family."

Ralph and Iris laughed. "You're making us feel very good," Ralph said.

"Iris, I feel like an ass," Helen said, then, looking at Ralph, "I'm sorry about your mother. I hope she'll be all right."

"Thank you," Ralph said. "Can we drop you off?"

"If it won't be any bother."

They seemed, all of them, reluctant to move. Iris studied her brother. He reminded her of their father—tall, stooped, and thin of face, but less broad than Big Ralph. His hair was cropped. She remembered when he had worn it long, brushed into a pompadour and greased heavily. Like herself Ralph had their mother's soft brown eyes. She kept thinking, over and over to herself—he's made it.

Ralph had begun a study of his sister from the terrace, the very first moment he had seen her. She was tall for a woman; tallness ran in the family. She swung her body in a sort of swagger when she walked, held herself regally. She hadn't changed much in two years. Even from a distance, he noticed the luster of her hair, twisted neatly into a French roll. Iris had the strong features of their mother, but her face was less broad. Her prominent cheekbones made her eyes seem to curve upward, giving her a catlike look.

The skycap signalled a cab and placed the bags inside. Ralph said in a low voice to Iris, "You'll notice that all the porters have quit the railroads and moved to the airports. Whenever Sam cuts out the end's in sight."

The skycap moved back out of the way, glancing curiously at Iris.

"He must think you're Jo Baker," Ralph said with a smile as he sat back in the car.

The taxi edged out onto the main highway and the driver accelerated.

"How's Adela?" Ralph asked.

"I started to bring her," Iris teased.

"Why didn't you?" Ralph said with a smile.

Iris said, "Why would I bring a hamburger to what must be a banquet for you?"

Helen glanced from brother to sister, then turned and kept her eyes on the landscape.

9

"At one time," Ralph said, "I had an overwhelming taste for hamburgers. But now, being an old married man—"

Adela had been one of Iris' friends, a dark-haired, unusually slender Catalan with blue eyes. When Ralph was leaving Barcelona he had asked half-jokingly, "Will you wait for me?" Adela had giggled and had looked at Iris. For months, Iris remembered, Adela had asked, "When will your brother return to Spain?"

Gently Iris said, "You might have sent her a card at least. Two years and not a word."

"I know." Ralph ground out a cigarette beneath his feet. "She was nice. Is she married?"

"Yes."

"Oh," he said, adding after a while, "good." He turned to stare past Helen at the traffic.

"And how's your wife? Your marriage? Are you happy?" Iris watched him as he turned toward her, smiling. Even before he spoke she knew what he was going to say.

"I'm happy." He opened his hands as if to say, What more can I say? "And you?"

Her smile was tight. "I'm a career girl, remember?"

They became silent.

The great bridge they approached soared up out of the ground and into the sky. "Is that the George Washington Bridge?" Iris asked, staring at the massive, snow-covered approaches.

"No, it's the Triboro."

"For Christ's sake, don't look at me like that. I don't know New York. Harry and I were only here three days before we left, and if it'd been up to him we'd have spent each of them in bed."

"Does it seem strange to you?" Ralph asked.

"Yes," Iris said.

They were speeding down East River Drive. "Were you very lonely here?" she asked. "I mean before Eve?"

"Yes, I suppose so," he answered.

The taxi peeled off the Drive and crept into a snow-filled street. Ralph and Iris said goodbye to Helen, settled back in the cab for the ride home.

The view of the mighty, hard, window-specked city, thrusting boldly up through the snow, jolted Iris. An old dread of this city, and of the continent to which it was the gateway, stirred within her.

2

"BIENVENIDO A SU CASA," the small, peach-brown woman said. Her eyes sparkled. "Ralph taught me to say that," Eve said, coming forward to embrace Iris. Iris liked her at once. "C'mon," Eve said. "You both must be tired and lunch is ready."

Ralph looked at Iris. She said, "Oh, man!" He grinned.

"Nothing new on the weather," Eve said, seating Iris at the table.

When lunch was over, Iris padded from room to room, a drink in her hand. Ralph was making telephone calls.

Iris had seen the dolls in Raphaella's room and the neat boxes of scarcely used toys. For the first time she thought of Ralph's child by his first wife, April; she felt a curious urge to see the child. Passing Ralph and Eve's bedroom she noticed one of his shoes turned so that its almost new leather sole was visible, and she thought of their childhood; in those days they had fitted meticulously folded newspaper into the soles of their shoes. She remembered also those rare, enthusiastically welcomed parades to the Modern Boot Shop where new shoes, restricted in style, color and durability by the yellow welfare order in Sissie's bag, were obtained for them. Sissie's tough thumbs, she recalled, would jab into the soles of the shoes and skim along the stitchings, feeling for inferior merchandise. Sissie always demanded the best the order could buy. Iris wore Italian shoes; she had had it on good authority that this mode would not get to America for another two years; the shoes were very expensive.

She paused in the alcove where Ralph's desk was and looked down at the typewriter. He hadn't had a machine when she and Harry left. She studied the titles of the books on the shelf above, as if they might reveal something of Ralph's secret self. On the shelf above the books was a photograph of Raffy. The ash tray was piled high with butts. Iris smiled. Eve was not allowed to enter this part of the room. The apartment told little about the people who lived there; its spare furnishings made her think of the monastery at Monserrat. Standing here where Ralph worked, she pictured him spending innumerable hours at the typewriter, in the small pyramid of light cast by the lamp above. She turned the battered, cane-bottomed desk chair and, seating herself in it, thought how wonderful it was that her brother now lived in the peace of such a home. Once more she glanced around the room and the life that he led there with Eve somehow became real for her. She needed a background against which to imagine things. Until his arrival in Spain two years before, she was not able to think of him as married to April, or as the father of a child. But April and the divorce were now all past: there was only himself and his bride of six months, Eve.

Suddenly she sensed that Ralph had come up behind her. "How's Raffy?" she asked without turning.

"Oh," he said. "You know kids. She's all right."

"And April?"

"Okay."

"Dad?"

"All right. I should call him."

Now she turned toward Ralph. "Do you think so?"

"Yes, don't you?"

She nodded. "You know," she said, "I like your wife; she's very lovely."

"She's all right," he said, sitting down in another chair.

Iris smiled at him. "Look, baby, how's it going?"

"So-so; could always be better."

"But you're making it?"

"*Got* to make it."

"Hey, I got a Ramirez for you."

"No shuck? Print or original?"

"Oh, come on, now. Nothing but the best for my Broth. I'll get it for you in a while." She stared at him. "You look better than you did when you came to visit me. I guess"—she glanced toward the kitchen, and, satisfied that Eve was still there, went on—"Adela got you straightened out."

"And you."

"Hell, I couldn't do what *Adela* did."

Ralph laughed. "No."

14

They were silent for a moment and then Ralph said, "I'm sorry it had to be this way. I wanted you to come on a visit and have fun."

"I might not have come back quite so soon," she said. "Not because I hate it here." She laughed. "I never knew that much about it except home. You know, I've made it over there. I don't know if I could bring all that here without losing something."

"I know."

She said, "I suppose that I would've come sometime soon to visit mother. That talk we had in Barcelona. . . ."

"That talk," he said, "and the other." He breathed heavily.

"And the other," she now echoed.

"Look," he said, nodding toward the windows. Great snow-flakes tumbled lazily out of the sky. "It's come. The storm."

From the kitchen Eve called, with almost a child's delight, "It's snowing!" And then, thinking what the snow meant for Ralph and Iris, she came out of the kitchen and said, more softly, "It's snowing, baby."

"Yes."

Eve looked at Iris. "Why don't you rest? You must be beat."

"I am, dear," Iris said, and turning to Ralph added, "I'd like to call Oliver."

"Sure," Ralph said.

"I'll get your bed ready," Eve said.

After Ralph dialed the number for her, Iris listened intently to the telephone ringing at the other end.

In Los Angeles, Oliver Duncan wandered aimlessly through the chilled, stucco house which had so suddenly become lonely. He heard the telephone ring and lifted it slowly to his ear, expecting to hear Dr. Clayton's high, womanish voice.

"It's me, Oliver—Iris. How's Mother?"

Almost immediately Oliver began talking of Sissie's illness. Sissie, Oliver said, had fallen ill, saying as she always did, that she was tired and hurting a little. But then had come that plunging moan which had not yet ended when he rushed into the bedroom, saying, "Sissie, what is it?"

"Oh, Lord. My chest and arms hurt. Call Dr. Clayton, quick, honey."

"Her heart," Dr. Clayton had said when he had come.

"She had just seen Dr. Clayton two days before," Oliver continued into the telephone. "She's still in the tent, but the doctor said she isn't requiring as much oxygen."

"It's snowing more heavily here now. Flights are canceled because of the storm. We'll be there just as soon as we can." Iris paused. "Ralph wants to talk." She passed her brother the phone.

"How you holdin' up, chief?" Ralph asked. "Sure. Yeah. Well, we'll get there as soon as we can. What?" His smile was cheerless. He said quietly, "Yes, we're all praying. S'long."

For a moment Ralph and Iris and Eve sat watching the snow which had now obscured the sky. Eve rose and left. Within a couple of minutes, Iris was startled to hear her own voice coming from the other room. Eve returned with a smile on her face. "I love that record," she said. "It's our favorite." She sat on the floor beside Ralph whose head rested on the shoulder of his chair, his eyes closed. His hands moved tenderly through his wife's hair; Eve stared at the floor. Iris turned her eyes away from the couple and looked out the window. Snow.

She remembered making the record.

While she had been singing, the white faces of the Swedish engineers had been a cottony blur in the background; the overhead mike had threatened like the sword of Damocles. Things had been bad then for her and Time. But when she sang ("I wish you love . . .") he talked to her on the piano. ("Yes, baby. Me too. I wish you love. You need it!") The chords he was playing were sharp and sardonic ("You need it, baby!") And the others knew; despite their impassive faces. ("I wish you bluebirds in the spring . . .")

Will their love never be over? Iris wondered, looking at her brother and his wife. Suddenly Time's image stood in the foreground of her mind, his skull reflecting the studio lights. So she had seen him in a hundred studios in a hundred cities over the last eleven years—Melvin C. Curry. When had he become bald?

Iris rose as the record approached its end. "I'd better get some rest now," she said.

And then, thinking that her departure was perhaps too abrupt, she said, "I would like to see the play tonight. It doesn't look as though we'll be able to fly out." Ralph looked down at Eve, and she smiled back at him.

Eve went into the kitchen and Ralph rose from his chair and walked over to Iris. He rested his hand upon her shoulder. "Would you mind if I sent you with Eve? I'm trying to get some things out of the way before we go. They're rather important—"

"No, baby, I don't mind. But why were you two smiling?"

He smiled again. "Eve's ex is the lead in the play."

"Really!" Iris laughed. "Does she mind seeing him?"

"I think not," Ralph said.

17

"But you didn't tell me. What's his name?"

"Catroux," Eve said, slipping an arm through Ralph's. "Henri Catroux."

"You were married to Henri Catroux?"

"Yes," Eve said.

"You're better off without him. An egotistical, no-talent—"

"Iris, he's got fine talent—"

"Yes," Eve agreed. "He has that."

"Henri's hot right now," Ralph said with a bitter smile. "He's hot because white folks realize that they can market a little anger. Henri's the Negro who finally meets violence with suggested violence; can't be too damned obvious about these things. I'm sure he'd like to stop playing these superficial roles. Something—a whole process brings a human being to anger. Multiply that eighteen million times over and you don't have a process anymore. You have history."

Iris gestured with her hands. "But Henri's personality completely destroys his talent; at least it did when I met him." She turned to leave the room, but stopped and said with a grin, "Good work, Ralph." They all laughed. Iris turned to Eve. "Seriously, you won't mind?"

"No. You get some rest now. Ralph'll go back to work and I'll think of something to wear tonight."

"Bless you," Iris said. She left the room. She was sorry she had used that phrase. It was one of those things one learned to say to people who rushed up and told you they liked you; eyes glowing, they played the humble role when it was you they really wished to humble. She shouldn't have said it to Eve and Ralph. It was phoney and she had no need to be phoney now. She was home.

3

SOMEWHERE IN THE BUILDING an oil burner vibrated gently. Iris sensed that the snow was still coming down, heavier, whiter. When she awoke it would be like Christmas. The stillness of the apartment was broken by Ralph's voice. Iris started at first and then, recalling where she was, whose voice it was, she smiled sleepily.

She remembered him best among the sights and sounds and smells of Barcelona. He had seemed just another amorphous child before his tour of duty in the Navy. It had been good to have him home again when the war was over. He had changed, had acquired form. The war had touched him; he had nightmares about it. But she had been delighted that this new form was one of rebellion. Had rebellion been smoldering there before? She couldn't be sure. Now he was curt with Sissie's friends, the ones who came by and wanted him to show himself off in his uniform and ribbons; he insulted Reverend Polk. He didn't seem to have any friends. It was at that time that Sissie, preaching "readjustment," spoke of God and Ralph's need to join the church. He threw a Bible at her.

One Saturday night, when Sissie had been brooding about a three-day absence of Ralph's, a neighbor had dashed breathlessly up the stairs to tell them that Ralph had been taken off in the paddy wagon for fighting in the street. Iris recalled Sissie's sudden concern about the neighborhood gossip, then their swift passage through the city to the station. The desk sergeant had been about to call the police psychiatrist; over in a corner Ralph was still struggling with two officers and vomiting in between curses. On his face was a rage Iris had never seen before.

Madge had come next—a woman twice Ralph's age who lived on the hill near the park. When Sissie had learned what was going on, she called Madge and shouted into the telephone, "Ralph's going to make something of himself, old woman; now you let him alone!" Iris had laughed. As if it had been poor Madge's fault. The affair had continued until Ralph met April.

Before the war he had been a series of nervous comings and goings: she remembered him running in and out with books, athletic equipment, stale jock straps and unbearably foul socks. He was finished with the Boy Scouts and the Boys Club and just about through with Sunday School picnics. When he was not running with breakneck speed or leaping

20

dramatically from roof to roof, he moped for days on end. Later, he had to leave school for a while and got a job to help out at home. No longer able to play with the other boys, he became despondent and resentful. But when he was working and had money he took Robbie and her to the movies on Saturdays. And it had been Ralph who stood between them and Sissie's tired rages, Ralph who hastily cooked another pot of beans if Iris had burned the first; Ralph who glued together the vases broken by the other children as they raced through the house; Ralph who seemed always there.

She remembered the way he had of silently observing things and people. She approached him always with a curious kind of respect. This attitude had had its genesis the summer he was fourteen and she eleven.

For several Sundays following the death of their sister Mary Ellen, he had stayed away from Sunday school, church and the rescue mission. The mission was a depressing-looking building where smelly white children with stringy hair met Negro children scrubbed clean so as to look as good. Invariably the Negro children looked better. The children sang uptempo church songs and stared at GOD IS LOVE signs painted in bold black letters on the dirty cream walls. Ralph would go downstairs, strap on his skates and disappear down the street. He would return two or three hours later.

"Where did you go?" Iris would ask.

"Skating."

One Sunday she asked to go with him. "I go a long, long way," he said. She was pleased that he wasn't angry. "Can't I go? If my skates come off you won't have to help me, I promise." So she went with him. They skated down the street, each weaving from side to side. Then they struggled up the hillside. The neighborhood at the top was nicer and quieter. Now they skated as quietly as they could.

"Where are we?" Iris asked, gasping for breath, for a moment sorry that she had been so insistent upon coming.

"The cemetery," he said, looking at her.

"The cemetery?"

"Mary Ellen's here. You remember."

She remembered the little white casket and the front room filled with silent people; Sissie and Dad, folks from church, and all singing without music. She remembered that just before they closed the casket Ralph, knicker strap loose and hanging, had bent down to kiss Mary Ellen's cheek. . . .

They skated down the road in silence. Iris knew from the caretaker's greeting that Ralph had been there many times before. It was green everywhere. The wind blew softly through the trees. There was no other sound. They arrived at the grave with its small square of marble. They squatted beside it. "This is Mary Ellen," he said, "and that's Juanita. You don't remember her. She died before you came. I remember her. I remember her funeral too. They're both here."

She watched him sitting there, his knees chucked up beneath his chin, his skates blocked with pebbles. Once in a while he smiled at her as if apologizing for not talking. Mostly he peered groundward and once Iris had the eerie feeling that he was seeing right into the grave. Then they skated silent again, his hand in hers.

All of this had come back to her the day Ralph appeared unheralded at her apartment in Barcelona. Time—her break with him final, it seemed—had been gone three months, but in only thirty days Iris had run out of things to do, places and people to see. Now her contracts called for long-term engagements. She could no longer enjoy traveling and had left the one-night stand circuit even before Time's departure. She was in her fourth month of a two-year stand in Barcelona. The memory of Time had begun to haunt her. It was good that Ralph came when he did, following by only one day Sissie's letter asking her to keep a lookout. At thirty-three, Sissie's letter said, Ralph was "hitchhiking around Europe like he was eighteen without a brain in his head, and broke, too, girl."

Beatrice let him in; it was odd that she was so friendly to the few colored people who came and so coldly suspicious to any and all whites. Iris came out, frowning. The stranger, Beatrice had said, would not give his name. Iris halted. "Ralph! Oh, Ralph!" she said running to him. He dropped his two army knapsacks to the floor. "Sis. Iris, baby. Goddamn, how are you?"

Iris said, "I just yesterday got a letter from Mother. Why didn't you write?"

"I wasn't sure I'd make it this way. I'm not completely broke, I don't care what Mother told you—Jesus, you look good, baby." Iris noticed how tall he was, how set his face had become.

"Want some bourbon?" she finally asked, not knowing what else to say.

"How'd you get it?" he asked, still surveying the apartment.

"A fan. Beatrice, my brother. Bring the bourbon and ice, please." To Ralph she said, "Sit down, you must be tired. Mother said you were hitchhiking."

23

"No," he said, pacing like a huge dog through room after room, pausing to stroke the keys of the piano. "You rehearse in this room, huh? No, I didn't do much walking. Trains and buses. That mother, boy." He stopped and his eyes danced with pride. "Iris, this is fantastic." He pulled her to him. "It's out of sight. I'm happy for you. Where's the bourbon?" he asked as Beatrice, smiling, brought in the tray. "Which room can I have?"

"Anyone you want, except mine, of course."

"Got one with a balcony?"

"Yes."

"Good, I'll take it." He had taken his first drink neat. Now he poured another, dropped ice into it, sat back and smiled at her. "You know you're a fine-looking chick, baby. How's it going? Tell me everything. When you coming home? Do you want to come home? The white folks are getting atrocious there, but come home anyway. How's it been eleven years away from the States . . . ?"

"No, you tell me about home. How's Mother, and Raffy and," she said softly, "April? Tell me about the white folks and the colored folks and what you're doing now. Tell me about Oliver and—" she started to say Robbie, but didn't.

"You heard about Bird," he began, pouring another drink.

"Yes, what happened?"

"Awww, the usual."

"Do you like living in New York?"

"I think if you have to live in the States it's the only place, if you're colored. April's okay. Still with her father. Jesus, he hates my guts. Raffy, that's my charm, that doll."

He talked on through the snack, through the time when Beatrice was laying out Iris' dresses for the show that night.

How frantic he seems, Iris thought, and then, interrupting him, said, "It's getting near showtime. Want to catch me?"

He rose quickly, snatched up his bags and hurried toward the bathroom. He emerged minutes later, all but dressed. "Drip dry shit," he said, patting his suit. "Synthetic, like America. Very big, drip dry shit in America."

She was playing La Casa Blanca on the Sarria Road, and that night with her brother in front and Beatrice in back, holding the dresses, she whipped the Citroën over La Travesera, blazed onto Avenida del Generalissimo Franco to the Sarria Road, laughing, talking rapidly (somehow she had been drawn into it) with Ralph. In the back, Beatrice, frightened by her recklessness, cautioned Iris in Spanish to be careful.

Oh, she remembered that night, singing down to Ralph, to that single, black uplifted face in the audience, urging her brain to sing something he'd remember out of their childhood. She decided upon "When you Wish Upon a Star," and she sang it tiny, as though her voice were a probe. As she sang, she was conscious of an overpowering sexual feeling. Strange.

When she approached Ralph in the wings, she noticed that he bore himself with a strange, proud dignity. She hadn't expected him to be so serious. "I'm glad. Happy," he said, "and proud. God, I'm proud of you, Sis." He kissed her on the mouth and Iris started. She remembered it was that night that Ralph had met Adela.

Adela had been a graduate student in music at the University; Iris and she had become fast friends. The moment Adela and Ralph met, Iris had known just how it would be. Ralph had smiled and Adela smiled back in a manner Iris had never

25

seen before. "My brother, Ralph," she said. "Adela, a very good friend." During the next set Adela and Ralph sat together.

She remembered those hazy, chilly mornings when, arriving at her apartment high above Paseo del General Mola, she would receive the usual frown from Beatrice. Ralph, she would discover, had been gone all the night—with Adela, she presumed. He usually returned later while she was sleeping, and Beatrice would explain to him how hard Iris had worked and how tired she was. Then Beatrice, having left for mass, the apartment would be quiet until late in the afternoon. Ralph and she would sit on the *balcón* and breakfast on coffee and rolls.

Iris had been grateful that Ralph hadn't seemed at all upset that she was living in luxury. On the other hand she had been somewhat surprised to learn that he had acquired manners and moved easily in sophisticated company. How had this come about? As time went on, she took pride in what he had become and was ashamed of her earlier preconceptions.

She was always conscious of him during those rehearsals at which she shouted at the musicians. He usually sat in a corner with Adela, watching Bobby or Leonard or Odell, the pianist who had taken Time's place. Mostly he kept his eyes fixed on her.

Holidays they spent on the beaches at Castelldefels, or went to the mountains. They brought along wine, cheese and bread, just like Europeans, they said, but somehow never got beyond the first resting place. Before, between or after sets, there were parties with the foreign musicians who came regularly to play at Jack's Jazz Club down in the Ramblas.

The week of Iris' vacation—and before she moved from

26

La Casa Blanca to Jack's—she had no trouble enticing Ralph and Adela to go off on a trip with her, to Salamanca and Seville in the south, where the Spanish were darkest. Ralph told her that these people were descendents of Senegalese slaves imported into Portugal in the fifteenth century. "Some of Sissie's family might be here," he remarked.

"And yours," she added.

"Yes, and mine."

Then they swung eastward in the direction of Granada and the Sierra Nevada. They traveled through the mountains to Murcia and northward on up the coast. Ralph insisted that they stop for a day at Tarragona so he could inspect the Roman ruins. But when the time came to go to the ruins he was nowhere about; the *sereno* said he had gone by himself, and on foot, to the Arco de Bara. It was early morning and there was no traffic on the road; as they approached they saw him in the distance, squatting beside the arch, staring up at it. When their car came to a halt in front of him, he still did not move.

"What are you doing?" Iris asked, suddenly angry. Adela and she had been running all over that lopsided town looking for him, and he'd hotfooted it out here to sit and stare at that stupid arch. He started to laugh, and leaned against the arch. "Can you imagine," he said, "Sissie's children here?"

Iris stared at him. His eyes traveled up the weather-specked browned structure. She saw Adela's dress rise gently in the wind. "Crazy Romans," Ralph muttered. "Here are Sissie's legions." Now Iris understood. Here they were on an empty road, a slim blue line of sea just visible beyond the edge of the parched land. Crazy collision, mysterious impact of past and present embodied in a ruined arch and Sissie's piss-potty children: fantastic! Iris began laughing and Ralph joined in. Adela, looking from one to the other, joined in too. Ralph glanced quickly up and down the road and then at the farm buildings standing on the long sloping hills. He tucked his bottom lip beneath his teeth, and started a time step. Iris danced also and Adela nodded her head from side to side rhythmically. In a few moments they were out of breath. They got into the car and drove on to Barcelona.

Ralph grew quieter as the time approached for his return to the States; spent long moments without speaking. Adela stayed close by. The *balcón* that faced the long avenue and from which the towers of the Church of the Sagrada Familia could be seen drew him to it. He wandered about the apartment as if loath to leave it, or took long walks by himself, returning as depressed as when he had gone out.

"You don't want to go, do you?" Iris asked, one night, and was surprised when he answered, "Yes, I want to go. Not happy about it, but I want to."

"You're lying."

"No."

"Will I feel like that if I decide to go?"

"No," he said quickly, positively.

Curious, she asked, "Why not?"

"It's different with you. You don't have to make it there; I have to. And if you don't like it you don't have to stay."

"Neither do you."

"Yes, I do."

"Have you a girl there?"

"Sort of." He gave her a crooked grin. "Sort of a sponsor." He showed her a cable wrapped around some pesetas, shoved it back into his pocket, distastefully. "I don't have to go back because of her."

"Then why?"

"I told you!" he said sharply; then, pressing his hands to his face, "Hell, I don't know, really."

"And Adela?"

"And Adela," he mocked her. "Should I take her back with me? So we could starve together? Besides, we couldn't make it in America. Not at all."

"So you'll stay with playwriting?" They had discussed it during less somber moments.

He said, "Yes."

She nodded, knowing she'd approached an area marked out of bounds. "Stay a while longer," she said.

"Can't. I've had my respite. I've got to get back."

"You can do what you have to here, in comfort, without starving, for God's sake. Look at you, moping around here because you say you have to go back home. Well, you don't have to and you know it."

"I know, I know. It's confusing for me to try to talk about America! I feel so many things about it, mostly a big sadness, and a fear, like a sailor must feel about a great, lovely ship that's still in pretty good shape when it begins leaking."

"Is it?"

"Badly."

"How can you tell?"

He laughed. "It's damp around the bulkheads, baby. It's the truth," he went on. "Oh, America had it once, and lost it."

His head was turned; she could stare at him. He turned back to her and went on speaking.

29

"It's funny how accidents have happened to America; I mean the Declaration and the Constitution—originally didn't take into consideration black men; didn't deem them worthy of mention even. They mentioned Indians all right: if they weren't taxed they didn't count either. The indentured slaves were considered people; they were white. The accident, of course was that the signers, even in their ignorance, moved, Sissie would say, next to God in their ideas. They could not go back on this godly concept when it became apparent that people who weren't considered people wanted to be treated as people. It was almost as if God had left that little loophole for history to catch up with Him."

"Talk that shit, Broth."

"Listen, the nonviolent business is an accident—funny! These damned fools have been so busy Christianizing Negroes that they can't fathom their use of the Christian ethic as a tactic. It shakes them! To think! They gave them this weapon and are getting their damned brains beat out with it. God must be getting his jollies about now over the whole business."

"Hush! Don't talk like that!"

"You sound like Mother."

"But just suppose—"

"I'd be one of the happiest cats on earth."

"You confuse me. Want a drink?"

"Yeah," he said, shouting after her, "the trouble with America is that she forgets that she's people and not just a goddamn brass whore symbol to herself." When she returned, he hoisted his glass. "To the tree."

"Oh—okay, to the tree."

"You know, Sis," he said rocking on his haunches and sipping his drink rapidly. "We don't raise statesmen in Amer-

30

ica. I guess the last one was Benjamin Franklin. We raise hacks. But things try like hell to work their way out."

She saw him frown. "Can I have another drink?" he asked.

"Get it, baby."

He got to his feet, walked to the kitchen, came back with a drink and sat down again. "She reminds me of a good-looking broad in my building," he said, "who smiles, digs your pants, you know, gives you the great glad eye and talks lots of shit and smells real good. But you can't ever get her to bed to bang her one."

"Who's that?" Iris asked absently.

"America."

"Oh, yes."

"What d'you mean, 'oh, yes'?"

"I mean you're right, I guess," she said hastily. She had been wondering what his life was really like there. She had heard so many stories from musicians. "Well," she said gently, "you know you're welcome to stay and welcome to come back."

He had had the nightmare late that night.

When Iris heard the noises in the predawn darkness, she thought that Adela had stayed the night, and that Ralph ought not be so obvious with Beatrice around. But the noises altered their character and when she rose, prepared to give Adela and Ralph a tongue-lashing, she found Ralph lurching around the kitchen like an undernourished bear, chasing Beatrice back to bed.

Iris stopped when she saw his face, and did not speak. He's had the nightmare, she told herself, remembering how he had been at home. She put on coffee and sat with him in silence. When he had finished his first cup, he shook his head from side to side, as if he were in great pain, and said, "Baby, I got to talk to you." His tone was unfamiliar.

"All right, Broth."

"You know I never liked the Navy," he said quickly. "But I was stuck and tried to make the best of it. In the Navy they let you know right from jump what you are and how you rate. Lots of shit, Sis. A whole lot of it." One of his fingers tried to dig into the table, then relaxed. "After boot we hung around for a while. They shipped me out alone. My buddies stayed behind or went somewhere else. There I was, just me. . . ." His voice started to fade. "On the ship I was alone. Can you imagine. Thirty-five hundred guys on the ship and I was alone, ain't that some shit? I made friends, but they soon fell away; lot of Southerners on the ship. You know, one day you're looking for your new buddies and the next they're breaking their asses to stay out of your way." He paused. "This is silly," he said, but he didn't look at her. He held up his arms in a gesture of hopelessness. "Sis, in the Navy I killed a man." Slowly he turned to her, his eyes veiled but expectant. Iris reached for a cigarette and she thought, How awful that you always thought him more capable of it than other people. He didn't have to tell her that the killing hadn't occurred in combat, but he said, "He was an American." He turned to the window. "He wouldn't let me live."

"You never talked about the war," she said. "Did you tell April?"

He shook his head.

"Mother?"

"No one. You know, I think I came all this way just to tell you. I could have done without the nightmare, though."

32

"Are they, have they?" She waited, exploring her innermost being.

"I am the only one who knows," he said. "Sometimes that's one person too many."

"You haven't told anyone all this time?"

"How could I?" he said.

"All these years," she said, looking at him.

He nervously tried to light a cigarette. "You think I'm nuts?" He got the cigarette burning. "He deserved to die. I don't mean to sound like God; he did. But he made something rotten begin in me. I guess I'll never lose it." He began jabbing the cigarette in her direction. "Iris! I tell you this man would not let me live. I could stand the being alone where guys going to die held on to each other, complete strangers. I tell you I could stand that. After all, wasn't I Big Ralph's and Sissie's boy? Yeah! Can you imagine, I kept telling myself that, like it would bring me through! Goddamn fool, I was! No one to even shout encouragement to so that *you'd* feel better, and no one to care, no one to be offended by your not having lived your eighteen or nineteen years as fully as the next kid . . ." He stopped to take a big drag of the cigarette, then crushed it out. "But I stood it," he said proudly. The door to Beatrice's room opened slightly and Iris waved Beatrice back. The door closed; Ralph hadn't heard.

"Ralph—"

"This day," he said, " we were on Saipan. God, it was hot. There were Seabees around, building something. A cracker outfit. One of them was a guy called Doughnut. A big red guy, and loud, like the world was his. They said he sometimes wore a string of Japanese scalps in his belt. I avoided him.

33

When I heard him coming, I cut out; if I saw him from a distance I took another trail. It wasn't that I was afraid of *him;* he was something evil to me, like a Fate."

Behind Ralph the day began to break in the east and the first rays of the sun stretched golden lines through the mists.

"This day I went to the water tank. The water was always hot and lousy, but it was water." Iris passed him a lighted cigarette. "There was a mess cup chained to the tank; everyone drank from it." He sighed. "Doughnut walked up while I was getting ready to drink. 'Drop that cup, nigger!'" Ralph's voice boomed. Startled, Iris watched his face; he seemed to be watching a screen set just above and in front of him. She could see the cords straining in his neck. "I stood there a minute, then went on with what I was doing. Iris, he was on my ass like white on rice. He knocked me down; felt like the top half of my head had lost itself. I got up, and funny—I started for the cup again. He hit me once more. Suddenly I knew that I had to get my hands on that cup. The hell with him; I won if I could get my hands on that cup and fill it with water. There was no way to stop this man short of shooting him. I kept trying to get that water. Once, realizing what I wanted to do, he waited and let me fill it up. I lifted the cup to my mouth and the world fell in on me again. I lay there. I couldn't move. I lay there in that coral dust and looked up at the coconut trees and that blue sky and I knew I had to kill him."

A smile flitted across his face. "I ached for days. I was in torture, killing him so many different ways. I killed him a million times before I really did, and all the while *I* felt like I was dead. I couldn't begin living again until Doughnut was

34

dead. I ran a fever thinking of ways to kill him. I couldn't eat and I spent my nights thinking. . . ."

"How?"

"Does it matter?"

"Yes. He should have died horribly." Iris found that she meant it.

Ralph raised his eyes slowly; they were filled with gratitude, but he said, "Don't say that, Sis."

"I mean it." She felt a slow burning anger at this man, this dead man and his kind, that they had intruded so far into her family, had disrupted it so.

"No you don't." He got up and went to the window; his body was silhouetted against the light. He said quietly, "In the nightmare I see his eyes big and scared, like I was *his* Fate as he was mine, and he always says, 'Hey, nigger! what are you—'"

Iris waited. Ralph turned. "He's frightened when he says it. I'm not one black man; I'm all of them. All their strength and hatred and fury—it's in me." He turned back to the window. "I let him see me, of course. He would have known anyway. I want to hurt him and then push him off that cliff. I got a piece of coral rock in my hand, waiting by that path that overlooks the sea. He comes. I jump out, and that second when I let him see me is the longest God ever made. I start to push and he moves back, then I let him have that coral rock smack upside his head. Again! Pushing all the time, and he's grabbing. . . . He goes over, but I'm on the edge too, digging with my toes. I can feel the cold air the sea pushes up against the face of the cliff. I listen for him to hit the rocks below. I hear a sound, but I don't know if it's him or the waves."

In the silence that followed, Beatrice's cough sounded unnaturally loud.

"I'll warm up the coffee," Iris said to him.

He shuffled to the table. "Oh, God, Doughnut, let me be!"

Adela came while they were drinking the coffee. Ralph sprang to his feet and embraced her, and Adela, surprised, looked beyond his shoulder to Iris, Iris nodded and Adela knew that for the first time since he had arrived Ralph had real need of her.

The doors to the past had begun to swing open. Whenever they were alone now, Ralph and Iris pieced together their pasts as in a puzzle. Time was her secret; she did not mention him. Most of the memories were painful. Ralph had one other secret which he did not tell until a week before returning to New York.

It was a warm night and they sat on the *balcón*, watching the traffic on the *paseo*. Adela, reluctant to be far from Ralph, dozed on a couch inside; Beatrice pattered about in the kitchen tunelessly singing one of Iris' songs.

"Looka here," Ralph said after a long silence.

"Tell me, what?"

"You ever miss Dad?"

She looked at him, surprised.

Without waiting for her answer he said, "I used to say 'so what,' then all of a sudden—I can't explain it—not having one seemed to mean a helluva lot."

Iris placed her forearm on his shoulder. They continued to stare down at the street. "Honey, I don't think so. You were always there and then Harry. . . . No, I don't think so."

"It's all very funny," he said. He lit a cigarette and tossed the match over the rail, envying it its almost weightless descent to the street below.

"I miss Mother the most," Iris said. "Not *her*; something *about* her. I mean she didn't really seem like a mother to me."

Ralph nodded. "I know." A leaping wind caught the tip of his cigarette and hot ash went flying across the *balcón*. "But you survived; we all survived." He looked at her, she thought, with a peculiarly gentle smile. "In a way you shouldn't have, baby."

"What do you mean?"

"You remember One Seventy-Nine?"

It was habit, this remembering the houses where they'd lived by their street numbers. "Yes. That's where you used to climb up and down the roof all day and tear up the attic floor."

"And where you used to be afraid to hang clothes—"

They laughed.

Ralph put out his cigarette; Iris watched him narrowly. "I found some letters up there one day, all tucked up beneath the boards. Mother used you—there's no other way to put it —for the sickest kind of revenge possible."

Iris reached for his cigarettes and he held a light for her, shielding it from the wind. "What on earth are you talking about?"

"You said you felt Mother wasn't like a real mother. You said it. She couldn't have been because you're not supposed to be Dad's child."

The wind brought them the sound of trolley bells.

Iris laughed. She roared. "So what the hell's the difference? I'm here!" She flung her arms outward. "And it's too late for anyone to do anything about it."

37

Ralph said softly, "Yeah, I know the feeling." He waited until her laughter had dwindled. "Mother had this guy Arthur. Arthur thought you were his child. Mother was angry at Dad —seems as though nothing worked out the way she wanted— and she let Dad think you were Arthur's child."

"I—how come we—"

"Apparently they were separated; you weren't even born at home—"

"I know. I just thought we'd lived for a little while in Chicago—"

"—and Dad asked her to come back. He didn't care if you weren't his. I guess he loved her that much. You always looked so much like her, he couldn't tell, and she had to be—not so close—because of Dad, you see; he would have been jealous because of me, Robbie, and later Mary Ellen. All those years she had to pretend that you were not really Dad's child. It was the one concession she made. Maybe when the time came when she could love you and it was all right, it was too late; she had trained herself too well."

"But Dad—Daddy"—she hadn't called him that in years— "you mean he—oh, God, Ralph. Are you sure?" she asked, her eyes searching his face.

"I've never been more sure about anything."

"That——!" Iris said through her teeth. She flung her cigarette over the *balcón*. "That bitch!" She leaned forward on the railing and stared at the ground. "And all the time—" The wind caught her words, tore them away.

"What?" Ralph said, leaning forward. Iris sat back.

"—all the time she was talking about what a bastard Daddy was!"

"Yeah," Ralph said. "She gave that cat a fit. Don't be too

38

hard on her. You do what you have to do or you aren't yourself. You know that. I guess she was strong in her way, stronger than any of us will ever be. I think she had to be. Dad, I think, was strong in a way people soon forget. He gave you your music, remember."

"He never said a word against Mother." Iris turned to him. "Did he?"

"Not a word that I know of."

Now Iris saw the lights almost all the way down to the pier and she thought, Time, Time!

Ralph was speaking softly. "I thought you should know. I didn't think it was one of those things better left unsaid. You felt something was wrong, now you know. Have to see what this tree Sissie's always talking about is made up of. When I get back I'm going to start finding out some things I should know. About myself."

She looked at him curiously. "You've got a lot buzzing around up there in your little head, haven't you?"

"Not much. It only feels like too much sometimes."

4

"SHE IS AS LOVELY AS YOU SAID," Eve said to Ralph. He had been staring at Iris' photo on a record jacket.

"Yes," he said, absently. The eyes, he thought; it's the eyes that never change. The face grows fat or lean; the hair falls out; the lips get a little fuller or thinner—colder or more sensual—but the eyes, they never change. "Yes," he said again, hoping that his sister was sleeping well, "she's always been very lovely. Tough, but lovely."

"And what's more," Eve said, wishing to dispel the sadness which had come to her husband, "I like her. You know, women don't usually like other women who are lovely."

"You always were kind of special, baby." He winked at her.

"Now wasn't that what you wanted me to say, something like that?"

Eve rose. "I just wanted you to be not quite so sad, Ralph."

"I know. I know. I'm sorry. I knew all my life that it would come, and I think I even practiced carrying on with the show or the conference—you know, all that yo-yo crap. But it's here, suddenly, and I guess I'm the only way I can honestly be."

Eve waited. Good for him to talk, she thought.

"If I were asked," he said, blowing out a great cloud of cigarette smoke, "if I loved her, I would have to say that I didn't know. Love? What is that? Giving love to children was a luxury she couldn't afford and when she could, she had got out of the habit. I don't mean that she didn't *have* the feeling. Love? You know, that's whipping the crap out of your children so that they don't crack their heads against the walls that make up this labyrinth, and if they don't, they might live and make out somehow. That's a kind of love, isn't it, Eve? Isn't it?"

"That's what you said in *Shadows*, Ralph."

"Yeah. I guess so."

He was through, she saw, all through talking for now, and was, as usual, embarrassed. Eve smiled. "I have to get some things together for dinner. Can I get you anything?"

"You've got everything," he said. "Why don't you come here?" He put on a mock leer.

"You nut," she said, pleased nonetheless. "You've got work and I've got work. Let's sublimate and do lots of good things in work—for the time being."

He shrugged, and when she had left the room, he turned

again to the record jacket. The eyes. He wondered if his own eyes revealed as much as Iris'.

What a surprise that was coming home from the war and finding Iris holding the door open. So well-developed for her age. Reminded him of the girl he'd known on Fillmore Street in San Francisco while he was awaiting discharge from Treasure Island. A little. Same size. Maybe even the same age. No, the girl in San Francisco was older. At least he told himself at the time she was older. No. He hadn't even thought about age; big enough, dammit, old enough. That Iris wanted to sing was an even greater surprise. He remembered only that she'd taken some piano lessons. But sing! And then he remembered their father crooning around the house. Before.

He had heard her for the first time in 1946 in Simpson's. He'd been sitting with April, his girl, fiddling with his drink, feeling again the onset of the malaria and the depression which always came with it. Iris appeared. On the stand those players of music who in small towns pass for musicians, were noodling, getting ready for the next set. Ralph watched his sister obey the summons of the pianist. She stepped upon the platform and glanced out at the couples, the single drinkers of Seagram 7 and beer. The pianist began the introduction. "No," Iris said. Her calm voice carried clearly over the open mike. She reached back and touched a chord twice on the piano. The pianist nodded. The group began to play again. She sang gently, simply, and her voice carried like a sheen of crystal water, without vibrato. Her head was raised and she stared with amused insolence at the audience.

Poise, Ralph thought, she had poise.

"... in that small café
the park across the way,
the children's carousels
the chestnut trees,
the wishing wells. ..."

Maybe it was good because he liked the song, the song re-membered from a rest area on Espiritu Santo, far from the northern islands, far enough away to make you homesick.

Her body (and Ralph grew uneasy with the wholesomeness of it, the glittering male eyes watching it) began to move.

"I'll be seeing you
In every lovely summer's day,
In everything that's bright and gay,
I'll always think of you that way. ..."

She stepped back from the mike and dropped her clenched fists to her sides. She took a deep breath which thrust her bosom invitingly forward and brought the side of her mouth back on mike.

"I'll find you in the morning sun
And when the night is through,
I'll be looking at the moon,
And I'll be seeing you."

After surveying the audience with a sly smile, she stepped down. The musicians went into the chorus again, still cap-tured by her mood. Passing, Iris touched Ralph on the shoul-der. Outside, he knew that old Mason, the lecherous bastard of a cop, sitting with his partner in Car 26, would make some smart crack when she went by. Ralph didn't know to whom she went or where she went then; he never asked.

Soon after that night at Simpson's, Lieutenant Harry Stapleton, stationed at the fort on the lake, met Iris, and when Ralph discovered that Harry was going to Germany with the Army of Occupation, he knew somehow that Iris would be going too.

Glancing at her occasionally during the wedding reception, Ralph found himself wondering just how long the marriage would last. Harry was not fast enough for Iris. Sissie seemed pleased. Her job was done; she had raised her daughter to marriageable age. Harry's mother kept getting in Sissie's way, but Sissie was polite to her. It was hot that day too, hottest day on record, the radio announcers had been saying all day.

Iris stood beside Harry at the bridge tables which had been piled with gifts. The photographer hovered about gathering people in groups and taking their pictures. Iris was perspiring; from time to time she wiped her forehead with her hand or with her handkerchief. She looked beautiful in white. Glancing at April, Ralph knew she was imagining herself in Iris' place and with him as the bridegroom. Inevitable.

In the kitchen Sissie bustled around, blunt, quick. A fine wedding; people would be talking about it for years; this or that happened the year that Joplin girl had the big church wedding. Yeah, she married some army officer.

Sissie said, "He's an only child, that Harry, and a little spoiled." Ralph knew this was his mother's way of saying that she was a better woman than Mrs. Stapleton; Sissie had had five children. "Two dead," she said. "God's will."

44

Sissie believed that the wedding would kill Iris' notions about singing in the clubs where those "no account" men hung out. Like his mother, Ralph didn't want his sister to come up big. Nor did he want her to have a marriage where the babies came every year. No, he wanted something special to happen to her. The marriage would take her out of town, and he suspected that she wanted to get away. The town had nothing to offer; it seemed to revolve around sex and liquor.

That evening after the wedding as they stood in the station waiting for the Empire State Express, Iris gave Ralph a brief smile.

"It's time, Mother," Iris said, as the crowds began to surge into the hall and up to the platform.

"Yes, honey, I see it is." Tears came to Sissie's eyes.

"Mother, please. You cry at the drop of a hat," Iris said, glancing at Ralph.

"Well, I can't help it. I'm supposed to cry," Sissie said. Both Ralph and Iris laughed.

Iris wiped her mother's eyes with her handkerchief.

"Aren't you afraid," Sissie asked, "going over all that water, all the way to Germany? I was afraid when I left home. I was younger than you then and didn't have a husband—"

"I know," Iris said.

"I guess you do," Sissie replied.

"Mother?" Now the tears welled up in Iris' eyes. Ralph turned away.

"There, there, baby," Sissie said.

"I am a little afraid."

Sissie said, "No, no you're not. You're just saying that to make me feel good."

Iris' eyes had grown even larger and more luminous. . . .

The eyes! Ralph thought again, searching them. He lifted the jacket cover and stared at it. Yes, there was a sadness in her eyes now; you had to gaze deeply into them to see it. He replaced the jacket and listened to Eve in the kitchen. Odd how a woman goofing off in the kitchen could give you a sense of comfort. He lifted his eyes to the windows. Snow. He allowed the fact of snow to sink in slowly. He felt that he should be shouting, railing against it, anything.

"You're not working," Eve chided from the kitchen. "I don't hear the typewriter."

Eve went on chopping vegetables.

5

IN HER BEDROOM Iris lay fighting for sleep. She heard the soft murmur of the voices of her brother and sister-in-law; heard his footsteps, heard the place settle into silence for a time only to be broken by the sound of Ralph's typewriter. The soft clatter went on and on to a small *bling!* of a bell, then on to a rasping sound. The vaguely satisfying odor of freshly made coffee was in the air. She glanced at the window. Snow. Still snowing, and why hadn't she been able to sleep? Why couldn't she sleep? For a moment she considered taking a couple of sleeping pills. They'd leave her groggy and perhaps even more depressed than she was now. Relax, she told herself. Relax.

But as soon as she tried she thought of being in New York,

of being in Time's city. He had once lived in New York. Before the war. He'd wanted to return sometime, he'd said, but he hadn't. Instead he'd stayed, located in Paris where, she had been told, he was seen often in Gabby and Haynes or if not there, hustling along Rue Manuel on his way for his weekly ration of barbecued spare ribs.

She wished he were in New York. Now.

Time, she pictured herself saying into a telephone, *Time, I'm here. Take me back. I want to come back.*

Perhaps not.

Time, I'm in town for a few hours. My mother's dying. Please take me to dinner.

Not strong enough.

Time, baby, I'm here. God, let me see you; I'm sick to see you. I'm sorry, sorry, sorry. Time—don't tell me now. . . .

But she had never, never been like that.

Iris turned in bed, disgusted with herself. Time was not in New York; he was in Paris. How could she work up such a fantasy now when he was so far away? No, she doubted that he was in Paris; probably in Monte Carlo playing for the wealthy and keeping warm. And women? No one ever spoke to her of the women he had been seen with. Perhaps it was because everyone knew, after eleven years together, their break-up couldn't be final; eleven years was a long time.

Thirteen years, the first two being merely a conveyance because they were spent with Harry. He was all there was the first two years; Time was not there then, only Harry, young and bright-eyed, reminding her of the Negro students who studied on the Hill. He had close-cropped ungreased hair parted to one side; he had one of those eager-to-please expres-

48

sions forever on his face. Harry stood and walked ramrod stiff, and his voice, though he was man size, was that of a boy.

They were many days aboard ship after leaving New York, and she had just begun to feel at home when the trip was over. At the precise moment when the ship docked Harry appeared at her side, like Columbus claiming the land. His chest swelled; his golden bars seemed to give off flashes of light; his eyes grew keen and hard. Down on the pier at last, she looked up; the ship was massive and she could not believe that it had rolled so violently. It was held down by its puny, looping hawsers; they sparkled with their ratguards. Beyond the ship she saw the sea, green close to shore and a dull blue farther out. She felt cut off, stranded.

Escorted through the demolished cities, then past them, along a long line of mountains, they came to rest at last among a dull yellow perspective of barracks. Flags fluttered and troops in varnished helmet liners marched by. Tense sentries mounted the gates. Cadence calls rolled out endlessly and jeeps whined through the streets. Junior officers, off duty, marched down the walks to the barracks which had been partitioned off for married officers quarters; they marched softly calling cadence—"Hup, two three four!"—and took the salutes of the EM with an offhanded snap. At first Harry practiced the kind of salute he would give, deciding finally on a general officer's slow, threatening half-snap, half-wave. There was unrelieved darkness in the quarters and she could always hear the couples in the rooms on the other side. The dances at the Officer's Club were always the same and so were the trips to the Post Exchange for souvenirs to send back home. And in their quarters she cooked, visited, and washed

49

and ironed uniforms and placed them in the closet where they hung above Harry's boots, which looked as if he were standing in them. There was no time for music. The summer vanished and the fall came and more Germans clamored for work so they could buy food for their families. Then winter and spring far, far behind.

A year and a half passed, a vague restlessness, a dissatisfaction growing like a tumor within her. Sissie, Oliver and Robbie had moved to California (leaving her with no frame in which to imagine them), and Ralph and April had married and were expecting a child. But her life remained static, deadeningly static. It was clear that Harry didn't give a damn whether she ever sang again. She felt like one of his uniforms, useless except when worn; meaningless until removed from the closet and patted down to conform to the lines of his body. The bridge parties, the dances and the outings continued; most of the wives had been to college and they used this against Iris because she was more attractive than they. Once or twice there was a race riot which was quickly squelched but not before the junior officers placed the blame on their men for chasing the German girls. "They didn't do it home," Harry said indignantly, "why in the hell do they think they can get away with it here?"

The months fled and Iris' despair transformed itself into various aches and ennuis. Raphaella, Ralph's child, was born and Iris sent the usual silver spoon and cup. Pictures came from Sissie, taken at Yellowstone. She and Robbie (how big he was now!) stood arm in arm. Old Faithful was tardy, Sissie explained, and therefore unseen behind them. Suddenly it was spring again.

And then one day, as she trudged sadly through the still

rubbled streets of the town, the sound of music came to her and she stood still, head lifted in the pert manner of an Italian greyhound. She hastened to the restaurant from which it came, her little aches and pains forgotten. She paused a moment, then pushed the door open. Darkness, but the sound was all around her; she wanted desperately to move with the music, to open her mouth and let the sounds glide out; she wanted to take it, gather it to her bosom, dissect each note and put her own meaning into it. Her eyes became accustomed to the darkness and she saw a tight huddle of bobbing figures. Off to the side—at the bar—stood a bent old man whose white hair glowed in the dusk; he seemed a hermit in a cave watching playful animals scurry about. At the piano was Time. No, Melvin C. Curry (transposition: a present when she came to know his name to a past when she hadn't.) Smiling, trying to restrain some bubbling eagerness, she slipped across the floor unmindful of the browned vegetables which lay in the basket on her arm. She sat down, lightly, as though about to rise the very next moment. As soon as she was seated, the old man was wiping the table with a filthy cloth and asking in a cancerous voice, "Beer, fräulein?" The old man vanished and returned in a flash. It had not been a flash, of course, she thought; it had seemed so because of the music.

The musicians smiled at her, pleased by her presence. They even seemed to swagger a bit more. The pianist, the man with the thin hair, looked at her and smiled; smiled even more broadly when Iris, ignoring the beer, rose and approached him.

He said, "Hello, Homefolks."

"Let me sing. Please," she said, hardly recognizing her voice as her own.

"Sure." He took a look at the men behind him. "What?"

Iris was grateful that they hadn't laughed or even smiled. "Lover Man."

"Key?"

"G."

They swung with her; she could tell that they liked what she was doing. The pianist stroked the keys possessively. "Take your time," he said. "We got you." She liked his voice, the familiarity of it, his face, and especially his hands. She watched them. Sometimes he frowned. The dim lights reflected his scalp through his thinning hair. Prematurely balding, she saw. All of the musicians were dressed in clothes sent from home, pegged pants and long jackets. Veterans discharged in Germany; she hoped the war had gone well for them. Now the bass player nodded in encouragement; her chest filled with air, and she knew the notes were coming out right even before they issued from her lips. The drummer touched kisses to his cymbals; the trombonist studied her face, her chest for signals of breaks, stops and rests. She felt that she was with them; it went well. The pianist began his solo and Iris found that she could not remove her eyes from his hands; she wondered how old he was. Certainly a little older than Harry but not much. He turned to her. "Not bad, Homefolks. Nice. Let's do it again." He led her in again and too quickly it was finished.

"Take a crack at 'Waterfront.' That seems to be your style," he said. They seemed more at home. In the early bars she felt them groove behind her. The beat was solid; she smiled at the bass player; he really brought you on. Great! she thought, and before she knew it she was snapping her fingers. Mad, absolutely *mad*. The pianist took off again on a long, golden passage. They did the number a second time and then broke.

"What's your name, Homefolks?"

"Iris Stapleton."

He touched the keys, simulating the accents of her name. "Iris. I—ris." He looked up quickly. "Want a job, Homefolks?"

"Singing?" she said, not believing, cautiously, waiting for the inevitable punch line to the joke. But none came.

He nodded and then smiled. "I'm Time—Melvin Curry, and these—"

"Oh, I couldn't!" Iris said, while wanting to say yes she would, for she wanted to sing beautifully of love and happiness, even sadness, the way she felt they should be sung. But Time had meant it; she saw his eyes cloud for an instant and felt compelled to say, "Harry—my husband—he's a lieutenant—"

Time held up his hands and behind him the others pretended a wide-eyed, withdrawing fear. Iris did not finish. Her mind fled pell-mell back to the barracks and to her ramrod Harry, and she thought of all the years with him and foresaw only a vast emptiness for herself.

"Well," Time said, tossing his head in a that's-too-bad manner, "stop around sometime. We'll be playing this place for a while." He barked over his shoulder and began playing at a rapid tempo. "Hey!" he said to the piano. Iris felt that they had suddenly been pushed away from her and that she was watching them grow smaller and smaller. She was dismissed; they were romping along without her, just as they had a half hour before. Iris retreated to her basket, stood a moment, then left, the sounds of their music teasing in her ears all the way up the street.

She did not recall when the sullenness set in, she only knew that she was never in a good mood. She knew that it had nothing to do with what Sissie, with her neat pigeonholing would have called "a woman's evilness." She began to nag Harry about her lessons; she let his uniforms go; prepared his meals late. In bed she put him off by saying that it was her time or that she didn't feel well. The sterility of their daily living produced a horrible ennui.

That afternoon when Harry strode in, crisp in dress OD's, he stood silently, legs spread. "Let's go to bed," he said.

"I don't—"

"To hell with that!"

Iris glanced at him, turned back to the stove. "I'm fixing dinner now," she said calmly. There was a silence, like that which surrounds the movements of great cats circling for advantage. And suddenly she knew she never wanted to go to bed with him again. Selfish; it was always for him. He always finished quickly and uncaring, like a boy doing it hastily in a hall. Only once had it been all right and not since, but once done, she wondered, why not again and again? "Harry, for the last time, what about my lessons?" How could you tell your husband that he's no damned good in bed?

"Look, Iris. I'm a career officer in the Army. Why should you want to stand half-naked in some club singing? To hell with that. Now, come on. I want to go to bed." He stalked into the bedroom. She heard him undressing. Thoughtfully she turned and followed him; she undressed slowly. The bed sighed beneath them. There was singing on the other side of the thin wall; it was Janet. Her husband was a first lieutenant. When he went home, Harry would get promoted. Iris tried to hold herself in, but Harry's kisses were warm and long and moist. A faint odor of sweat came from his body. His hands clutched her breasts, searched clumsily below and she felt herself letting go. She tightened her arms around his neck and kissed him, hoping suddenly that it would be all right, that what was clouding her mind would vanish. She began to move expectantly. Quite clearly, and all at once, she knew that this time would be like all the others. "Oh, Harry, *wait!* Harry, *please* wait!"

But it was over almost as soon as it began. Harry slumped to his side, smiling but more embarrassed than pleased. Iris' cry hung still in the air, pulsed against their ears. Softly, enunciating clearly, she cursed him and pulled him back to her. He was surprised and then frightened; he became Lt. Harold Stapleton; he frowned. But Iris was furious. She climbed atop him, pressed her hands tightly against the surfaces of his shoulders, near his neck. "Be still! Don't move!"

She did not look at him; she moved and moved; disgust grew with her desire; her contempt for him was massive. But the desire was growing; it was becoming overwhelming and it seemed that she had never before felt it. She felt his eyes on her face, but she didn't care. He tried to make a salvaging juvenile movement. "Be still!" Iris panted sharply. He became still beneath her. Now her body was wet and his hands slid limply from her. Her neck was tired and her head drooped, letting her hair fall, obliterating his face.

"Iris? Iris?" he said, his voice sounding more like a child's than usual.

She didn't answer. On the other side of the wall, Janet tried

55

for a high note and missed; from outside came the ominous
tread of a company marching by. Harry seemed far away
now. Then, a plaintive animal sound, the bark of a big cat in
the darkness, escaped her opened mouth. She folded gently
upon her husband, still remembering to hate the touch and
smell of him. She felt him moving away and when that lovely
paralysis ebbed, she looked at him with hard eyes and a defiant
smile that showed only around her lips. His eyes were filled
with hatred. Her eyes laughed him down. Wordlessly he rose
and went off.

They avoided talking about it for days. In bed they lay
apart. But they kept up the pretense at club dances and parties;
and then, one night, drunk and weary of the question, they
tried it again and it was the same. Iris said into the blanket,
after allowing him to have his way, "You don't love me. Why
don't you love me?" She had said it with an edge of finality
in her voice. The morning after, their speech was studied.
Iris walked about in that purposeful, vicious stride she remembered Sissie using. When Harry had gone on duty, she
took the bus, rode past the great gray slopes of mountains to
the restaurant. Time and his group had gone to Munich. She
posted a letter and returned home. The waiting was gray and
boundless, filled with risings and going to bed. Bed became a
place for a jagged kind of sleep, nothing else. Sometimes she
was glad that Harry was there and then she tried to tell herself
that it didn't matter about how he was. But that didn't make
it any better. She thought of Sissie and Oliver and Robbie,
moved; Ralph and April with the baby. There was no place
with them for her. She considered becoming a whore, thinking that a colored prostitute would make a lot of money in

Germany. The thought made her feel better for the day. But surely, Ralph and April could squeeze her in somewhere for just a little while until she got settled. This thought made her feel even better, and carried her over into the next day. That afternoon, Harry came in, his eyes accusing. He threw the letter at her. She picked it up and retreated to the bedroom and turned on the light. Harry straddled the doorway. Iris laughed and ripped open the letter. She read it quickly, sighed, looked at Harry and laughed harshly again. Time wanted her; his group needed a singer.

Early in spring, 1949, the marriage over, Iris boarded the train at Frankfort. She studied the big, light-haired corporal who was to share the compartment with her, and considered that for the very first time in her life she was alone. It was morning. The proper time to begin anew.

The train began to roll smoothly out of the covered station; crept cautiously across a bridge. Once over the Main River it gathered speed and roared southward into the Rhine Valley. As the train approached Darmstadt, the mountains of the Oden Forest came into view.

"Are you going to Bavaria?" the soldier asked politely. He waited for her to reply, his hands resting lightly in his lap.

Iris smiled, closing her eyes and shutting out his image. "Is Munich in Bavaria?"

"Oh, sure," he said. He glanced out the window. "It's about fifty kilometers from Dachau. You're going to Munich then?"

"Yes. Where are you going?"

He hesitated and then said, "To Innsbruck." He reached into his pocket and brought out a pack of cigarettes. "To

57

look up some relatives." He extended the pack for her and laughed. "Micronite filter. Newest thing in the States." He lit her cigarette. "Are you from New York?"

"No; my husband."

"Husband," he said, peeking over his cigarette; "you look almost too young to be married."

"Well, it's over," she said. Now she glanced out the window and saw his reflection in it; he was looking at her.

"Was your husband in the Army?"

"A lieutenant," she said.

"The Army," he said. "I'm on furlough and damned glad of it. I'd like to get out of this country altogether and not ever have to come back."

"You don't like the Army?"

"No, I don't like it. I don't see how anyone could like it."

"Harry likes it."

"Your husband?"

"Yes."

"Listen, my name's Jack." He smiled with assurance. "What's yours?"

"Iris."

He repeated her name softly. Iris could hear the wind rushing past the train.

"And you," Iris asked, "are you from New York?"

"No, Chicago." He unbuttoned his jacket and loosened his tie.

As they left Mannheim and Heidelberg behind, Jack remarked, "They really shot the hell out of these places. It's a pleasure to see them. Was your husband in action?"

"No."

"I wasn't either, thank God."

She could see how his chest strained against his neat khaki shirt. She dropped her eyes and began to stare out the window.

"Look," Jack said with a sudden enthusiasm," I've got time and time. How'd you like to stop at Ulm, have lunch there instead of on the train, and go with me to see the Weydmann collection?"

"I can't," Iris said, embarrassed because she didn't know what the Weydmann collection was. But now Jack was leaning forward touching her arm. "It's a great collection of things from medieval Africa, really fine things, I understand. . . ." His eyes pleaded. "Or have you seen it already?"

"No," she said, watching his hand grip hers, looking without any of the emotions she thought she was supposed to have because of the white skin. "I haven't seen it." She guessed that Harry would leave Germany without ever once going to a museum, without ever once doing anything which was not covered by Army regulations. She wanted to go to the museum; she wanted to do anything to fill up the emptiness that she felt. "I just can't," she said again, watching him as he lifted her hand to his lips and kissed it. "I'm taking a job in Munich. I'm going to—*sing*."

"Sing?" he looked at her.

"With a small band. My first job."

"That's great," he said with a big smile. She saw that he was studying her face. "So you're a singer."

"Yes," she said, loosening her hand, "I'm a singer."

"I was thinking," Jack said slowly, "that I'd stop in Munich for a day or two. Maybe I could catch you sing. . . ?"

Iris smiled out the window at the valley through which they were passing. She found herself saying, "I'd be glad if you would. I don't know anyone there...."

"Then I will."

"What about your relatives?" she said.

"My relatives." Twice he opened his mouth but did not speak. "They might not be alive," he finally said.

He looked at her for a long time and then, flicking the ash from his cigarette, said, "How can I say it without sounding sorry for myself?"

"You're Jewish."

Jack nodded slowly.

"I'm sorry. Were they close relatives?"

"Not very. Cousins and the like."

"I hope you find them," she said, remembering that Harry had never liked Jews.

Jack said softly, "I want to go to Dachau and see for myself." His tone changed. "Where will you be staying?"

Iris gave him the address of her hotel. She felt happy that she was not alone any more. For the time being at least there would be Jack. The reason why didn't matter. And she, she thought, stealing another of those surreptitious glances at him, wanted him. He stood between her and the world.

The hotel, they discovered the next morning, seeing it through the slight mist that came with the warming sun, was a narrow, steeply gabled building. Great dark beams laced across the upper part of its light-colored façade. The street upon which it stood was cobbled, clean and narrow, between the university and the park.

The desk clerk's eyes brightened at Iris' approach, and Iris, hesitating for a moment, grew cold, fearing that the job

60

had fallen through. She drew nearer; the clerk spun around, reached into a box and picked out a small white envelope. Smiling, he tapped it against his fingers. "Miss Stapleton?"

"Yes." She took the envelope, ripped it open.

"Dear Homefolks—Just got a quick gig, very good bread in Zürich. Four days. Relax. Everything's cool with the hotel. Go over the arrangements I left with Herman (the clerk). Cool it, Time."

"It's all right, isn't it?" Jack asked gently, seeing her smile. She nodded gratefully. "They're out of town until Tuesday." The clerk was holding her keys and the music. "Thank you."

"I'm glad it's okay," Jack said. Then in a lower voice, "What's your room number?"

"Thirty-one."

"I'll call for you in an hour. We'll walk and have lunch somewhere."

"All right," she said. An old porter was picking up her bags and shuffling away, his head turned toward her. "In an hour."

Within that hour Iris had lost her fright. Once again she was able to see in the mirror that she was an attractive woman.

In the city it was the festive time of the *Marzenbier*. Strolling around the city with Jack, she felt the delightful sense of the unreality of things. People stared at them, curious about the big man in the uniform and the woman on his arm. Iris and Jack noticed, smiled at one another.

In the English garden of the Aumeister restaurant, Jack said, "I'm glad I came."

Iris nodded. Her eyes sparkled. "Yes, yes." A chilly wind blew from the Isar and ruffled her hair. After lunch they went

61

to the Theresienhohe and climbed the statue of Bavaria and saw the city stretched out beneath them. Then they hurried back to Schwabing, and had dinner in a brown little tavern—Moselle wine and Klopse. Tipsy, they found their way to a half-empty club where musicians played violins, then to a cellar filled with students who were the friendliest people they'd met so far.

When they got back to the hotel she kept laughing and saying no to him, wanting him to insist. "No." He staggered down the hall to his room. Iris stood in the doorway. He turned at the door of his room and pouted, "C'mon, how about it?"

"See you at breakfast." She closed her door, leaving it unlocked. Two hours later she rose and viciously threw the lock.

She did not see him at breakfast; on her way back to her room she saw the note in her box. She read it in her room before she went over the music. He had left for Dachau. What a fool, she thought, then was sorry. She spread out the music and opened the bottle of Scotch she'd stolen from Harry; it was the first bottle she'd ever owned. The morning passed slowly.

Jack came back late in the afternoon. He was drunk. She kissed his lips as if to warm him. When he took her hand, quickly, pressing it so hard that it hurt, he cried with fierce, dry sobs which seemed to come from the deepest cave in the world.

The next day, the third, they walked. They crossed the Reichenbach Bridge to see St. Mary's Church and then they lunched in the Rosenheimerplatz. Neither knew how to say goodbye. When she looked at him Iris thought of the lean, bony feel of him, the strange and somehow hideous hair on his body. They returned to Schwabing in silence. When he did not knock at the door of her room later, she knew that he had checked out, perhaps to search for his relatives.

Iris studied her music very hard that night; she studied until very late and did not drink.

"Everything cool?" Time asked, sticking his head in the door after breakfast. His eyes dropped to the music she held in her hands, then rose back up to her face, pleased.

Iris got up quickly, smiling. "Come on in. How was Zürich?"

Time entered. The others thrust their heads in through the doorway.

"Hey, baby, you lookin' good," the bassist said.

The drummer growled, "Lord, looka here."

"Get the hell outa the way, man, so *I* can see," the trombonist said, shoving his way through to stand in the door his mouth agape. "Baby, you don't know how good it is to see a *black* woman!"

Iris heard them moving down the hall. Time looked at a piece of the music. "Got it, you think?"

"It wasn't hard," she said.

"Naw, it won't be hard. You try the things you think you'd be great with. Figure about three numbers. Introduction, you come on in, we groove; I'll do three and there'll be one across; trombone comes after me—" He smiled. "And that's all." He rose and went to the door. "Bread's a little tight now, but not bad." He told her the pay.

"All right," she said.

"We're going to get some rest. See you at dinner and we'll

go over the itinerary. We've got to travel; got to go where the money is. Glad to have you."

"Thanks, Time." When he left she put on her coat to go out. She walked slowly to the park, then across it to the Chinese pagoda and to a shop where she had coffee. Later when she had the itinerary she would write Sissie and Ralph and tell them about Harry and about the new job.

She heard the door of her room open softly. "Broth? Eve?" she said.

"Me, baby," Ralph said, waiting at the door.

"C'mon in. Getting late?"

"Yeah. Eve said you ought to think about getting up. Rest okay?"

"Yes," she lied. She twisted around in bed holding the sheet up before her and smiled. "Fine."

"It's still snowing; snowing like hell." He paused. "No calls."

"Oh," she said, turning to look out the window. When she turned back she said, "Is that drink for me? What is it?"

"It's not for you and it's the straightest bourbon in the world. Want one?"

"No, a Martini."

"Eve thought you'd want one. She's mixing some now. Still feel up to the play?"

"Of course. But—"

"What?"

"What if something happens while we're gone?" She did not like the idea of being away from the telephone.

Ralph looked into his drink. "Then it's just happened, Sis. I mean, what can we *do* about it?"

64

She watched him finish his drink. "Anyway, I'll be here and I can get in touch with the theatre."

"Hello!" Eve said with a smile, holding a Martini toward Iris. "Thought this'd help get you up."

Iris took the drink with one hand and held the sheet up to her with the other. She tasted it. "What'd you do, dip the vermouth cork in and out?"

"Too strong?"

"Oh, no!" Iris laughed. "Fine!"

Eve said, "We'll get out so you can get yourself together —"

"And hurry up, will you, Sis?" Ralph said feigning hunger, rubbing his stomach. "Eve's got some real solids: fried bird, biscuits—you ought to come around more often."

"That sounds *mad*!" Iris said. "Okay, okay, I'm getting up, but you have to leave, Bro."

"I have to finish up," Eve said, going out with Ralph, who stuck his head back in to say once more, "And hurry up, for Christ's sake, baby. I'm starved."

Iris went into the bathroom, swallowing the drink in quick gulps. The bathroom, like the rest of the apartment was neat, filled with crystal jars with colored soaps in them. Eve's, of course, she thought, touching the thick towels. Eve seemed so right for Ralph. Ol' Ralph, she thought fondly.

6

THERE HAD BEEN SOMETHING STRAINED ABOUT DINNER.
Now they were painfully making their way through the dessert, with coffee still to come. They could sense the ghostly shadows of huge snowflakes still sliding secretly down the night. Their conversation, as it had throughout the meal, rose and fell awkwardly.

Eve struggled to keep the conversation going, but she could not help noticing the glances between brother and sister. The radio had been playing all day, but now, with the announcement of the weather every half hour, Ralph called for silence. Suddenly the phone rang.

Brother and sister exchanged quick, frightened looks. Eve rose to answer.

"I'll get it," Ralph said softly. Eve halted. Ralph walked from the room into the hallway.

Eve and Iris strained to hear what he was saying. Both were sure that they could tell by his second spoken word whether it was Oliver or not.

"Barney," he called out to them. Iris crushed out her cigarette and promptly lit another.

"More coffee?" Eve said. Iris nodded. Eve went to the kitchen, returned with the coffee.

"Everyone dies," Ralph said grimly when he returned to the table. "Do you remember that picture, baby? Canada Lee was in it and John Garfield; they were boxers and Canada had a blood clot on the brain or something and died, and Garfield crossed up the mob and they were going to get him in the end, in the Garden, and he said to them, 'Everybody dies.' Remember?"

"Yes," Eve said, "I remember." She passed him his cigarettes. He took one and lit it.

"We'd better get ready," Eve said to Iris.

Ralph was staring at the table. He pointed toward the hall. "I hate that goddamn phone!" He dragged deeply on his cigarette. "Iris, I don't know what the hell we're sitting here crumbling up for; I mean she's a tough ol' broad; you know that, and that it'll take a lot to chisel her loose—I mean"— and his head came down in one powerful nod of confirmation —"she's tough!"

Iris said, "Yes." She felt her eyes blurring. "Let me get my face on," she said, rising without looking at the others. She walked quickly from the room.

"What's Barney talking about?" Eve asked, clearing the table.

"Just wanted to know how it was going."

"How's his little boy?"

"Forgot to ask." He watched for a moment. "I'll get the dishes."

"All right. Just leave them in the sink for Mrs. Phipps, okay?"

"She here tomorrow?"

"Yes."

"Tell her not to mess around the desk."

"Baby, she knows already."

"Oh, she does? I forgot. Okay, I'll leave the dishes for her."

"Ralph?"

"Hummm?"

She hesitated and then asked, "Are you all right?"

"Yes, I'm all right. What the hell did you think, I was going to fall on my ass on the floor?" He smiled.

Relieved, Eve giggled. "I didn't know *what* you were up to."

Ralph said, "You're not supposed to know everything. Go on, I told you."

"You've got the seat numbers?" she asked.

"Yes, yes, but I keep telling you I won't need them. You'll see. That Sissie's tough, girl—" His voice fell. Eve was now out of the room. "*Tough*," he said, gathering up the dishes.

Iris returned to the room, ready, waiting for Eve.

"You look good, baby."

"Ralph, now I don't know if I should go. Doesn't seem right—"

"You go. Let's not have the wake before it's time." He

held up his hand; she had lifted her chin preparatory to speaking. "Please, Sis."

"Okay. I've packed a bag already. And I'd like to speak to Dad when we get back. I feel guilty that I haven't already."

"Well, you had to rest, for Christ's sake. Sure, we'll call him. I haven't called to tell him what's going on. You know he still might love her or some yo-yo thing."

He walked them to the door when Eve came out. "Both looking good," he said, kissing them. "Try to enjoy it, will you, Iris?"

"Okay, hon. I'm sure I will."

As soon as they had gone Ralph went to the phone again and called the weather; there was no change.

"Will there be an audience?" Iris asked as they rode in the taxi.

Eve laughed. "Sure. It's only the commuters who won't come because of the snow and they usually get their tickets for weekend performances. The house'll be full enough; you'll see."

Iris nodded. She liked the smell of the snow and the way its falling dulled the street lights and curtained the immense buildings. She had not walked in a great snow in a long while. If they did not leave that night or in the morning, and if it were still snowing, she would walk in the snow and feel again that universal cleanliness, neatness.

They crept down the block past theatre marquees, flashing colors, movement, sounds. "There!" Eve said, leaning forward in her seat, "See it?"

"Yes," Iris said softly, nodding, reading the words stark

black against the background of white, so bold that not even the falling snow obscured them:

SHADOWS ON THE SUN
a new play by
Ralph Joplin
Directed by Paul Lancer. Produced by London
Petit. Designed by Ma. . . .

Iris' eyes swept back to the first three lines. She grinned. "Yes, I see it." Now the cab came to a stop beneath the marquee. "It's like showtime," Iris said breathlessly, feeling excited by the lights, the people, the noise. She thought, as they hustled through the door, into the plush warmth of the theatre, of her first years of success—of those years with Time.

It was funny. Funny that how much you learned depended in great measure on how much you suffered. And funny too that just when you realized that you were paying, you understood how much more you owed.

She had not realized this until she had become one of that tight, sometimes desperate group of musicians shunting back and forth across the continent. In that first year of her success she became accustomed to the feel of a re-emerging Europe. Not even the shame of an occupied France, Time said, lingered longer than necessary to create the illusion of grief. Germany was like the bully who had been caught again in the act of beating a hapless victim. And those free nations that lay outside the arc which had closed from the hinge in the East picked themselves up and began again. The countries inside the arc, ringed in the twilight of the war by Zhukov and Konev were never considered much anyway. Wherever they went there were whispers about the Jews, the Jews, like an orgy one stumbled on and participated in, perhaps, or wished to but didn't.

Graves registration teams still functioned. One came upon them in little hotels in the provinces east of Paris, Caen and Le Havre; they were found in Rennes, Avranches, Alsace and in Germany, where the camps with their smokeless stacks stood tall above the barbed wire. At one period Iris' troupe seemed to be forever in sight of military cemeteries with their geometrically neat rows of white crosses interspersed with occasional Stars of David. The pianist complained that every fourth man in Reims was one-armed.

But Time was above all a businessman. He demanded "front money" (an advance) and was uneasy over "back money" (arrears). He haggled unashamedly over money and halls ("Got to have something that'll give back the *sound*.") He was band boy, manager, leader, father and brother, and he was indefatigable. He would schedule a trip to the end of the farthest province if it paid well, and never had them play above his audiences or, if he did, he managed not to be condescending. Some of the trips were long and terminated in cold hotels run by wizened, unkind concierges; sometimes at the end of long second-class-coach trips there were hissing audiences who didn't understand. Then Time gave the group a little nod and they played for themselves. More and more frequently there was that beautiful teamwork, when theme and melodic line, furiously nurtured by Time, passed from him to the horn and then back again, clicking dynamically. Iris knew that behind her the rhythm seemed every turn, every revolution of the world; seemed a reaching beyond for the greatest, unscored beat, the inexplicable vibration of being and doing. And when those moments, held as long as humanly possible, were over and they had sensed exactly what they had done, the dull, disappointing, slightly bewildered feeling of having been rudely jettisoned in flight came to Iris; the feeling was to come many times.

Even more than as a child she now felt herself part of a wild, happy family. The musicians surveyed her dates and commented on them; she in turn destroyed their illusions about women. She slept with her room doors unlocked; they came to her to talk of their women, their sisters or mothers back home. Sometimes they just talked. Iris found it very strange and wonderful that she could speak to them and not feel somehow that they wanted to sleep with her.

For a period of several months she drank too much, then suddenly not at all. She had clothes, perfume and shoe binges —above all she loved shoes. She became exhilarated with Europe as she never could have been with Harry. She came to know that she was a desirable woman; she knew it from a hundred phrases and by the way she was looked at. She remembered when she sang, arching her body, curving her arms in the spots, that the men who came, came for her and not her voice. Iris became European; she belonged to the Continent.

They came, the jazzmen, rich with talent and ideas and an awareness of America which could not be separated from their disgust of it; the only America they referred to was New York.

The greatest of them was Charlie Parker, who arrived that first year and played the Salon du Jazz, the Salle Pleyel, the St. Germaine clubs, and, like the others, moved all over

Europe. Some, like Jax, the bass, new to Time's group, were deeply scarred psychologically.

Toots Jones, an old-time trumpeter who could no longer make it in America was Jax's victim that year. Toots was considered the swingingest by the Paris squares, but had said "Yessir" and "Nosir" to a white American record company executive kicking it up on the town. Jax and Iris, on the club route, saw it, heard it: Jax called Toots an Uncle Tom, and Toots said he couldn't be like the young cats who'd been raised to kick asses—he couldn't change the way he was raised up so he could survive. Jax, short, bull-like, with fierce yellow eyes and the bassist's strong hands, cried, "It's never too late!" They began fighting, gasping and punching in the street, the Arc de Triomphe in the distance. Toots died a year later and Jax cried when he heard about it in Stockholm; it was just about the time the Korean War broke out.

She remembered that year because of Jax and Toots; Charlie Parker, high on champagne, had made a pass at her in the Hotel St. George V. There was a sudden new phase which began with the letter from Robbie. It was one of those half-cool, half-patriotic letters, the kind of letter Iris remembered Ralph's having written once, filled with quiet reminiscences and youthful philosophizings. Then nothing else until the letter from Sissie arrived saying that Robbie was in Korea, caught in the two-year Army. Iris wondered: would the war affect Robbie as it had Ralph?

But that war was too small, too far away and too soon after the big one. Few people noticed it or cared. Even Sissie, given to War Mother's bouquets and Service Stars in the window, made it sound like a two-week sojourn in a Boy Scout camp. Iris remembered the parties Robbie had gone to; they had been like the parties her own group had held. He had grown up so quickly.

One summer day in Amsterdam she sat in a café reading the papers. "The war's a year old and no one's much concerned with it," she said to Time, sitting opposite her.

"Why should they be?" Time asked.

"Just wondered to myself."

"Brother still there?"

"As far as I know."

"Tough," he said without hardness. "He'll be all right, if he's like you."

"Thanks."

"Wars," Time said, "are for fools and the desperate."

Iris was silent.

"I went into the line a few miles north of here," Time continued. "I volunteered. Me and thirty-five other fools. No, we weren't fools. Yes, we were fools," he said again. "We were all colored. We went from there all the way into Frankfort with crackers behind us and Germans in front of us. A whole platoon. Well, that's not much in a big war. It's enough, I guess, though. There were only two of us left; two out of thirty-five men, my sergeant and me. His name was Moody and he cracked up." He brought his eyes down to hers and they smiled at her. He called for *jenever*.

"Oh, you liked it," Iris said, teasingly.

"Sure." When his drink came he said, "We had to steal guns to fight with when arms gave out. We had to—" He was chuckling. He turned toward her. "You know what we did? They put us on the point, our lousy little platoon; we had to hit every objective first, take it out or bring it down to where the cracker boys behind us could handle it. My God.

We lost half the platoon on our first two assaults. Then," he said slyly, "we got slick. We'd run up to the Germans, fire away like hell, making all the goddamn racket in the world, but not getting too close, and then we'd run on around"—he moved his arm in a big, slow semicircle—"and on past. Those crackers would come charging up, thinking we'd taken the Germans out, and—Lord!" Time smiled. He straightened up. "The lieutenant would ask Moody what had happened and Moody, face all straight, would say, 'We took 'em out, they must've brought up more troops!' "

"Is that why you didn't go home?"

"Why go home when you have this?" he nodded toward the street. Three girls were walking in their direction. They whispered to one another when they saw Time and Iris, and smiled. Time smiled back; Iris studied the girls as they drew abreast and her eyes followed them as they passed.

"Stop kidding," Iris said.

"I only have my mother at home," he said. "Home is the furthest thing from my mind. That reminds me: I wish you'd stop showing pictures of your niece around when you get them. You shake everybody up. Slim's talking about going home."

"Slim's always talking about going home."

"Yeah, but he's talking more about it lately."

Iris stood. "Thanks for the tour."

"My pleasure."

"Didn't think those Indonesian chicks would let you out of sight long enough for you to get some culture."

"Ha, ha."

"Ha, ha, hell." She glanced meaningfully at him. He shot her a glance, dropped his eyes to her body. "S'long, baby."

75

"Like that?"

"Now," he said, "you stop kidding."

She turned, smiling, and picked her way over the cobblestones. He would be taking a new look, she thought, at her backside.

Nine months later she received the letter. She stared at the postmark; it wasn't from California, it was from home, but it was in Sissie's handwriting. Have they returned East? Iris wondered. She opened it and scanned the bold scrawl.

Dear Iris,

Surprised? This is a sad day. I'm here to bury Robbie next to Juanita and Mary Ellen. Oh, I knew about it three months ago, I just didn't want to upset you. I asked for him and they sent him to Los Angeles and then across country. I rode with him all the way and now he's with them, where I think maybe we all should go. Ralph wanted to come, but I told him no. Wouldn't even let Oliver come. I called your father and we went together. Seems like that cemetery's got half of us already, but I know the Lord is working His will.

Suppose now that Robbie's gone I can tell you. Told Ralph already. Maybe you knew it though, that Robbie was my favorite. Don't be mad now. All mothers got a favorite. And I was rooting so hard for him after you and Harry messed up and then Ralph and April. Seems like nothing was going right, but I knew it was God's will. A hard one, but His all the same. You know Robbie wanted to be a doctor and how bright he was in school. Don't seem fair. Not for me or the family, for the Government to take all the colored boys and send them out to be killed and not let them have any rights. God will have His vengeance. Thinking about moving back East. Don't know. All the folks are still the same Willa Mae and Louise and Edward. Ain't changed a bit. Shiftless. I suppose I should be grateful that Ralph wasn't killed

*too. And I am, Lord knows I am, but Robbie was my heart. You
and Ralph was scrambling to get out of the way of Juanita and
Mary Ellen. Robbie was the last. Lord, I wanted this family to be
a great strong tree, like some of those oaks on your grampa's place.
But something is eating that tree from the leaves and branches
right down to the roots. And I just left another branch in the
ground. God willing, see you before much longer? Going back
to Cal tonight. Wanted you to know, and don't grieve, child. Get
right with God then you can take anything.*

Mother.

Iris could only think of Robbie in the postures of dancing
to "After Hours," tall, thin, crouched over whispering in
some girl's ear. Or him looking at her, his eyes brighter and
more hopeful than they had a right to be. Bold, beholding
limitless faith in himself. Sissie had given him that, that seem-
ing careless ability to stride through the world.

She thought of him but could not cry. How unfair, she
continued thinking, that once here you expected the process
of living to carry you with a certain degree of casualness to
an ultimate end.

God's will. She wanted to curse, but could not. Poor
Mother, she thought. Poor tree being eaten leaf by leaf,
branch by branch, down the trunk and into the very root.

Robbie gone. One less face to smile up at her when she
returned home, and perhaps by the time she got there, there
would be another missing and another, but that was, as
Sissie said, Iris thought with a bitter smile, God's will. . . .

The months continued to pass and too quickly became
years. Time and Iris, though drawn to each other, achieved
no strong relationship, as though each knew it was not yet
the proper time for that. The influx of American Negroes

77

had become a steady trickle. The club circuit grew from a dozen cities to twice as many.

Jax was the first to return home and was replaced by Leonard, a thin, reserved young man with a leaning toward the classics; he was in fact a better cellist than a bassist. Iris liked the classical touch. Slim, always on the point of going home, finally booked passage and told Time at the end of a rehearsal.

"Man, what's wrong with you?" Time asked, upset.

"Nothing."

"What're you going back for?"

"I just want to go home, man. Why we have to argue about that?" Slim and Time were good friends.

"You want to go home to get kicked in the ass? They beg you to come back? They tell you, 'Slim we need you'?"

"Time, let's not argue. I'm going."

"You're a goddamn fool!" Time said sharply.

"Easy, Time," Slim warned. He was slow to anger.

Time didn't leave off goading him. "Cats getting their black asses out of there as fast as they can get coins and here you're trying to get back in."

"Oh, man, go 'head," Slim said, turning away.

"Damn, Slim." The anger had suddenly left Time's voice. "That ain't no place for us. We're musicians—artists. We got to be free."

"Lookit Bird and JJ. They're doing all right."

Time scoffed. "You sure ain't Bird and you ain't JJ. If you took the time to listen you could hear the hurt in their music."

"Well, the troubles 're in my music." Slim was slipping on his jacket.

"You're a fool."

"Maybe," Slim said with patience, "but how come you like to look at ships too? You ain't shuckin' me none."

Time took a deep breath. He had met Slim in a Frankfort bar; they had been discharged the same day and had been together since. "Man, don't go."

"Melvin, I got to go."

Time nodded. He placed his hands in his pockets. "Okay, baby, if that's the way it is." He turned and, snatching his jacket, walked out. Iris went after him.

"What the hell are you following me for, Homefolks?" he asked without turning.

"I'm not. You're just going my way."

"Well, come the hell up beside me and walk like you got sense."

"Okay."

"He's a fool."

"Yes."

"I'm a fool for wanting him to stay when he said he's gotta go."

"Yes."

He glanced at her. "And you're a fool."

"Yes."

"What'd you have, 'yes' for breakfast?"

"Yes."

"To hell with him. I'm never going home. Raggedy-assed States. I suppose you'll be going soon too?"

"Not right away."

He stopped quickly. Iris had already moved on a pace. "You're working, Homefolks. You're cookin'. Been getting some nice write-ups. I think we'll be playing behind you soon." He paused. "That's what you want, isn't it?"

"Yes," she said.

"That's what I thought." They started walking again. "Pretty soon it'll be Iris Stapleton in big letters. C'mon," he said swerving off into a bistro, "let's drink on it."

When Slim left, Time dropped the horn altogether. Chubby left next, to eventually return home after his new American wife finished her tour of Europe, Africa and the world. Isabel, Chubby's wife, was fifty, had unlimited sums of money and was so tanned that she looked like papyrus that had lain too long in the sun. Crinkly. Bobby, the new drummer, was young too, and had been eager to leave a mixed Parisian group and go with an American Negro combo.

Iris could not know as she stood shimmering in her cones of light from Birmingham to Berlin, Copenhagen to Capri, Bordeaux to Berlin, which of the Africans or Arabs were igniting the torches of nationalism in their homes. When she and Time listened to them they exuded the sense that all of Europe had died and only Africa, her deserts and savannas and mountains and jungles lived and would be free of the French and the British. They bellowed it out in the club cellars and from the various colleges and quarters to which they had been assigned *de facto*. But they cried, Iris and Time always noticed with amusement, in better French than the French and in better English than the British. And when they cried, one arm raised to pound against the sky, the other arm lay softly upon the shoulder of a colonial daughter.

"How mad!" Iris said.

Time shrugged.

They were in Rue Biscornet and it was dusk. All evening they had been rather silent, their laughter forced. At times their hands had touched and bounded away as though they were brown squirrels. When their legs had touched under the table there had been an instant's shock and then a casual drawing away, an averted gaze, a sudden, too sudden animation. They had raved about the dinner, though it hadn't been special, and about the wine, which had been worse, and had spent too much time discussing the arak served by the Arabian restaurant. And they both drank too quickly and too much, so that Time occasionally bellowed, "Hail, Jomo Kenyatta!" at which point the Arabs turned and smiled and the two or three Africans, who looked, Iris had observed, like the British version of the Mau Mau, turned, nodded, smiled and sipped their milky liquids in a toast.

And so, walking along slowly, their bodies loose and listless Time said, "Girl, why don't you stop messing with me?"

"What?" Iris said, and then walked on at a more rapid pace, but he caught up and pulled her back by her shoulder. She stopped and leaned backward. "I'm not messing with you," she said. "You're messing with me."

They stood motionless, he straight, she leaning against him, faces pointed in the same direction. Iris looked up at the sky, the stars; Time looked at her neck. He said, "I'm not messing with you. . . ."

"You're very high, aren't you?"

Time said, "You're looking damned good tonight."

Still motionless she said, "Lookin' pretty good yourself, boss."

Now they began to walk again; she watched him but he wouldn't look at her until they arrived at the hotel. Standing at the door of her room he said, "Okay, let's stop messing with each other. See you tomorrow." He turned and climbed the stairs to the second floor where Bobby and Leonard also had their rooms.

Iris sat a long time in her slip. When the phone rang she accepted an invitation to go out with the editor of *Le Jazz Revue Hot*; it would help her publicity, she told herself as she dressed. When she was ready and standing at the mirror, letting the editor wait in the lobby, she told herself over and over again, Goddamn right I'm looking mighty good tonight. She slammed her door hard when she went out; she was sure the noise could be heard even on the second floor.

Iris was fond of Stockholm and always hated to leave it, but they had to that evening after closing at the Koncerthus. But at the moment they sat in the Stallmastergarden, working their way through the smörgåsbord lunch. She was already on the meat course and paused to stare around at the pools and the gardens. Several faces looked familiar; they might have been the same jazz-loving faces or the expatriate faces that she had seen all over Europe, rising up out of the darkness like the white bellies of fish.

She felt a curious impatience; why was she no further along than she was? How long did it take to become—*what?* A star. She was a star, but she meant a bigger one; big enough to cause a tight fit to the image she'd already formed for herself.

"What're you thinking, Homefolks?" Time asked. In the past months he had devised a way of turning his face toward her when he spoke, but without really looking at her. She noticed this again.

"Nothing," she said, and then she noticed that he looked

at her, really looked at her, briefly to be sure, but for the first time in months.

When they finished at the Koncerthus they moved overland to Göteborg to play the Green Hat. The third day there Time called a meeting; he had received a telegram from Stockholm. Iris sat beside him on his bed; business meetings were always neutral things. Leonard and Bobby sat opposite in chairs. The long, long hours of daylight and the still too bright night had left them tired, but they knew something of importance had happened even before the waiter pushed open the door to bring in the champagne.

"We go back to Stockholm," Time said, "when we finish this gig."

They waited politely until the waiter had poured the wine.

"Man," Leonard said when the waiter had withdrawn, "we aren't drinking champagne for Tivoli, are we?"

"No, Berns." He looked at Iris. "Josephine Baker is closing. Patachou was there before her."

Bobby and Leonard were also looking at Iris, who dropped her eyes and remained rigid. Iris wanted to bounce to her feet and scream with joy. She already saw herself standing before the couple of thousand people Berns held. And, at last, she was close enough behind Baker to be compared to her and to be proved better or different, at least. Baker was an institution; Iris raising her eyes and smiling a little, knew that she could only be different.

"Yeh, baby," Bobby was saying to Time, "but how's about the bread?"

Time emptied his glass, poured another. "Great."

"Nice," Leonard said, rising. "I don't much give a damn if I never leave Sweden. These broads are too fine.

83

"That all?" Bobby asked. He stood too.

"Yeah. We'll have to work out some new stuff. Later."

Bobby and Leonard went out.

"The Swedes like you, Homefolks. This gig at Berns should make you. I've got some ideas about your songs."

"Do they really like me?"

"Listen, Berns wouldn't pay the bread they're paying unless they did." He hesitated. "Everybody likes you." He looked at her. She was staring into the space across the room.

She said, "Time?"

"Yes?"

"Is this what we've been waiting for?"

He didn't speak; he refilled her glass.

"Hold me," she said. "I feel so good."

"What do I want to hold you for?" He finished his drink in a gulp.

"Can't you ever stop being wise?"

They studied each other. Time rose, and as he pushed the serving cart outside and locked the door, he said, without looking at her, "Iris, you're going to mess over me; you're going to shake me up." Now he returned. "But I'm through messing around."

"It's you who's going to hurt me," Iris said. She wasn't sure that she meant it, but his words rang softly inside her. "But hold me anyway."

She waited in the wings and snapped her fingers. Bobby flashed a smile at her. The warming up was Time's idea. Let the trio work out for three numbers, loosen up; they'd be ready when Iris came on, just in time to change the pace.

Applause sounded on Time's dying chord. A tuxedoed announcer strode out, addressed the audience in Swedish. Iris swept out on stage with what Time later described as a cool majesty.

"Do it, baby!" Time whispered as she went by, gown rustling. It was in the air that night; whatever magic show people look for. The clapping died away. Iris dropped her eyes, inclined her head forward ever so slightly, and when she raised it, right on cue, Time began the intro to "Lover Man." Iris waited, raising her eyes outward to the farthermost reaches of the house, taking in the splotches of white faces fuzzy against the darkness; they were like dulled silver trophies fastened to a wall. She listened to Time and knew that he felt it too; they all did. God, he's wailing, she thought with a smile. When she began to sing she recalled the tradition which she had never considered before: the tradition of Bessie, Dinah, Lena, Jo and Ella.

"Work, baby!" Time whispered. "Work!"

She sang beyond them, far past their upturned, blurred faces; she sang out there and delighted in the tremolo which crept into her voice in the low registers as though it had been there always awaiting a summons. And then, softly pursuing the ending, she was aware of her posture, as though standing before a mirror and being pleased with herself. She wove through *"where can you beee. . . ."* her voice dying at the uttering of each word. She drew a deep breath and felt her breasts rise slightly, straining against the new fitted gown. The applause began, expanded and went on and on. Out there in the dark, people were standing beside their tables calling to her.

"Thank you. Thank you," she said into the mike, feigning breathlessness. She turned to Time, who sat erect, a wide grin on his face.

"Man," Leonard said, "listen to *them* cats, will you?"

The applause continued, but Time had begun to play again. The house became quiet.

"My ship has sails that are made of silk...." She sang. Iris knew when she had finished that this number had gone over even better than the first.

Later when it was all over and Time, his arm around her waist, walked with her down the carpeted hall to their room, neither speaking, she knew that through him she had made it. That they had made it.

It was as if she had all her life rehearsed being a success. She stepped gracefully, commandingly into it without a conscious change of pace, pausing only occasionally to wonder with some amusement what Sissie would think of the suites she demanded and into which she allowed Time. As the years passed, she began to feel irritation at the free-swinging way he came and went. What would Sissie think, she wondered, of the brocaded cloths and the long perspectives of silver; the porcelain and Dresden and bone china? What would she think of the maids and the butlers, the tailored suits and the closets filled with shoes, of the bowing and scraping—that's what Sissie called it when people went out of their way to be nice to you just because you were important—which went on wherever Iris went? Sometimes on the beaches—Algarve, Monte Carlo, Rapallo, Costa Brava—it all seemed to Iris a betrayal of her past. Time, suspecting her mood, would ask, "What bag you working out of, baby?"—

or a penny for your thoughts. She would smile. "What bag am I working out of?" And relapse into silence.

They flew more often as the schedule became heavier. To the same clubs to perform before the same audiences. The same people asked for the same songs. Everything was the same. Except Time; he was always looking for the new, discovering new numbers, talking to strangers. Iris wondered why he would stay constant to her. Why do I let him upset me? she asked herself. But why do I feel cut off when he's with me? God, she thought, don't let him ask me to marry him.

Ralph and April had been divorced; the thought of them recurred to Iris constantly. What was he doing in New York? Why didn't he ever write what he was doing?

She sat down that day and wrote to Ralph.

There was a point at which boredom set in, and more than that, anxiety. There were constant rehearsals. Iris and Time fought more often. The week-long stands continued with their two, three performances a day.

It took five years for it to get to Iris. Suddenly, at Monte Carlo, angry tired and bored, she told Time to cancel out for the next three months. She saw in Leonard's and Bobby's eyes, and even Time's, a silent contempt; they think that I've become a prima donna, she thought. "Suddeny I've become exhausted," she said.

"No, nothing ever happens too suddenly if you're colored," Time answered sadly.

"All I know is I'm tired. I've got to rest."

Bobby and Leonard returned to Paris and Iris and Time went to Castelldefels, within easy reach of Barcelona. Here near the sea that she loved she was able to rest. She took long walks along the coast; sometimes with her maid Beatrice, or with Time. The mountains loomed in the background. It was off-season and so they were alone. Afternoons they sat on the *balcón*, reading and talking or just listening to the ocean licking across the beach. Time allowed no music except for the radio; he even did without his piano.

Mornings began with the sound of Beatrice working in the kitchen: soon after the pop of the milkman's scooter echoed among the pine groves. No sooner were they at breakfast than they saw through the window the one-armed postman coming down the street on his ancient bicycle. The postman was a veteran of the war; they paid him a peseta for each piece of mail he brought. The important mail they picked up in town, for outside the larger cities of Spain mail was treated as casually as everything else.

"*Mañana* my ass," Time muttered from day to day.

During the siesta they invariably wound up in bed, talking, smoking, resting and once more making love.

Time was fascinated by the bullfights, particularly the matadors. "We could make a fortune if we only had a colored bullfighter to manage—*El Matador Negro*—we'd be working out of some bag, Homefolks!"

A letter came from Ralph saying he was thinking of traveling; if he did he would look her up.

One day they were sitting on the *balcón*, watching the mountains change color. Above them the clouds lay in soft whorls, the sea misted. The shadows of the pines grew longer and in the sunken garden surrounding the house the insects became quiet. Iris sensed that Time was thinking, thinking that she would certainly say yes. She turned to him, seeing the dying sun glisten on his bald head. She was suddenly aware of how swiftly the years had passed. He had had some hair when she had first met him.

"Time," she said.

"Yes, baby?"

"I don't want to get married yet."

"Why not?"

"Because I haven't made it all the way."

"Oh, I see! What way are you going?" he said sarcastically.

The two great German shepherds that lived in the house down the road began barking.

Time stared at the mountains. "I knew it. I knew it a long time ago. Listen, I wanted to marry you and maybe even go back home. It's something I always looked forward to. I never wanted to be an old jazzman dropping dead from a heart attack. But goddamn, Homefolks, why would you do this to me?"

"I'm sorry. I've thought about it for a long time."

"You've thought about yourself. You had that when I first saw you."

She said, "Time, I do love you—"

"I know all about *that* kind of love."

"Why can't we go on like this?" she asked.

"I wanted more," he said.

"There's only the difference of a piece of paper."

He looked directly at her. "That's the difference I wanted."

She could only say, "And I don't. At least not now."

"When, then?" he asked, his voice low and filled with humiliation.

The tears came. "I don't know. I can't tell you because I just don't know!"

"Beatrice is waiting," Time said.

The applause was dry and hesitant, then burst into a sustained explosion. Iris sat realizing that Ralph had made it, and on his own terms, here in America. Her hands hurt from clapping. The entire play had had the kind of symmetry she would have known instantly as Ralph's.

"Like it?" Eve asked gently.

Iris nodded. Her eyes were wet. Where had it come from, she wondered. Why had she been unable to see this talent in Ralph? How much had April and Eve to do with it? Adela? The one who sent him the money? And Sissie and Dad, had they contributed anything?"

"I want to call him," Iris said nervously. "I wish I could have been here opening night. And I wish he could have been in Stockholm the night I got lucky." Iris paused. "Most of it's luck." She hoped she didn't sound jealous.

"He tried so hard to get Sissie and Oliver to come," Eve said. "He took it pretty badly."

"I can hear Mother now: 'Come all that way for a little ol' play?' Didn't she say something like that?" Iris lifted her coat; they were standing now, waiting to get into the aisle. "They never seem to understand," she said. "Or maybe they are afraid."

Eve didn't speak.

"A drink after I make the call?" Iris asked.

"All right," Eve said.

But Iris was already shoving and squeezing through the crowds, anxious to get to the phone booths.

PART

॥

|7

"I'M SO PROUD, RALPH, SO PROUD," Iris said into the telephone.

"Thank you, baby."

"Any word from California?"

"Not a word."

"See you later."

Ralph hung up and lingered a moment at the window. He turned up the volume on the radio, and then he thought of Iris as he had created her in his play and of her in the audience, watching. The play had cost him a lot; how much he was only beginning to know.

He had had one dollar, two escudos and ten pesetas when his ship had docked two years ago in New York. He had also had a single slug. When he had finished in customs he walked out of the buzzing pier building, past the porters, through the line of yellow cabs hurtling in from the avenue between the steel beams of the West Side Highway, to a phone booth across the street. He placed his knapsacks on the ground, took out the dime-sized slug whose hole he'd covered with Scotch tape and called Sherry. When he finished the call, he picked up his sacks, walked to the corner and lit a cigarette.

He stared across the avenue at the ship. Tomorrow it would be gone. Ralph wondered how long it would be before he would leave the States again. He was suddenly weary as all the sounds of the city began to assail him. Then came the final whistle of a liner about to depart; impatiently he turned, looking for a cab. There were none.

He had thought much about Sherry the last three days. He hadn't wanted things to work out as they had, cabling her for money from Venice and later from Côte d'Azur and Barcelona. But they had and what the hell.

A helluva way to come back, he mused. Unmet, penniless. No crowds, no limousines, and the same harsh West Side façade of the city. He thought about Sherry again, and knew then that she knew him better than he knew himself, the bitch. A cab approached, slowed and swerved to the curb.

"Hello, Ralph," Sherry said, standing beside the cab, holding the door open.

"Sherry," he said, and he started to smile, and then he was upon her, kissing her. When they stepped apart she looked at him strangely.

In the cab she said, "Are you so glad to see me?"

"Yes," he said, taking her hand. He was surprised that he was not lying.

"I stayed home yesterday and today, of course, to straighten the place up. It's been a mess since you left."

"Has it?" She was telling her version of the truth. Sherry was an orderly woman.

She turned to him. "Ralph, I missed you *so* much."

"And I missed you."

When they pulled up before Sherry's Village apartment, Ralph busied himself with his bags until Sherry had paid the fare. Instinctively, Ralph looked at his hand to see if he'd remembered to place the wedding band on before he left the ship. He had, and now he noticed that Sherry was wearing hers too.

Graham, the doorman, approached to take the bag. "It's okay, Graham, I have it," Ralph told the doorman. The blue-uniformed Negro smiled.

"Have a nice trip?"

"Great."

"Good to see you back."

"Thanks."

Sherry had got the apartment when her white roommate married. Only occasionally, when new personnel from the renting agent came around was there some minor testing. Sherry stood her ground and became known as "the colored girl," or the "nice colored girl in number thirty-four in our number ten building." Then she got "married." Now the agent was hoping Sherry and her "husband" would move before they started having children. But all in all, from the agent's point of view, the Joplins were not bad people. Ralph, the agent understood, was a playwright and she was a social worker. Couldn't quibble with that too much. Anyway, not as long as the rent was paid and the parties weren't too wild.

"It feels strange," Ralph said as they rode up in the elevator. "You look," he said, "delicious."

"And you," she said, when they left the car, "look equally delectable. A little thinner, no?"

Ralph shrugged. "I don't know." He watched her walk into the apartment ahead of him. "And you look just as fine as you ever did," he said, sliding his bag across the floor and reaching for her, "maybe finer."

"*Did* you miss me?"

"The last three days," he said, pulling her across his lap, "were hell. I wanted to be here already. Before then, sometimes I was so busy looking . . . but I'd always run into things, landscapes, and I'd think, Man this would knock ol' Sherry out."

Sherry smiled. "I wondered if you thought often of me."

"You have my letters."

"Yes, but I didn't know if they were the being-kind type of letters or not."

"Did they sound like it?"

"No." She pressed her lips against his neck. He waited. "It's always been hard to tell with you," she said.

He had spent a lot of time writing the letters. There was so much to see and do that he early found it hopeless to sit down and work on the plays. All of his creative effort went into the letters he sent to her. He shook her; she had settled dreamily in his lap. "Let's go for a walk," he said.

"Dinner's ready," she answered. "I know it's too early, but I thought you might want a good, home-cooked meal."

"And so I do, but we just finished lunch. Early, before we came in."

"Ralph?"

"Yes, Sherry?"

"Are you restless so soon?"

He rose and walked to the window. The Women's House of Detention was across the street. It looked like an apartment building; you didn't notice the bars until you started looking upwards. He pushed the curtains back in place and stood looking at Sherry. The fan hummed, for though it was late in the fall, Indian summer had come.

"Yes," he said. "I am restless already."

"I make you restless," she said.

"I make myself restless."

"That too."

"Anxious to get back to work." He glanced at her. "Nothing, I suppose from Anna?" Anna was his agent.

"No. I'd have let you know right off."

"Sure."

"Have you changed?"

"Me? No."

Sherry rose. "Watch out, New York. Ralph's back. He'll cultivate you and use you and grind you underfoot."

"Oh, drop it."

"Does it surprise you that I know?"

"No."

"I haven't done wrong?"

"No. Maybe you've been more honest than me."

She shrugged. "You've been as honest as you can be. That's a family trait, isn't it, making mincemeat out of people?"

"Shut up."

"Sorry."

"I didn't write the rules."

"I know. I understand."

"C'mon, don't give me that superior, black middle-class pity."

"That was supposed to be understanding."

"Somehow, when it comes from you it sounds like pity."

"That's because my mother was fair and my father a doctor. Don't you remember? Did you forget to say that?"

"I didn't want to say it."

She pretended surprise. "You have changed."

He stepped toward her and held her by the arms. "I didn't want to fight with you the first day back; I didn't want to fight with you ever again, but since you want to lay cards on the table—*could* I take advantage of you if you didn't want me to? Aren't you trying to justify your behavior, your taking me back? I mean, baby, you transfer the blame from yourself to me, and I suppose it'll be all right in a few minutes, but those 're the cards."

"I hate your ass," she said, trying to twist away from him.

"Look," he said, feeling very safe because what he was going to say seemed a long way off. "I need to know that you and I can make it, that we can go from here to maybe something better."

"Maybe! Maybe! *Maybe!*" she said her eyes bright with both hope and anger.

"My whole life is maybe. What do you want from me?"

"Ralph, I hate you. *God*, I hate you."

He struck her. Startled, he stared at her, wanting to touch her, but knowing by the look on her face that he shouldn't. "Pull yourself together," he said. He left the apartment. He took the stairs down two at a time. At the street he hurried to Sheridan Square and sat down on one of the half-empty benches.

He wished he hadn't come back. A silly wish; he had to come back. Why had it all gone wrong? Why? Because he had crawled back under that masculine guise used in the phone booth ("Baby, pick me up at Twelfth Avenue and Forty-sixth Street. Just back. Hurry.") when there was nothing, not a goddamn thing under it? A man made his own way. He thought of the clinic. He would get into one in a hurry; a big hurry.

Sherry walked into the park from the Seventh Avenue side. She had put on slacks and she wore white sneakers. Her eyes were sad, and she was pouting. She sat down beside him and dug for her cigarettes; he held a light.

"Did I hurt you?"

"You," she said, puffing at her cigarette, "always manage to hurt me. Listen," she said, pulling out sun glasses and putting them on, "Ralph, do you think we could make it? Maybe?"

He didn't look at her. "What do you think, baby?"

"It's never been all up to me. Not once."

He said softly, "I think it's always been up to you. Now, if you want me to answer the question . . ." His mind leaped and buzzed with image crowding on image: City Hall and maybe a honeymoon (borrow a cottage from a friend who owned one in East Hampton) making it up with Sherry's folks (tolerating her father who drank too much and yapped about the Omega Psi Phis) her readmission to her society of balls, benefits, comings-out, dances; her ever-diminishing interest in the things that mattered to him (there had already

99

been her refusal to go to Europe with him) his work, and finally the unvoiced demands upon all of his time, taking him from his work even though she would want him somehow to keep it because *successful* artists, even street niggers like himself, became in-group noble savages; there would be children and they'd be set in her crown of womanhood as little jewels, proof to the world (but mostly to herself) that she'd been capable of motherhood. Children being what they were, *poof!* what little time there was left, *gone!*

Well? Wasn't it time to indicate some form of payment for food, shelter and some clothing and, yes, some affection at times when it counted? He looked at her and knew that he'd never been involved with a woman unless he loved her for some thing in some way. "Yes," he said. "I think we could make it."

Nervously she said, "Let's say something definite—"

A quick retort sprang to Ralph's lips, but dribbled away unspoken when she said, "Like when your play is produced, all right?" She gave him a little smile and he stared at the ground, at the faded shuffleboard lines.

He thought, What an ass I am. She doesn't want it anymore than I do! Why the damned play is still under option and it'll take rewriting and two or three new producers, if then, and she *knows* it. I've told her. We are where we were. This nebulous arrangement is no arrangement. We both remain unshackled; there are no chains. Thank God! And I— *I* was going to make the big sacrifice of my life. . . . "It's a deal, baby," he said.

She embraced him happily; she kissed him and began to chatter, *like someone in love,* Ralph thought, just like someone who's supposed to be in love. Looking at her face on the way home, he saw an intense distant look about it, and on the elevator he wondered whether or not he should mention the possibility of her going to a clinic too. He decided against it as they prepared for bed to celebrate; he was going to have enough to take care of himself in the months ahead.

Even with "inside contact" Ralph expected to be turned away from the doors of Osgood, Overstreet and Edwards, Advertising, Inc., but he wasn't. He reported to the research department and began work as a hand-tabber. The hand tabulating section was made up of artists—actors, painters, writers, singers—who were at the moment out of work. Here all personnel were temporary. Management never complained of the frequent goings and comings of the "workers" off to auditions and meetings with agents.

The very first day at lunch the only other Negro working there introduced himself to Ralph. "I'm Barney Moore," he said. He was a small, agile man who walked as though he were a heavyweight.

"Ralph Joplin."

"It's lunchtime. I'll show you a spot. These damned Schrafft carts are too expensive and the chow isn't much."

"You a writer?" Barney asked.

"Yeah," Ralph said without looking up from his food. Sherry was having one of her fits; she hadn't fixed breakfast coffee. "You?"

"I try."

"What?"

"Novels."

"Plays," Ralph said. "Published?"

"Short stuff. You?"

"Nothing."

"Rough," Barney said.

"Yeah."

"Well, the agency'll keep you in a little bread; I mean a buck and a half an hour in these times isn't much. Holds you together. And the people in our section aren't bad. Everyone's scuffling."

"It's pretty boring work," Ralph said.

"Don't worry about it. You'll get used to it. You get in about nine-fifteen, nine-twenty, and grab coffee and cake from the cart. By the time you've finished it's approaching ten. Go to the john about eleven. Sit there, smoke. Come out, it's eleven-twenty. Take late lunch, about one or one-thirty. An hour. Three or three-thirty they send out for coffee or tea. You nuts with that for a half hour or so and already it's four or four-thirty. You start clearing your desk—slowly—about ten to five—and that's your day. Somehow you manage to get some work done too." Barney lit a cigar. "Then you hustle home and go to work." He shook out the match. "Married?"

"No."

"That's a break."

Ralph grinned and thought, this guy sounds just like me.

"What's funny?"

Ralph shook his head. "Just a thought I had."

"I guess we'd better get back," Barney said, glancing at his watch. "Ready?"

Ralph learned that Barney was twenty-eight, lived in the Village, and drank heavily. Each assured the other that they'd have to get together for a good talk.

As the weeks passed Ralph became accustomed to OOE. The agency was located on Madison Avenue, in a dull-red-brick building. Sometimes when he worked late and passed the rows of cleaned desks, it seemed to Ralph that the next morning would bring an entirely new group of automation assistants and they too would fill the desks with Kotex, Tampax, Kleenex; red, blue, green and brown pencils; paper clips and the day's papers and the current pocket-sized best-sellers.

In his fifth month, as the end of winter approached, Ralph was transferred to a new job in the same section. The transfer occurred the week he had his first appointment with the psychiatric social worker at Riverside Clinic. This contact was a part of the clinic's screening process. Ralph was not sure they'd accept his case.

He was now working with the radio-television section of the research department, in Test Audience. Test Audiences were selected daily from the Manhattan, Bronx, Queens, Brooklyn and Richmond telephone directories. Ralph listed every other name and address up to fifty or seventy-five people, then gave the list to a typist who addressed the same number of envelopes. Dated tickets and form letters were enclosed. Three times a week Ralph worked late. Audience members usually showed up in full strength unless the weather was bad; the form letters had promised an "inside view" of television and most attendees felt honored.

Once inside the auditorium the audience was given a book-let to check its reaction to the commercials and to write answers to a variety of carefully compiled questions. Many members of the audience had come expecting something more than this, but few complained. At the end of the showing of the commercials, the booklets were taken up and souvenirs were distributed. The following morning Ralph would go over the questionnaires.

At home, Sherry's period was late as usual and as usual she vacillated between abortion and marriage. As he did every month, Ralph waited and tried to ignore her dire predictions of pregnancy. But this time she accused him of planning to desert her if she were pregnant.

"Sherry, dammit, I'm trying to work." He glared at her. "You *see* me trying to work."

"I looked for your shirts, where are they? Tell me that, if you aren't planning to leave."

Ralph turned back to the typewriter. It was ten-thirty and he'd just got in from a Test Audience. "In the laundry," he said.

"Show me the slip, show it to me!"

His voice trembled. "Bring my wallet."

She brought it and started to open it. He snatched it from her. "Don't *ever* open my wallet!"

"Why?"

"Because," he said, fishing out the receipt, "it's the only private thing I have and you keep your goddamn hands off it unless I ask you for it, and when I do, leave it *closed!*"

She looked at the slip and tossed it back on the table. "What about your bag?"

"What damned bag?"

"Your *suit*case."

He took a deep breath. "That bag's been in the shop with a broken handle ever since I came back. You took it there your*self!*"

"I don't care. I'm going to have my belly all puffed out

104

and I know you're going to leave me, and I'll have to tell the child it has no father and—"

Deliberately he turned back to the typewriter a second time and began pecking at the keys. He stopped once to say, "Will you be quiet and go to bed? *Please?*"

"I'll go," she said, "but I'm going to leave the door open so I can watch you. I don't want you slipping out of here."

"Baby, go to bed."

The next day the psychiatric social worker called Ralph on the job. An appointment had been made with the psychologist, and after evaluation, analysis might begin.

The following day Sherry got her period.

And the day before his appointment with the psychologist Ralph moved out.

8

THE PSYCHOLOGIST WAS A HUGE LUMPY MAN. His face was too pale and had a perpetual film of sweat upon it. He had cold eyes. "Come in," he said, moving back from the door. His voice matched his appearance: dry, quick, toneless. Ralph reacted more from the situation than from the words of the man.

When they were seated, the psychologist picked up some papers and looked across the desk at Ralph. "I'll explain this to you. This series of tests will take three hours. I'll time you for each segment of the series. Now. At the start of each segment I'll give you instructions. If when I've finished them, you don't understand, tell me and I'll give them to you again. Is that clear? When you indicate that you've understood,

I'll say 'Start' "—he held up a timer's watch just then, like a pitchman, Ralph thought—"and then you begin. Clear?"

"Clear," Ralph said.

"Let's begin with word association," the psychologist said. "I will call out a word and you will answer it with the first word that comes into your mind. Understand?"

"Yes." Ralph tensed.

In a second the warm, half-shadowed room was filled with staccato exchange of words.

"Mother," the psychologist said.

"Father," Ralph answered.

"Man."

"Woman."

An hour passed. Ralph's body ached. He began to sweat.

"People," the psychologist said.

Ralph said, "Fight." He saw the psychologist's eyes flicker. The heavy hand, holding the pencil, did not check; it scribbled.

"Fear."

Ralph hesitated and then said, "Rats," and as soon as he said the word he knew there was something odd about having said it, something he did not understand. He answered the next words automatically, still thinking back to "Rats."

"Masturbation."

Ralph groped. "Sleep," he said.

Later when "Fight" was mentioned Ralph anwered "People," and again was disturbed by the strange association.

While continuing to lean forward in his chair, the psychologist put aside one of the papers. "Why did you answer 'People' with 'Fight' and 'Fight' with 'People'?"

"People fight," Ralph said. He watched the man scribble.

"And 'Fear' with 'Rats'?"

"I don't know why." But then Ralph began to explain. "One morning when I was a kid, I woke up and looked at my sister—"

"You shared the same room?"

"Yes."

"How old were you?"

"Ten and seven."

"Go on."

"A rat was eating her."

The man waited.

"The side of her face," Ralph said.

"Now the next test," the psychologist said. His voice was still dry, his eyes cold, and Ralph was angry that he had had to explain to this man.

"I hesitated for another word," Ralph said.

"I know it. Let's get on, shall we?"

Another hour had passed. Ralph stared intently at the cards passed to him one at a time by the psychologist. "What do you see in that one?" His voice conveyed a sense of urgency, strain.

"Two servants. Their clothes are not very good. Torn, in shreds. They're on their knees."

The psychologist scribbled, took the card and handed Ralph another. "And this?" Ralph took the card and turned it slowly around. He tilted his head. What he had perceived upon first looking at the card remained.

"Yes?"

"They are"—Ralph said, slowly, hating the sound of his words,—"caricatures of—of guffawing Negroes. They're

grinning. Their heads are wrapped in rags or handkerchiefs or
—something. . . ." Ralph wiped the sweat on his forehead.
He frowned. The psychologist wrote. He took the card from
Ralph, glancing sharply at him. His eyes seemed softened.
"We're almost home," he said. "Take a break." He handed
his pack to Ralph. "Smoke?"

Ralph was exhausted when he concluded the tests with the
blocks and arithmetic segments. As he walked out, his shoulders sagging, his forehead and armpits wet with sweat, the
psychologist, writing hastily at his desk, said, "Good luck."

One week later Ralph had his first session with the psychiatrist assigned to him. The doctor's name was Bluman. He was
a short, broad-shouldered man in his fifties. He was bald and
his unusually translucent skin made his blue eyes seem even
more intense than they were.

There was no couch in the office. Ralph sat in the chair
beside the small oak desk. Dr. Bluman took the desk seat. He
pursed his bottom lip and the sharp lines which curved from
the edges of the nostrils down to his mouth tightened. "Well!"
he said, smiling at Ralph; he'd been well aware that his patient
had had him under scrutiny for the past thirty seconds. Dr.
Bluman said, "Suppose we get started, Mr. Joplin, hmmmm?"

Ralph smiled. The doctor noted: *The patient appeared
self-conscious at the beginning of the initial session. . . .*

"Freudian or Jungian, doctor?"

"Freudian."

"Can I ask what school?"

"Cornell and Columbia. Want the hospitals too, Mr. Joplin?"

"Is this irregular?"

Dr. Bluman shrugged and waited.

Ralph studied the stocky figure. "Ever play football, doctor?"

Bluman said, "No, tennis; but you've played football, haven't you, Mr. Joplin?"

"Yes."

"You've made your point, I think," Dr. Bluman said. "Can we get started now?"

"I feel a little awkward about this," Ralph said.

"Ummm, yes?" Bluman gave Ralph an interested, open look.

"I feel a little defeated too"—Ralph turned his eyes quickly toward the doctor.—"I mean, finding it necessary to come here."

"Why did you find it necessary?"

"Sounds corny, but—"

"What's that you say?"

Ralph coughed into his fist and shuffled his feet into a new position. "I said, it sounds corny."

"What do you mean, 'corny'?"

"What I'm going to say."

"You haven't said it."

"I intend to if—"

Bluman's eyes twinkled. He waited this time.

"I'm out of dreams. I'm not thirty-five and I'm not dreaming any more. I'm at a dead end—" He broke off, thinking with a sudden suspicion that even his speech patterns would be under analysis here.

"Dreams?"

"Confidence in myself."

"Oh. Then you don't mean dreams; you mean your confidence is gone."

"I guess so."

"Why is it gone?"

"Because I'm Negro." Ralph waited for a reaction; there was none.

The patient seemed to have given some thought to his problem, but may have evaded the real reason for it. . . .

"But I exist; I breathe and think, and I can do; I want to do. I want to live. I want everything that living means. I want to be useful. I want to look at people and not wonder when or with what foot they'll try to kick me in the tail." Ralph found himself looking down at his shoes as he said, "I want to be able to love."

The tiny clock on the desk ticked in the silence.

"I am a human being," Ralph said, still looking downward as if in casual meditation, "and therefore I am important, not only to myself, but to every other human in the world. I am due a chance at the life I conceived for myself if that conception is harmless to others. But there is a force, doc, which activates wherever I go, whenever I do anything or say anything. It says, no." Ralph raised his eyes to the doctor's, indicating that he had finished.

"I see," Bluman said.

"Do you?"

"I mean—you've stated what you think your problem is. . . . Why did you preface your remarks with 'it sounds corny'?"

"It seems unmanly to talk about these things; to me it does. The game seems to be that you pay for the privilege of getting a shot in the head, but you never squawk about it; you take it until you can't do it anymore. Then you start getting rid of yourself. Quietly, out of the way, in some place that's proper, like, for me, Bedford-Stuyvesant or Harlem, preferably with a police bullet or of an overdose of heroin. People feel better if you go that way, uncomplaining."

"Do you think you're unmanly, Mr. Joplin?"

"Hell no, just goddamn desperate."

The clock ticked on. A cold draft blew from beneath the closed window. Ralph turned to the window and watched the branches of the tree in the yard below sway menacingly.

The patient insists that the origin of his problem is racial. . . .

"Had you thought," Dr. Bluman asked, "that your problem is a result of your personality rather than your race?"

It was spring now. The office window was opened and the low afternoon sun appeared to lie on the sill. Work at OOE had run out and Ralph was working desperately, excitedly, on the last phases of the current rewrite of *Shadows;* the prospects of an actual purchase seemed imminent. Even Anna was excited; she had taken Ralph to lunch three times that week, and always, after the third Martini, she luxuriated in thoughts of a long run on Broadway and a movie. Her mood was contagious. The excitement helped Ralph get over the fact that he was unemployed. He had spent the night before drinking with Barney Moore; unemployment had finally brought them together. Barney had had a good nibble on his novel, and thus, when together, they talked with new assurance about many things.

Ralph's stomach rumbled; he was eating one big meal a day now. "My personality?" he echoed. "But doctor, the point is, isn't it, that my personality's been molded because of my race!" After the first month of therapy Ralph had called him "doc," but had quickly returned to the more formal "doctor" in order to re-establish the barrier Ralph wished between them.

"We're interested in the area of your personality," Dr. Bluman said. "Now why did you eat garlic in school?"

"So the teacher wouldn't keep me too long after school. It was only after school that I ate it."

"You were always sent home early?"

"Yes."

"With notes?"

"Yes."

"Did you destroy the notes?"

"No. I gave them to my mother."

"Your mother?"

"Yes."

"And your father?"

Irritated, Ralph said, "I told you, he'd gone by then."

"Oh, yes, that's right." *Patient showed signs of checking his temper when asked again about his father. . . .* "Well, what'd she do?"

"She raised hell."

"She spank you?"

"Once or twice she beat me."

"Beat you? Didn't she spank you? What do you mean, 'beat'?"

"We seldom were hit with her hand."

"What then?"

"Straps, boards, switches. . . ."

"All right. After she beat you, then what?"

"After a couple of times I guess she got tired. Looked disgusted."

"What'd you do to be made to stay after school anyway?"

"I don't remember; now it seems no more than anyone else."

"Using the garlic to get out of staying late—wasn't that a bit extreme? And didn't you suffer somewhat yourself?"

"Well, I got used to it. It didn't bother me and—"

"Mr. Joplin, consider: you took the garlic to school with you; you set up a chain of events in which you did something to make the teacher keep you, and when she did you ate the garlic and she sent you home with a note. To your mother. You weren't just carrying garlic around in your pocket every day, were you?"

"Dr. Bluman, you see—"

"I guess our time's up for this afternoon, Mr. Joplin. See you on Friday, same time."

Patient has moved from the general to the less general; he is discussing his family....

"It seemed that what I wanted to do was some sort of violation of family ethics; all I wanted to do was learn. I didn't know what the hell I was going to do with it. My teachers encouraged me; but at home, nothing."

"Your teachers were white?"

"Yes."

"All of them?"

"Yes."

"And they gave you the only encouragement you got?"

"Yes."

"Are you sure, Mr. Joplin?"

"Dr. Bluman, I'm quite, quite positive."

A pair of sparrows streaked past the windows; a soft, hot wind stabbed into the room and the bright green leaves of the elm tree rustled. "I can't pay the clinic this week," Ralph said. He looked down at his shoes.

"Oh," Dr. Bluman said. "Do you want me to pay the fee for you this week?"

"No!" Ralph shot straight up in his chair, staring.

"Wasn't that your thought, Mr. Joplin? If I pay your fee, encourage you, you'll go on to better things? I'm white, Mr. Joplin."

"That's not what I meant," Ralph said unsteadily. "Money's always been a problem for me. I have an obligation to pay for the services here and I can't. I want a solution, not charity. The thought just crossed my mind."

"Then why didn't you discuss it with the young woman in the office?" The doctor's eyes swept swiftly to the clock on the corner of his desk. "That's all for today."

Had that been his thought after all? Ralph wondered as he walked slowly to the clinic office. He had thought that he had down pat all the methods by which a problem comes to be stated through free association. In his mind he traced the conversation, checked the points in it where his direction had been specifically marked. But he refused to believe, even when he acknowledged the obvious path, that his thought had been to have Bluman pay for his hour.

The young woman Dr. Bluman had referred to was clearing her desk, but paused when Ralph entered. "Mr. Joplin?" she said with a smile. Then Ralph remembered seeing her in the office before.

"Hello," he said, and saw that she was waiting for him to speak. "Look, I can't pay for the visit today. And maybe not for the next one."

"Oh, that's all right," she said. "Pay when you can."

"Really?"

"Yes, didn't anyone tell you?"

Ralph straightened. "I suppose so. I just forgot about it. I'll keep account."

"That'll be fine, Mr. Joplin. Don't worry about it."

Ralph wondered if she had access to his files; if she had read them and what she was now thinking of him. "Were you leaving?" he asked.

"I'll say," she said, glancing at the tiny string of gold, her watch. "It's after five." She rose.

"I'm just going myself," he said, moving away, staring down into her eyes.

"Good, you can walk downstairs with me."

He stood aside to allow her to pass. He looked at her shoulders as she preceded him down the steps. On the walk outside, she stopped to smile goodbye.

"Which way do you go?" Ralph asked.

"I take the Seventh Avenue."

"Up or down?"

She hesitated. "Down."

"So do I. Let's go."

She hesitated again and glanced up at the building. "All right."

"What's your name anyway?" Ralph asked.

"Miss Cannady."

"I guess I'm not supposed to get the first one."

"No."

Ralph stopped. She walked on a few steps. When he had rejoined her he said, "Well, what is your first name?"

"Why do you want it?" she insisted.

"Oh, for Christ's sake. What's the big deal with your first name? To hell with you." He lengthened his stride, moved quickly away from her, but when he got to the corner he stopped and waited. "I'm sorry," he said. "Sometimes it's so damned hard to get to know people."

She gave him an arch look. "You've got yourself a temper, Mr. Joplin."

"Ralph," he said.

"I know."

"I thought you knew."

She blushed. "My name's Eve. We're not supposed to be involved in any way with the patients."

"Am I supposed to be violent or something?"

"I haven't read your chart. Are you?"

"No," he said.

"I'll look tomorrow." She looked at him. "No, I won't. I couldn't if I wanted to." He seemed relieved. "How's it going anyway?"

"I don't know yet."

They went down into the subway and sat in silence until the train got to Fifty-ninth Street. Eve rose. "This is where I get off," she said.

"Me, too," Ralph said; then, because her eyes showed that she didn't believe him, he said, "Honest. I change and take the D train here."

"Where do you live?" she asked, moving close to him as they made their way through the restless crush of people.

"Third Street," he said loudly, so she could hear him.

"Oh, no," she said.

He started to smile. "You live down there?"

"Yes!" she shouted. The A train had just come hurtling in.

117

"Where?" he asked, when they were in the passageway beneath the tracks.

"I've told you too much already. Listen you, I have a boy friend, anyway."

"Oh, yes?"

"An actor!" she shouted.

"Too bad!" Ralph shouted back.

She glanced at him quickly, and smiled. On the train, he said, "Have some coffee with me when we get off. Second Avenue, right?"

She nodded.

"Good," he said.

"No!" she said, terrified. "I meant I get off at Second Avenue too."

"Well, what about the coffee?"

"No. I have to rush and dress for Henri."

"Henri Catroux? That your boy friend?"

She nodded proudly.

"I got a thing for Catroux," Ralph said.

"What do you mean, 'thing'?"

"A play."

She looked at him carefully.

"What's wrong, am I dirty, or black or something?"

"No. Are you kidding?"

"No," Ralph protested with a smile.

"Henri's been looking for something with teeth in it."

After a pause, Ralph tapped her on the shoulder. "Isn't Catroux supposed to be in England finishing up something?"

With a sigh she said, "Yes."

"Did you have to lie?"

"Well, we are supposed to be going together."

"You don't sound too happy about it." He paused. She said nothing. "Now how about the coffee?"

"What's the big deal about coffee?" They both laughed. "It's really not the coffee."

"You should go to the clinic every day instead of only twice a week."

"I'm nuts?"

"You're nuts."

"And the coffee?"

"All right already with the coffee. Are you always so persistent?"

"Never before," he said as they got off the train, and started up the steps.

Patient indicates a willingness to explore his relations with siblings. . . .

"You went every Sunday?"

"Nearly every Sunday. Roller-skated. Once I took my sister Iris." He waited a moment before saying, "That Mary Ellen. She was sweet, happy. She liked me best of all. She'd laugh and crawl for me when I came home from school. It made me feel good. Looking back, that was a crazy thing for a kid to do at thirteen or fourteen, wasn't it?"

"You can't explain?"

"No."

"Come now, Mr. Joplin."

"I've tried!"

"Perhaps you didn't want to admit the truth to yourself, Mr. Joplin. This child—your sister Mary Ellen—you avoid using the word 'love.' Didn't you feel that she *loved* you?"

"Yes."

"Then why didn't you *say* it? And didn't you, perhaps for the very first time, find that you could love someone too? I think, while you know love is a good thing, you basically feel it's a weakness."

"No I don't."

"You still won't tell me why you roller-skated nearly five miles every Sunday to sit beside your baby sister's grave?"

"I don't know why!" *Patient expressed controlled anger again when pressed for an answer....*

Ralph stared past Dr. Bluman to the print of the neat schoolhouse on a green lawn. The picture was framed with polished black wood. "Could it have been that you wanted to join in death the little sister who loved you and whom you loved in return?"

Ralph was silent.

Dr. Bluman said quietly, "It's not uncommon, Mr. Joplin."

After a brief hesitation Ralph said, "Can we cut this one short, doctor?"

"Don't leave it," Dr. Bluman said. He had considered using "run"—*Don't run,* but a small goad would perhaps do more harm than good at the moment. *The patient's tendency to react angrily could make what was coming into focus recede.* "We might put the time left to good use, especially since this is the last session until fall."

"I've nothing more to say."

"You have. Why did you take your *other* sister, Iris, with you? You didn't go back to the cemetery after that Sunday you took her with you, did you?"

Ralph flashed a look at him; he thought, then said, "No."

"Why not?"

Ralph spoke haltingly. "Because I accepted the love she had

for me"—he looked up questioningly at the doctor's impassive face.—" and I transferred the love I had for Mary Ellen to her."

Dr. Bluman nodded.

"It was a good thing, wasn't it? Otherwise. . . ."

Now they sat in silence. Ralph smoked. His mind was unclear—turbulent. Dr. Bluman's eyes flicked to and from the clock. "Our time *is* up now. I suggest that you call the office if you want to continue in the fall. If you do, you can be fitted right in."

Without looking at him Ralph asked, "Will you be back, doctor?"

"Yes, I'll be back."

They shook hands and Ralph walked slowly into the first days of summer, everything in turmoil.

During the summer he thought of his sessions with Dr. Bluman infrequently but when he did, became fretful and anxious. Ralph sat in the almost unfurnished flat on Third Street working twelve hours a day. The sun poured in through the uncurtained windows. The noise on the street below never stopped.

Twice Sherry visited him and they fell upon one another hungrily. But somehow or other she always departed in a temper, and always she teased him about money.

He needed it. His unemployment checks brought him twenty dollars a week, leaving thirty dollars a month for food. When the superintendent of the building quit, Ralph took on the job. This paid him a small salary and he got his rooms free. Ralph collected the trash and put out the heavy steel cans in the early morning. Barney helped him mop the hall floors once a week. One of the first tenants he became acquainted with was Mrs. Scalzone. "Good morning," she would say as she passed him walking her Pekinese. She left notes in his box asking him to repair the lock on her door, a shelf in her pantry, the handle on the gas range. Mrs. Scalzone was a widow of fifty. Her eyes and hair were dark; she had a pretty, round face which had begun to wrinkle slightly.

One hot summer morning, Ralph sat at his typewriter sweating out another drunken night with Barney, who hadn't stopped talking about his quiet, golden girl from Pakistan. Barney had tried everything to get Jane to marry him—had even jabbed holes in her diaphragm. Then Barney had confessed with some embarrassment that his novel had been bought. The statement left Ralph jealous and disconsolate; Anna hadn't yet completed the deal on his play. Now she doubted that it would even be sold.

"What's your novel about—that old tired nigger shit?" Ralph had said, but had not meant it to sound as bitter as it had.

Now he sat in the heat, his head buzzing, thinking of the night before. The heat made him conscious of his poverty; anyone who had money fled New York in the summer. As he sat, not wanting to work any longer, he thought of sex. But with whom? The thought of Eve entered his mind. But Catroux stood between them, even though he was out of the country. His mind came to rest on Sherry. He had only to call her office and say into the phone, "Sherry, I must see you!" Ralph frowned as he thought of Mrs. Scalzone. There was nothing wrong with her shelf; the handle of the gas range? They were made so they could be slid off and replaced. Ralph put out his cigarette, wiped the sweat from his

122

face and torso, pulled on a shirt and went downstairs. He knocked on Mrs. Scalzone's door. Her Pekinese barked.

"Who is it?" she sang out.

"The super," he answered, not too loudly.

"Oh!" She opened the door. "Come in." Ralph heard the lock snap shut behind him.

"I wanted to look at your shelf again," he said, realizing for the first time that he had no tools with him. Mrs. Scalzone was wearing a close-fitting blouse and dark shorts. Ralph saw a harsh, dark vein running down the inside of one of her thighs.

"Go right ahead," she said. The Pekinese sniffed belligerently at Ralph's trouser cuff. It looked at its mistress, then guardedly pranced alongside Ralph as he walked to the kitchen. "Very hot today," she said, following him.

"Yes," Ralph said, examining the shelf.

"Like some iced coffee? You've been working since seven this morning in all this heat."

He was touched by her concern. "Fine, thanks."

She wore a light, conspiratorial perfume which wavered above the scent of prosciutto. Ralph allowed his hand to drop from the shelf. He turned slowly. Her face, strained with a close-lipped smile, was less than an inch away. He watched her eyes drop to his lips; he saw the slender dark veins in her lowered lids. Her throat pulsed. He moved his face all the way down that endless millimeter which separated their mouths. He felt her welcome when he kissed her. The Pekinese retired to a corner and curled up.

"I don't even know your name," she said later, "but it doesn't matter. You had the look of loneliness about you and

123

now you look *content*. I—I am happy. I was alone too." She sighed. "In a few years those things which made you only content will make you happy."

Ralph wanted to say I love you. I *was* lonely, and I was tired. You *saw*, you were *there;* you understood. You're rare. Instead he said, "My name's Ralph."

"Georgia's mine."

"I must go," he said.

"Yes."

"The people in the building...."

"Yes."

The Pekinese sniffed the air with its puzzled expression. Ralph took her hand. "Goodbye, Georgia." He restrained himself from saying Thanks. She looked at her telephone. Ralph looked at it.

"Goodbye," she said.

He kissed her lightly; her kiss was light also.

Toward the end of a dull succession of summer days and nights, Ralph received a call at three in the morning from Barney.

"Barney, dammit, you're drunk."

"So what? Disaster strikes at ten and you bug me with being drunk."

"What's happening?"

"I need you for my best man. We're getting married at ten."

"You," Ralph said, "and Jane?"

"Yeah, man, me and Jane."

"When did you decide this?"

"Got the license last week, but I got chicken. Jane caught

124

up with me last night, Man, you don't know how hard I've been running the last week."

"I noticed you weren't around to help with the mopping, you bastard."

"Get off me. I've been had."

"Stop crying. You wanted to be had."

"Will you, man?"

"Will I what?"

"Be the best man?"

"Sure. Why the hell not?"

"Thanks. Meet us at St. Philip's about quarter of, will you?"

"Sure."

Barney was late. Jane asked again, "Are you sure he wasn't with you last night?"

"No, I *told* you he called and asked me to be here, that's all."

"Where can he be?"

"Here he comes!" Ralph said, and down the sun-drenched street Barney came loping, his face drawn, his eyes puffed. He hung his head as he came up. "Hello. I'm late." He glanced at Jane. "Let's get it over with," he said gruffly. She straightened his tie. "Are you ready?"

Barney looked hopelessly at Ralph. "I'm ready."

They walked silently to the pastorate, and the minister, a young man with half-lens glasses, settled them in appropriate positions and then, bidding time and the world to note the union in crisp but solemn words, completed the ceremony. Perhaps, Ralph thought, as they returned somewhat bewildered to the street, this was the way it should be done; unnoticed. He shook Barney's hand.

"Man, I guess that was *it*," Barney said. Jane watched, smiling slightly. Ralph kissed her. "Good luck, baby," he said, thinking sadly that Barney had at last obtained this substitute for the white girl he wished he could have married.

"Now," Ralph said, leading them across the street to a bar, "a toast."

When the drinks had been brought, Ralph raised his glass. "To my friends Barney and Jane, who pretended, but not well, that there was no love between them." They drank. Because Barney had problems did not necessarily mean that he did not love Jane, Ralph thought.

Ralph walked quickly away from them and dashed into the subway. He passed a Negro derelict lolling on the steps. The man's eyes leaped with hope as Ralph approached. "S-s-*say*, man," the derelict said, "lay somethin' on me, please." Ralph sidled past, murmuring, "Baby, I'm clean as chittlins." The derelict laughed and shuffled aside. "G'one, jum, you the goddamn best." His appreciative chuckles followed Ralph all the way down the steps.

Ralph wondered what the derelict's reaction would have been had he not uttered an element of the idiom with the proper inflection. Passwords. Not just what you said, but how you said it. That's where the white boys fell down; they didn't know how. He passed through the turnstiles; in this part of town the subway entrances were unencumbered by the great steel U-bars which were attached to the turnstiles in Harlem, and which sounded like great cell bars being lifted when people went through. During the rush hour the bars rattled so loudly that the trains could hardly be heard. All those Negroes; ghettoized.

9

IT WAS TEN O'CLOCK when Ralph sat back in his chair, lit another cigarette and waited tensely for the weather report. When the announcer said that the last of the storm was in sight, Ralph ran to the telephone.

"Reservations for Joplin, two, Los Angeles; they were canceled this morning because of the storm," the reservation clerk said. Ralph's voice rose in anger "For Christ's sake, didn't you say you'd call back as soon as you got the word? You people ought to know better about storms than us—are the reservations valid for the first flight out in the morning or not?" He slammed the instrument down.

He walked to the bathroom, his hands shoved deep into his pockets. Ralph let the water run hot while he fixed a drink and lit a fresh cigarette. He stood before the mirror lathering, and thought with some surprise about the amount of temper he'd shown talking to the airlines clerk. Bluman would have found it most interesting, he thought with a smile. Then he grimaced. What the hell was he thinking? Of Bluman and that whole crazy time; nutty time.

The heat of the summer days had begun to ease; there had been more people in town and the sting of being compelled to stay in the city had lessened. Henri Catroux had lain heavily across letters which Ralph received from Eve. She didn't say so, but she intended to marry Catroux in the fall, he knew. He had known it from the beginning; why had he persisted? Because he knew, with the instinct that was still strong in those that fight for survival, that she was it.

What in the hell was Anna doing?

Why didn't she call, ask him about a million things, tell him two million things and finally say calmly that *Shadows* had been sold. Anna! You bitch! And then perhaps . . . Eve?

Wearied of the city, haunted by the sounds in his apartment and the thought of Eve, Ralph left New York and went to see his daughter. He had planned to go for a week, but after an hour decided to stay only three days.

Each time Ralph saw the child he was overwhelmed. He remembered that June night when April told him to call the doctor. In the hospital he had sat alone on a cold enclosed terrace, listening to April's piercing screams. The labor had taken until morning. Inside the glass the nurse held up the child for him to see. It looked small and pale and red and not at all like either April or himself. It had been one of the rare times in his life when he had felt truly humble.

Now when he looked at her, the wonder was coupled with reality. At what age would she have her first man (or boy)? Would she know what to do? In his mind he formed up a boy here and one there, then quickly a park with high hedges. After, a shabby hotel room. God, he thought, let April not be afraid to tell her when the time came. Raphaella was already curious, he realized with a shock he didn't disclose when, sitting upon his knee, she reached matter-of-factly between his legs, felt around, grasped and then squeezed his penis, let go and busied herself with something else. He told himself that she merely wanted to find out if he were different. Yes, yes, of course, and now she knows.

Ralph did not visit his father before he left, so depressed had he become with the town and its people. Had he seen Big Ralph they would have drunk beer and talked of football. What else did they have to say to each other?

Ralph was happy to leave town. Within a week of his return to New York he had signed at the clinic for the fall and accepted work with another temporary hand-tab crew at OOE.

He looked at his flat for the first time, it seemed; it was as though he were just emerging from narcosis. The place was depressing. He looked at his rooms, then at his body which had gone slack with months at the typewriter. He started straightening up the place, picked up the soiled clothing, cigarette butts and wrappers, balls of typing paper. The sharp obnoxious smell of stale cigarette smoke disappeared. Georgia gave him some old drapes which exuded the scent of Parodi cigars and fichi secchi, an insistent Mediterranean perfume.

Two days later, going to the first session with Dr. Bluman, Ralph thought back to the spring and the tests he'd taken—he'd been an abysmal failure at the blocks, a blundering ass with the arithmetic.

What must they have written as his diagnosis and tucked away deep in the files to be pulled out after every visit and added to? The solution to the matching of the blocks and to the problems had been etched in his mind just from visual contact, but he hadn't been able to solve the problems by *doing*. Instead, like items in a closet, the answers had remained in his mind. Relentlessly speeding time and an exceeding, strange weariness had caused the jam. . . . What was it he'd read (for he was reading hungrily) . . . the failure to manipulate the blocks and solve the problems indicated an inability to (deal? cope?) *relate* to reality. But mightn't this also call up a rejection of that reality as being unworthy or unsuited or in itself unreal to the (subject? person? patient?) Who or what made it mandatory that the reality delineated in a clinic be accepted anyway? Wasn't reality relative in the final analysis? (Damn that word!)

Thus armed, Ralph bounced into the office, shook hands briskly with the doctor and sat down. Dr. Bluman automatically noted Ralph's manner. Ralph, on the other hand, found the doctor tanned to the very crown of his head. Then, still studying the doctor, Ralph told about the happenings of the summer. It seemed to him that his voice carried more authority, that he even spoke with greater fluency. He thought, I sound like a man who has his problem in hand. But Eve. Eve. She hadn't called and she wasn't at her desk.

"Why didn't you see your father?"

Ralph found himself brought up short.

"I wasn't feeling too hot up there. Sort of depressed what with my daughter and the same house and my friends. I almost always feel like that."

"But sometimes you visit your father."

"When I feel well."

"What does 'well' mean?"

"When things are going all right."

"Like having money?"

Ralph paused and said, "Yes."

"Did you have money?"

"Not a lot." They fell silent for a few seconds.

"What're you thinking of?" Dr. Bluman asked.

Ralph had been thinking of Eve, but he said, "Could it be that I'll only see my father when I'm superior to him, when I have more money than he, when my position is unshakable?"

"What do you think?"

"Yes."

Dr. Bluman cleared his throat, placed his hands together on the desk. "One of the things you've said most often is that you're a better man than he ever was, in many respects. You haven't proved that to yourself yet; you want to. But now—you talked about your father and then went on to your friend Barney, the fellow with the new book—have you felt anything about his—success?"

"I'm very glad for him. He's worked very hard."

"So've you."

"Well, he deserves every break he gets."

"Don't you? Wasn't that your premise when you began here?"

"I suppose so."

"You haven't felt any envy? You haven't been comparing

131

the roads both of you've traveled? You haven't felt jealousy that he got there first?"

"I'm human!"

"What does that mean?"

"Of course I felt something!"

"What did you feel?"

"I told you."

"What did you really feel, Mr. Joplin?"

"Look, doctor, success is relative. . . ."

"You *did* feel something about his success then."

"I felt happy for him."

Dr. Bluman leaned back and sighed. "It's a human condition to be reasonably jealous of the other fellow's success, Mr. Joplin. There is a tie-in here between your feelings for your father and your friend's book." He paused. "And also on quite another level, consider the success of your sister in Spain."

"I don't resent her success," Ralph said quickly.

"We've discussed her rather often. I think you have some feelings about it. However, this is not the important area. We're working on your statements today."

"Why in the hell should I be jealous of my father? What kind of success has he had?"

"Time's up for now, Mr. Joplin. But I want to say: Give some thought to thinking in less literal terms. You might consider our discussion today and try to relate it to Mrs. Scalzone; you've mentioned three times that she was fifty years old."

"I have?"

"That's all."

Eve was waiting at the subway. But his elation died when he saw the somber look on her face. He pulled her to him and then pushed her back slowly so that he could see her eyes. She would not look at him. Instead she crossed her hands, fingers stretched across her breast; he saw the band. "Oh, you've done it?" he said.

"I told you I would."

"I know. I guess I kept hoping."

"I won't be at the clinic anymore."

"Well, if you were married to me you'd have to work your can off."

"What about the play?"

"Still cooking. Hasn't sold yet." He glanced sharply at her. "Happy?"

She did not look at him. She shook her head. "No. I don't tell you this to make you feel better. I'm not happy; I didn't expect to be."

"Then why did you do it?"

"I've known Henri for a long time; when we were kids and he'd just come to New York. He's always made me feel that he needed me, even when I didn't want to be needed so much. It got to be habit with all the guilt attached."

"Eve, I need you."

"Not in the same way. I'm not your life; I never could be. I'm Henri's life. The theatre is nothing without me. Nothing is anything without me and it's a pity that I've known for so long."

"How can you hurt yourself so?"

"To keep from hurting him."

"You've hurt me."

"You allowed yourself to be hurt if you truly are. I told you how it was from the beginning."

"Will I see you, ever?"

"I want to," she said simply, rather defiantly. "If it's all right I'll call you; please don't refuse me, though you have every right."

"I can't refuse you."

"I wish you could, but I'm glad you can't."

"Eve...."

"I couldn't tell you all this in a letter. I'm not much of a coward."

"You look so lovely...."

"It's good to see you, Ralph. It doesn't seem so bad now that I know I can talk to you. Would you still want Henri to do your play?"

"No."

"I didn't think so."

"I wouldn't have anything to say about it."

"I guess I'd better go now," she said.

"Let's go, then."

She said, "We live on the West Side now."

"Oh," he said. And now fury and despair gripped him, tugged mercilessly at his intestines. He would have his phone number changed first thing the next day. "Goodbye then."

"Ralph...?"

"What?"

"You've changed your mind about my calling, haven't you?"

"Yes."

"I saw it on your face. Please don't. We aren't very comfortable there. We need a lot of things. It's just the West Side. . . ."

"What're you talking about?" He knew. Eve was bright that way.

"All right," she said. "I won't call if that's what you want." She turned and stepped into the street to hail a cab. He stood waiting until one came, then frightened, terribly frightened, he called, "Eve! Yes! Yes!" and then he took the subway home.

Patient has become sullen, defiant, evasive. . . .

"How old were you when Juanita died?"

"Three."

"Do you remember her death?"

"No, but I remember the funeral; it was at home, like Mary Ellen's; it was kind of dim. Smelled funny."

"What do you mean 'funny'?"

"Like—like—fish!" With some amazement Ralph's mind had drifted back to that somber funeral room. It was fish, and potato salad," he said. "After that the next thing I recall is —the train." He pulled his eyes from the past and looked at Dr. Bluman. "It ran right down the street in front of our house. I guess I'd never been out before, and this day I went out and the train came down street, rumbling, its bell was ringing, the steam coming out—I was scared as hell. I screamed and ran up the stairs. My mother heard me and was on her way out the door. I ran right into her and she picked me up and held me." Ralph drew hard on his cigarette and mashed it out. "After a while I wasn't scared anymore. Next, I remember the fight."

135

Dr. Bluman watched the simulated tough smile. This was the first session in weeks when he hadn't had to push his patient.

"I don't know what caused it. But they were fighting and bumping into the walls; my father was shouting and my mother screaming. She was on the floor and he was standing over her, something in his hand. I think I screamed too. I'm not sure, not sure. . . ." Ralph looked helplessly at the doctor. "Then nothing. A big hole. Next thing I knew my mother— I didn't know who the hell she was then—was coming up the porch with this damned baby in her arms. A few days later, I knew she was my mother. After that I got all the pieces."

"What about the gap?"

"I never worried about it."

"You were blocking out something unpleasant."

"I don't remember."

"Try."

"How can I recall something I don't remember?"

"You have to work your way through the unpleasantness."

"How do you know it was unpleasant?"

"Because you can't remember it."

"It could have been something very good."

"No, Mr. Joplin."

"Anyway, I don't think it's so goddamned important!"

"Then why don't you say something about it? Toss it out like you've tossed other things out here."

Ralph sprang to his feet. "I've had enough of this crap for today!" He glared at Dr. Bluman and the doctor saw, for the first time, a plea—camouflaged as it was by anger, rage— in Ralph's eyes. Dr. Bluman waved his patient with gentle movements of his hand, back into his chair, fascinated (or frightened?) by the danger he had sensed. "Very well," the doctor said. "We won't talk about it right now, but do be seated. Time is valuable and something might come of it if only you'll sit it out. There're a hundred others waiting for your chair—"

Ralph shot the doctor a look, dropped his eyes and asked in a less angry voice, "Am I so bad, then, that you had to take me right away?"

Dr. Bluman frowned. His patient's brief rage had unsettled him. "That's not at all what I meant."

"How much time have we?" Ralph asked.

"No more. See you Wednesday."

"Yeah, sure."

Ralph went out into the raw New York winter.

Patient has tried to by-pass the working out of his problems....

"We'd been on this bit for weeks," Ralph said, "and I got tired. I was spending all my time on the job and at home thinking about that gap and getting nowhere. So I called my mother."

Dr. Bluman darted forward in his chair. "Mr. Joplin, I've cautioned you about reading psychiatric works and certainly you should've known that calling your parents was along the same line. These things've got to be worked out. You haven't really helped yourself, you see."

Ralph turned to the window. "Spring is coming again, doctor. I felt it in the air today. I feel like I've been here an awfully long time, and I want to *hurry*."

Why was it, Dr. Bluman wondered lazily, that the clinic

patients were always in a hurry while the private ones lingered on and on and on, waiting to be told that nothing more could be done for them? "What did she tell you?" he asked.

"She said my father went away. For almost a year. Jail. She left town for over a year and came back with my sister."

Dr. Bluman watched Ralph frown. "Where were you during this time?" Dr. Bluman suspected where he had been.

"She put me in a city home." Ralph's voice was incredulous. "For nearly a year. My father took me out. I might have spent —a *lot* of time there," he said wonderingly. He got a grip on himself. "She tried to make me remember something about the place, but I couldn't. I still can't. I guess I was pretty rough with her."

"But why?"

"I don't know. As she was telling me I had a sense of having been betrayed."

Dr. Bluman said quietly, "Our time's up, Mr. Joplin."

Patient dreams....
Ralph said, "I was walking around with these two girls, just ambling around. Suddenly we're in the make-up room of a newspaper. I see a banner and it reads *The New York Times*. While I'm reading it a guy comes over and says how great I am and wouldn't I like to work for him. I turn him down. The two girls are still there. I look up and I see ropes hanging from the ceiling. The dream sort of goes after that."

"What do you make of it, Mr. Joplin?"

Ralph shrugged. "The ropes make me think there's a sexual connotation, but—"

"But what?"

"I don't think so. The whole dream goes back to what we've been over many times. I don't believe it's sexual. I think it's racial."

"How so?"

"In a way the girls are alike; I think Georgia and Adela. The ropes are lynching ropes." Ralph chuckled. "I'd like to be offered a good job by *The Times*; but that's only a symbol. A good job, period. Then I'd be accepted. But as it is, I'm not. In the dream I reject the job without thinking about it twice; I'd like to be able to do that."

"You've given it some thought."

"Sure."

"It's been quite some time since you've seen Adela."

"Yes."

"When did you last see Georgia?"

"This morning."

"I mean, to sleep with her."

"This morning."

"And Sherry?"

"Last night."

"What?"

"Last night."

"Oh," Dr. Bluman glanced at the window. "Oh," he repeated. "I see. Did anything unusual happen?"

"What do you mean?"

"Anything that hasn't happened before with either one."

"No."

"No?"

"No."

"I thought you and Sherry had broken up."

"We go and come," Ralph said, thinking about the pun, and thinking, a little about Eve. "Do you think the business with the ropes is a little paranoid?" he asked.

Dr. Bluman gazed at him. "Well, it's too early to tell—"

"Too early? Even after a year and a half?" Ralph broke into loud laughter which lasted until the end of the session.

It was this last exchange which had started Ralph again thinking of leaving the clinic. But it was not until Anna called, her voice calm and matter-of-fact, as he had expected, to tell him that *Shadows* had been sold, that he made his decision; he would quit sometime soon. For the next few sessions, however, he contented himself with toying with Dr. Bluman. He would begin the session with a topic "somewhere out in left field" and watch while the doctor followed along. Then building on free association, he would move smoothly from topic to topic, "problem" to "problem." But Dr. Bluman had noted: *Patient appears to be marking time. . . . It appears that his recent good fortune has considerably alleviated some of his most pressing problems. He has engaged therapist in mental exercises which have little or nothing to do with his presence in the clinic. . . .*

10

WITH SOME RELUCTANCE he went home one Saturday to see his daughter. He had neglected to call April and learned that she and the child were out of town. April's father told him this with great relish through clicking, ill-fitted false teeth. The old man did not invite him in. Concealing his anger, Ralph left the presents.

He borrowed a car and drove aimlessly around the city, and finally came to a greenhouse. He bought a dozen roses, then drove to the cemetery, turned off the asphalt road and onto the gravel. He stopped the car and gazed at the patches of snow, the tough, short grass. He took the roses, got out, and trudged through the snow and mud until he came to the three graves. He was glad he hadn't worn a hat. He'd have felt foolish taking it off.

Beloved Son
Robert Joseph Joplin
Corporal, Army of the United States
1930–1951

This, the newest grave, was closest to the road! Sissie no doubt had had it arranged that way so that Rob could protect Juanita and Mary Ellen. He remembered how they had gone down to the Union Station in Los Angeles to receive the lead-sealed coffin. The United States flag had been draped over the coffin and an honor guard had been in attendance. Sissie had stared at the guards; they were alive, those white boys, and Robbie lay dead. "Goddamn them," Sissie had said, but she hadn't cried.

Ralph walked to the grave, the roses in his hands. Perhaps Sissie and Big Ralph, separated for so many years, had stood here together in the rain, getting Robbie laid away, to use Sissie's expression. What had they been thinking, each of them? Ralph knelt before the grave. He set the roses at the head and rose quickly. Three-fifths of the family rested here, and not one of them had had a good or a full life.

He knew that he must see his father, but remembered that Big Ralph worked late even on Saturdays. Football would be their only topic of conversation.

He drove back to the city, returned the car, and walked slowly into the downtown section. He stopped for coffee. The farmers from the country were in with their broods. He moved through the rustic crowds and came to a stop before the window of a store and stood looking in just to waste time.

"Hello."

He knew it was Jeanette even before he turned around. "Hello, baby," he said, in a tone devoid of emotion; he reached for her hand and kissed her cheek. It was as if they had seen each other only the day before.

"Why are you smirking?" she asked, smiling herself.

He said, "I'm not smirking. I'm smiling because I'm glad to see you. Surprised." He was not. He had always expected her to appear again one of these days. Behind them the main street traffic moved slowly north and south. The street reminded Ralph of those small Western towns one sights suddenly coming around a curve.

Once more she tilted her head and said, "I'll bet," and they both knew what she meant. She was heavier now, fuller through the hips and bigger in the bust. Her skin was still pale, but hinted of deeper browns. Her eyes were stark brown against the clear whites; folds sagged like the scabs of sores beneath them. Ralph found himself trying not to stare at her mouth.

"Have you had lunch?" he asked.

"No. Is this an invitation?"

Jesus, Ralph thought. All of this was too old to have anything to do with the present. She had been a convenience in that period just after he had broken with April; he knew that she had regarded him similarly. "Yes, let's go eat."

"O-kay." Nothing ever changes here, Ralph thought. Neither the town nor the people.

"Heard you had a child. How old?," Ralph asked during lunch.

She had been speaking about *Shadows*. She had heard that

he was living in Greenwich Village. Yes, but he was thinking of moving out. And yes, he was already working on another play.

She appeared embarrassed. Her child had been one of those "errors" he guessed.

"And George?"

She shrugged her shoulders. "The same." Surely she could not still be teaching her husband which fork to use at dinner, he thought, and by now George must be picking out his own clothes. Ralph felt a pang of pity; George had committed the hellish sin of marrying an educated Negro woman who felt contempt for his own lack of education and sophistication.

"I have to go," Ralph said suddenly, taking her hand again. "But I'd like to see you later. Can I?" He waited patiently.

"Where are you staying?" she asked.

"At the hotel."

"Ralph, I'm afraid."

"It'll be all right."

"What time?"

"Any time after nine."

"I'll be there."

"I'm glad."

She laughed. "I'm glad you're glad." It was like her to make that kind of joke. "Byyyyyyyyye . . ." she said.

Why was he bothering to do it, he asked himself. Certainly he got no pleasure from it. But there would be a kind of satisfaction for him. He was no longer merely a promising young man as he had been before. He was now, in her eyes, one of the wielders of power. He laughed.

"McCarran," Ralph told the receptionist at the paper. It had been Anna's idea, this stopping by the paper, just to say hello. "Might noodge things a bit," she'd said after her third Martini.

The receptionist said, "Go ahead in."

"Thanks." Ralph felt her eyes upon him. None of your goddamn business what I want, he thought. He walked across the city room with its dulled marble floors. The ink from the presses downstairs was not so keen here, only the soft smell of too much copy paper. Back near the wall the teletypes chattered on and on, bells ringing at the end of each story. Ralph did not look in the direction of the managing editor, but could see Addison out of the corner of his eye. McCarran, florid and looking tired, waved at Ralph from across the room. As Ralph approached McCarran's desk, the phone rang. Ralph smiled. Addison. He'd be calling asking McCarran: "Is that Joplin out there?"

Ralph sat down in the chair beside the desk. "Yeah," McCarran said into the phone. He studied Ralph, then let his eyes drop to the desk. He hung up. "How y'doin', buddy?" McCarran held out his hand, playing the role of the tired, hardbitten reporter. "Congratulations," McCarran said. "That was Addison on the phone. He wants a feature and a couple of pix. Okay?"

Ralph shrugged. "Sure, why not?" Everybody owns you when you've made it, he thought. Perhaps the *Express* did own a little of him for each of those nights he checked in and then back out to cover what was happening in the Pork Chop, that section of the city where the Negroes lived and clamored to get out of, and where most of the policemen on the force

145

supplemented their salaries with a graft which provided a decent living. Perhaps the *Express's* ownership had been invested in that ragged little desk with its miserable light where he was allowed to work up the crime news—the murders and vice-squad raids; the wife-beatings and the stabbings.

Later he had risen on the staff, and had interviewed Negroes, those who were sincerely concerned with their lot in town and those who sought only for those sticks of print which gave their names and addresses. From the latter he had taken money, which had been willingly given, but he had almost never used their names—mostly because of the paper's policy but also because he had not wanted to. Brotherhood Week had been different; then he had been able to get in all the names he wished. Since his leaving, there had been no other Negro at the *Express*.

Now for Addison and his feature. Was it not possible that the *Express* had helped make Ralph a playwright? Maybe, Ralph thought, watching McCarran clean his typewriter (it was a fetish, done before beginning each story). Yes, Addison was right. McCarran slipped the sheet of paper into the typewriter. When the interview was over, Ralph, reading the rough, noticed that the *Express'* style hadn't changed—there was still the same provincial lead:

"A former *Express* employee and native of the city today returned in triumph, his Broadway play, 'Shadows on the Sun' scheduled to open this fall. He is. . . ."

Later, when Jeanette came whirling into Ralph's room, she said, "I felt just like everyone in the lobby knew." Ralph laughed and gave her a drink. As always she drank little, like a whore who has to be right on top of it all the time. Jeanette, of course, didn't think of herself as a whore, but she gave away what she had with a furiousness that would have shocked any self-respecting prostitute.

When they were in bed together, he was glad he'd had a few drinks. Her body was coarse and unsymmetrical. Protoplasm. When she kissed him (moaning with the theatrics of a Fourteenth Street pickup) he thought of a series of small, feverishly wet gulpings. Her mouth gaped and strained for his tongue. Yes, she was flabby now. She was moving in his arms in a rhythm all her own, twitching, her hands all over him. Ralph felt almost as if he were a spectator. He began to move slowly, surely, forcing her from one position to another. Once he opened his eyes and saw that she was watching him.

He shouldn't have asked her, he knew. His body grew rigid; he was conscious of how strong she was. He let her go. Gone now was her caution, her fear of moral censure. Ralph had not been wrong. With a moan which was this time genuine she tore her mouth from his, scattering small splashes of saliva over their bodies; her lips and tongue searched his neck, fastened like wild leeches upon his chest; then they glided down over the curves of his stomach, lingering but a second on his navel. He felt a crazy desire to shout something like "Go, baby!" But he waited until she was where she wanted to be, then forced her head up and turned her struggling upon her back. Her body was stiff with anger, gun-hard. But he held her. It was as it had always been with her: penetration minimum. She clawed and quivered, he strained brutally to widen the breach, and then hesitated, knowing the struggle

147

would not end until she had her way. She rose to her knees, strong and trembling—all he saw was the nape of her neck. There was not the smallest part of love inherent in the act; and it was followed by no other. Through this her mind had transformed her into a man. Ralph forced her from him; "Don't," she whined. "Stop it, Ralph!" Her spine tensed. "Goddamn you!" He covered her mouth with his hand. He was turning her over. A pillow fell to the floor. She dug her feet into the bed and arched her back. Ralph let his body fall upon her. "Ralph! No! I never—!" She didn't stop fighting. He wrapped his arms around her and held on. She tried to bite him. Her eyes had grown large and she shook her head as if in disbelief. Jeanette rose in one great final effort to dislodge him. When finally she was no longer her peculiar kind of a virgin, Ralph stumbled to the shower. When he came out she was gone. He felt lonely.

Ralph lit a cigarette and walked to the window, and stared at the barren street below. He remembered sitting with his father on Jumbo's Back, the hill which overlooked the stadium; the hill where all the people without money came to watch the games. They sat on the hill and it was cold. Great cheers burst from the bowl below and a lone figure, clad in orange and blue, raced out of the eastern end of the stadium into view, speeding across the green, white-striped field. His father jumped to his feet, bellowing "Go on, Hudson, go!" The hill behind them rocked with shouts. "Touchdown!" his father cried, lifting Ralph on his shoulder. Below, a cannon sounded: Thoomp!

No alumnus had been more faithful to the Hill than his father. Impetuously Ralph walked to the phone. He was lucky enough to catch one of the last flights to New York.

The sessions with Dr. Bluman were becoming time-consuming, wasteful, it seemed to Ralph. Jeanette had been, Ralph said, like—and then he had stopped because he had thought of Doughnut. "Like who?" Dr. Bluman had asked, sensing that this was the time he could pierce that shield behind which his patient sat. But Ralph had avoided giving an answer and the session had gone on, others following. He could not talk about Eve. First, because initially he could not, and second because now, jostling around within the area of free association, he felt slyer, superior, because there was something which he after all could retain of his own. Bluman insisted upon a return of self-examination, to a perusal of personality. Ralph, on the other hand, insisted that personality be explored in terms of environment. Then, three nights running, he dreamed of Doughnut, and sometimes Doughnut had the face of Jeanette.

Patient's hostility has returned....
"I dreamed I killed you, Dr. Bluman."
Dr. Bluman flicked his note. "Yes?"
"I just killed you."
"I think the reaction is normal after our last few sessions."
Ralph looked closely at the doctor and for the smallest part of a second wondered if he should not have told him the year before about Doughnut. He was glad when that second had passed that he had not.
"But tell me, how?"
Ralph looked blankly at him.
"In a fight? Gun?" Dr. Bluman had thought, Knife? but changed his mind.
"None of those."

"How then?"

"I'll tell you about the dream. I'm angry with you; you've done something horrible to me—"

"What?"

"Well—"

Dr. Bluman waited.

"You hurt me."

Dr. Bluman waited again, puzzled by a feeling of being aware of some vague inconsistency. "How did I hurt you?"

The patient's eyes came up, cleanly, innocently, but somehow masked over. "Sodomy," Ralph said.

"I see. Then what happened?"

"I decide to kill you. I have a hatred I've seldom had in my life. I wait for you. It's night. I push you off a cliff."

Dr. Bluman sat back. He glanced quickly at the clock. "A cliff, you say?"

"Yes."

"Where's the cliff? Have you been around any lately?"

"I don't know."

"New Jersey?"

"Don't know."

"*Try.*"

"I am."

"Upstate a little ways? There aren't any cliffs around here."

"I don't know!"

Dr. Bluman's voice came a bit harsher, more insistent. "This seems somewhat unusual, Mr. Joplin. Let's get to the bottom of it. Have you ever been involved with another man?"

"No."

"Never?"

"No."

"Not as a child?"

"No."

"Wanted to?"

"No!"

"All right, all right, *all right!* Now the cliff: Were there cars near? What was I wearing? Why didn't you shoot me—"

Ralph broke in. "There were trees." He thought, Have I given myself away by changing the thing? Have I *goofed?* "Tall trees, and it's hot. Tall trees," he said again," you know p—"

Dr. Bluman slid forward. "*What?*"

"Pear trees."

"Pear trees."

"Yes," Ralph said hopefully.

"But pear trees aren't tall. Not in the sense that—"

"I'm sure they were pear trees," Ralph said quickly.

"Why are you so sure?"

Even more rapidly, eager to pacify, Ralph said, "Because some of the coconuts are on the ground!" Ralph set his face sincerely toward the doctor. He saw a light go on in Bluman's eyes and Ralph speedily re-thought his last words, selected *coconut* as the impetus for that knowing light.

"Co-co-*nuts*, Mr Joplin?"

Ralph felt an urgency to yawn and he stretched his mouth, then reached for a cigarette and lighted it.

"We were in the tropics, Mr. Joplin?"

"Gee," Ralph said, "I just don't know, doc." "Doc" echoed in his mind.

"You were in the tropics during the war, weren't you?"

"Yes," Ralph said.

Dr. Bluman looked again at the clock. "Time's almost up," he said and Ralph knew by his manner that Bluman wished it weren't. "I must tell you, Mr. Joplin, that the pattern of your dreams, with the exception of perhaps two, has never been specific. There is something so specific about this one that it makes me think that it is no dream at all. You're hiding something. What, I have no idea—" Dr. Bluman stopped and looked at Ralph, thinking, Is it possible?

Patient missed two successive sessions.
Patient appears calm, more sure of himself than at any other time. . . .

"We've been making it in circles. You say it's *me;* I say it's *it.* You talk of *your* reality, the one you know as a white man, as a white therapist. I'm talking about *mine;* mine as a black man and we are not talking about the same reality."

Dr. Bluman studied his patient's hairline.

"There are things I've gotten here on myself, but they've all been things I've suspected or put together anyway, and they all go back to the *it* you've been telling me to adjust to, to accept. And I can't do it; I can't make that scene."

Dr. Bluman thought about his patient's last phrase and in context understood what it meant.

Ralph went on. "At every bend in the road there's been *it,* for me, for my family, all the way down the line, like weather affects birds, as currents of warm or cold water affect fish. Do you think my parents would have been at one another's throats if there'd been room for my father to behave even nominally like a man; do you think he enjoyed living a life without balls, letting his wife bring home the bacon? And further, would my mother have been my mother if they had

152

allowed my grandfather to live his life a man instead of a black man down there in Mississippi. The last recession—why are ninety percent of the men out of work nonwhite? You ask me to adjust to these conditions? The things which constitute your reality are nothing more than a psychic concentration camp for me. I guess what I expected here was someone neutral to spill my guts to so no one would know how much it all bugs me." Ralph halted, filled abruptly with the sadness of still another disappointment. "Well, I want to give this chair to someone who can put it to better use; someone who has a problem that can be solved in a lifetime." He waited; he had announced his intention to leave therapy.

"You've derived some benefit *because* you're Negro, Mr. Joplin." It made Dr. Bluman fretful to have a patient leave before he thought the problems all worked out.

"Those benefits, too often the result of guilt, are the very things that made me *know* times should be better, doctor."

The patient was using the term "doctor" rather patronizingly, Dr. Bluman thought. "Many Negroes haven't had or will never have your opportunities."

"Can you begin to imagine how much worse it's got to be for them?"

"Tell me, Mr. Joplin, when you say 'it,' what do you mean?"

Ralph thought, He's being patronizing with his "Mister Joplin." "Racial discrimination. When I first came here, I must have sounded like the Negro child who's spent his first year finding out what it's all about and blamed all his problems on it. But I *looked* at it, doctor, and it is so. Two things happen when you're able to see and say I'm what I am because of racial discrimination. First, when you reach this

153

conclusion, which seems to me inevitable, you're out of dreams, because the dreams you dream aren't applicable to you. Then you begin killing yourself in a hundred little ways. Or, having reached the end of *that* road, you start back, not really knowing what the hell you're going to do, but at least and at last unhampered by delusion. But there's life in understanding finally where you're at."

"When did you first begin to reach this conclusion? During the war, in the tropics?" There was something besides coldness in the doctor's eyes.

"Yes," Ralph said. He turned his gaze to the print on the wall.

Dr. Bluman blew out a puff of air. "You are leaving therapy then?"

"Yes."

"How do you feel about it? Leaving, I mean."

"I'm sad because the clinic doesn't have what I need."

"You've some loose ends, you know."

"I'll work them out."

Dr. Bluman stood. He picked up the clock, scowled at it. He jerked his head upward. "The time's all gone," he said.

Now Ralph stood. "It is?"

Dr. Bluman went to the door, held it open for Ralph. "Good luck, Mr. Joplin."

"Goodbye, doctor. Thank you."

RIVERSIDE CLINIC

TO: Dr. Morris Alpert   New York, June 18, 1959
FROM: Dr. Sidney Bluman   PATIENT: Joplin, Ralph, Jr.

Patient began therapy Nov. 3, 1957. Psychometric tests indicated high average intelligence, but with reduced intellectual efficiency; also evidence of paranoid thinking, grave anxieties and a hostile and evasive personality. Diagnosis: undifferentiated schizophrenia.

Patient has no previous history; however, he states that he feigned mental disturbance in order to get discharged while overseas. He further states that the attending physician accused him of being ashamed because of his race and then excused him.

Age given: 34. Occupation: Office worker—Playwright.

Patient has had a normal sexual life which began at age ten. Masturbation, infrequent prior to his marriage, has been nonexistent since. This marriage, which lasted seven years, was terminated by divorce five years ago. There was one child born of this union, a girl. Cause for the divorce, according to patient, was wife's infidelity.

Patient stated that he was beginning therapy because he "was at the end of his rope but only in his mid-thirties." He described this as being unable to obtain suitable employment, difficulties in obtaining housing, although he feels he is qualified for a number of positions because of his education and experience. He characterizes the housing situation as being "impossible." Patient blamed these conditions on his race; he is Negro.

Patient can be described as dark brown, tall, with a mustache and well-defined features. His demeanor is cautious and reserved. He appears unconcerned by what is going on around him, though he is implicitly aware of the events. He does not encourage friendliness. Patient is well-spoken and has charm. His anger is expressed by an aloof silence or by an unreasonable burst of rage. He has expressed some self-consciousness. His movements are quick, alert.

Patient is the eldest of two living siblings, born to parents who later separated. Two siblings died in infancy. A brother was killed in the Korean War. Patient's problems probably con-

155

gealed at preschool age when father was incarcerated for the attempted murder of patient's mother. The cause for the attempt is believed to have been infidelity. The mother placed patient in a public home and left the city. Both parents were absent for about a year, and after, a reconciliation which lasted some nine years took place. The mother dominated the home. In defense of the father, patient said, Negro women could always get domestic work where a man could not. Sessions indicated a high rejection probability as regards patient 1) because he was the eldest and the youngest required more care, and 2) because of the economic situation which patient has described in detail. Of the two siblings who later died, one was able to create affection in the patient who was entering adolescence. He later transferred this affection to the only remaining sister, now living abroad. Undeniably patient sought affection from the mother when the father left the household. Patient relates adolescent desire to assume the father's role, but denies this desire included sexual relations with the mother. The acceptable part of this affection rejected, patient turned to hatred of the mother, but therapy indicates that by early manhood the balance was achieved. However, his relationship with Mrs. S., a neighbor some twenty years his senior, may be a subconscious fulfillment of the adolescent desire.

Beginning sessions indicated a serious impairment of patient's affectivity potential, but throughout therapy his attachment (in a sense, neurotic) for another female, S., might indicate a desire to remove this obstacle. There is doubt that his marriage had any effect on this barrier. Returning to Mrs. S., patient's relationship with her might also indicate a working out of this problem. The affair with Mrs. S. is apparently without the Dollard motivations. Mrs. S. is Caucasian. There are, nonetheless, overtones of Oedipal origin. Patient is aware of the futurelessness of this relationship, and indicates in conversation that the

156

affair with S. (a female nearer his own age) has more depth. Patient himself drew comparisons between S. and his mother. She dominates because of her money. While this might be a minor factor, it is always with patient.

Patient is in competition with sister, a singer whom he visited abroad. She has had a highly successful career, which underlines his failures, according to him. Patient also expressed some distress at the success of a writer friend. However, his combativeness is within bounds, his envy within reason.

Throughout therapy patient has exhibited masochistic tendencies which do not run counter to diagnosis. He denies having a compulsion to hurt, just as he denies aggression which often has carried him into combative situations. His aspirations were high compared to what he could gain before the acceptance of a play. This factor has given him new self-esteem which in turn may remove the frustrations which have caused his anger. The other traits of low self-esteem, self-renunciation, cautiousness, ingratiatory behavior might also be removed. The removals would indicate in addition, a new lack of fear from retaliatory measures. Before the acceptance of his play for production, there had been either a marked lack of self-esteem or a void altogether; at present a redemption is taking place.

During the last of the current sessions, patient threatened therapist through the medium of a "dream." Prior to this, patient and therapist had been engaged in crucial talks involving his parents. Patient became visibly angry. At the next session patient disclosed his "dream." Details noted by patient were unrelated to "dream" as most details are. The "dream" incident which angered him to the point where he wished to kill therapist, that of a homosexual rape, indicates that patient has ignored admonition to avoid reading psychiatric material. The incident might be interpreted as a beating, or in patient's aggressive syntax, loss of manhood by virtue of the beating. "Dream" has the mark of a recurrent nightmare, one which had origins in adult life; details mature. It is likely that the basis for this nightmare was entirely real but unrevealed by the patient. Therapist believes it took place in the tropics during the war. Therapist attached significance to this disclosure because the patient missed the next two sessions and left therapy after the third, although therapist felt work remained to be done.

Conclusion:

Patient's progress was immensely helped by acceptance of his work. The rationale that his problems stem directly from his racial origins may have some validity; patient claimed no adjustment to an inferior status could be made when therapist suggested an acceptance of the reality of the situation. Patient states that he and therapist were at an impasse and that while he has learned something of himself, his great problem remained and could only be alleviated by the removal of the outside pressure which brought him to us.

Dr. Bluman pecked out a note to his superior and attached the summary. His note read:

Morris:

Is there really anything to Tappan's pilot study on the effect of discrimination upon Negroes? Let me know.

Many thanks,
Sid

P.S. How about that new dictaphone? This one's going fast!

11

IT WAS DURING THE WEEKS and months of Raph's postanalytical depression that Eve decided to leave Henri. *Shadows on the Sun* had opened and was a success; the play settled down for a long run after shifting theatres a couple of times.

Eve did not make her decision until she was given an ultimatum by Ralph: she would have to leave Henri or not see him at all.

They had been to another of those parties. Eve had arrived with her husband, but, as usual, had met Ralph afterward. Once they had left parties boldly, together. And there had been occasions when even Henri, drunkenly sarcastic, had asked Ralph to see Eve home. Eve had said that somehow the play had given Henri everything he now needed. She had asked Henri to release her but he had refused and she was reluctant to leave him.

Ralph had had a lot to drink at the party, but Eve had drunk little. He spoke very quietly, so quietly that his voice trembled, and then went to bed. She put on her nightgown, turned out the lights, walked into the bedroom and, jostling Ralph gently, told him all right, she would leave Henri.

Afterward, with a little sigh and a languid turning in his arms, she went to sleep. Ralph continued to lie awake.

The gray of a morning come too soon sat heavily within the room. The air conditioners which had battled the humid night continued their monotonous racket, tiny motors churning furiously. A great truck, lost, for the street below Ralph's apartment was not a truck route, bawled hoarsely with its air horn, hissed its air brakes and in a few seconds was gone. And then a stray, hungry pigeon galloped past the window, returned and fluttered down to the sill. It cooed; Ralph could see its throat puffing, its iridescent feather tips dull in the gray light. After a moment it flew away again.

So it was a new day, he thought. It was an important day, perhaps the most important in his life. Then he promptly thought of a dozen days which had more meaning than this one. But, he considered, they might have all existed only to bring him to this morning.

Which were the important days?

The day Anna called with the news of his play? No, he thought. You expected that day; you moved inescapably toward it, even if it never came.

The day Raffy was born? Ah, that had been a dazzling, mystical, irrational moment.

The day Doughnut thrust himself into his life or the day he ended Doughnut's? Yes, the first was important; it was as if he had been wound up then and had started ticking.

And he thought of the day when the Japanese officer on Peleliu had shouted to that pitiable little group of reluctant Negro Seabees, cargo humpers for the Marines, "What are you doing here? Why do you fight with them?" One of the men in the hole had fired his carbine screaming, "Shut up you yellow Jap bastard!"

It made Ralph sad to think of that day.

There had also been the day when Sissie had come at him with the broom. He had been only fourteen then and had taken the broom away from her; they had stood looking at each other and finally she had cried. That day Ralph had known that he was a man.

All of those days had brought him to this one. Staring at Eve, he wondered at the forces which coupled people.

"What're you thinking?" Eve asked, her eyes opening. About us?"

"Yes."

She said, "Don't be afraid."

He said, "I'm not afraid."

"I'm not either."

"Aren't you? You have my life and you're not afraid?"

"No. Are you afraid to have mine?"

"No." After he had paused he said, "How could it take me until nearly forty to know that to be loved is a responsibility and you until only twenty-five?"

"I don't know. And you're not nearly forty."

"Eve, be kind to Henri."

"This will be a kindness to all of us. I wish I hadn't met you, though. I could have been cruel all Henri's life and he'd never have known."

At noon, showered and dressed, silent over her coffee, his hand pressed tightly to her lap, she ignored his unblinking worried stare and said, "You shouldn't have dressed. There'll be no trouble."

"I hate you when you're so sure of yourself."

"Love me."

"I wish there wasn't this to do. But"—he gestured hopelessly with his hands—"do it. Do it."

"Yes, I know. I will."

"More coffee?" He held the pot poised over her cup, waiting.

"No." She pushed her cup away. "Am I what you want, really?"

"Yes," he said. "Yes, but don't make me kiss your ass." He wanted her to understand that they were done with games.

"No, I just wanted you to say it again."

"Words," he scoffed, "mean nothing today. They're empty. If you don't know by now that I love you, words aren't going to help."

He sat alone drinking coffee, meditating upon his new, tranquil condition: contentment. He did not deserve happiness. Doughnut, he thought. How the family would applaud if they knew! What glee! Served the bastard right! But violence was basic; it was always there, expected, met, bested if possible. The family had understood the nature of violence even as they were being shipped from West Africa aboard,

162

perhaps, the *Desire*, 120 tons, out of Rhode Island with its stink of slopping feces, urine, vomit, rotting bodies and stale blood. Perhaps that was where it began, that need which had become a lowering, concealed lust for revenge. Retribution for Doughnut? No, Ralph thought with an uncertain chuckle. The Shore Patrol would not come crashing through the door to charge him with murder.

Retribution coming maybe for April, ol' April.

He rose from the table and moved to his desk. He reached for paper. The typewriter was dusty; he walked across the room, secured a cloth, brush and cleaning fluid.

April—and Raffy, of course. The hospital: he'd worked there as a night orderly, often handling the corpses, shaving them, setting them into their refrigerated compartments. April hadn't touched him for months after she found out; death not only frightened but disgusted her. The foundry: he had driven his body against sand, steel, and time, moving with the perfect rhythm of the craftsman.

Then there was the end of school, and the foundry, and the resumption on another level of his work on the paper. And Raphaella had been born, planned of course. That was the way to do things: with a casual diligence. He was by then, everyone said, a fine ambitious young man, ambition meaning nothing more than working every day, and not being publicly drunk, being seen occasionally with his daughter and appearing at church from time to time. "Ambition" in that town was the barricade that blocked access to a vaster world.

Ralph looked up from the typewriter and wished Eve

163

would call to tell him that everything was all right, that Henri had accepted her decision. Once more, he looked down and resumed cleaning the typewriter.

He had not known just when he'd had enough of the *Express;* nor when buying a cheap house on a G.I. loan and paying off a Chevrolet became meaningless to him. He knew, however, that he couldn't say to April: I want out, it's no good. It's a mistake. April the Fundamentalist would have quickly suggested analysis. So he said nothing. Instead, little by little he began withholding. Little things first: now she had to drive herself to church, he didn't go at all, he stayed at the *Express* later than was necessary. When he had to speak, it was in monosyllables. There was another woman, April said. No, he answered. What then? Nothing. I don't know, he said, lying. Two months, three, five passed. He saw the resentment growing within her. April's revenge was swift, simple and predictable.

Ralph knew that what women carried between their legs was no particular prize. The models came like that, every one. He knew that he should have felt no emotion the night he came home early from the *Express* and stood outside his bedroom listening. After a moment he flicked on the light. The stranger scurried out of bed and clutched for his clothes. April just stared defiantly. "Get out, motherfucker," Ralph said, "or you're dead." The stranger, clothes in hand, scuttled into the hall and out of the house. April lit a cigarette. She moaned hoarsely, "I'm human, I'm human, goddamn you!" Ralph hit out viciously. Her nose bled. He washed it for her, without emotion. On the floor, damp and wrinkled, was the condom.

All right. Expected: retribution for April.

It was dark out now. Ralph hadn't realized it was so late. Why hadn't Eve called? Maybe Henri had punched *Eve* in the nose. The Fates: giving and taking back.

"I'm all right," Eve said when she finally did call. "I'm at Barbara's. Don't ask me to come over. I want to be by myself for a while."

"You're all right," he said.

"Yes, but I didn't tell you that I loved you."

"I know already. Have you ever felt when you spoke of love to me that you'd seen too many movies and plays and read too many stories that you're acting out? All of them handled with a language that seems inadequate?"

"Yes."

"Me too. I wish we had our own language, whatever it was. I'm sure it made more sense. You had to use the exact combination of grunts and things. I suppose once it was even hard to lie. Anyway—" He took a deep breath. "G'night."

He rose and dressed for a walk. Outside the sky seemed to be filling with stars, as many as one could see in the garishly lighted city. The great jets, outspeeding their own sounds, slithered and rustled through the night. Would the missiles, all those missiles hidden in all those secret, well-manned and well-guarded places come with a jet sound or would they come nosing heavily over in silence, solemnly dipping their noses and end it?

An end to it. Fantastic, incomprehensible that it should be so visible, the end, so pressingly present, neatly defining the denouement of the comedy. A flock of geese sharp on a radarscope; a Negro SAC navigator smarting under racial rebuff in Grand Forks, North Dakota, and seeking the ultimate subsconscious revenge; a radio out of control; a leader too heavily sedated; a crazed pilot or a sane one; a locked switch; a distortion of codes; a hot-tempered President—and bang!

And yet this—not quite an inevitability—was accepted universally as such. But then man had always fled from the great stalking animals and had hidden himself until the danger had passed, confident that it would be of its own accord. Sometimes man had to stand and fight because he was trapped; but the awareness of being trapped seemed to have been bred out of him.

Ralph's stride quickened with anger. Was this what the Fates had in store for him, for all the Joplins who had not died in the slave raids nor during the Middle Passage which had taken fifteen millions? Was this scorching and sundering of the earth to be their welcome when they joined those other survivors, not necessarily the fittest? Shit. Tttt! He wished he were able to get to those ugly gnomes who inhabited the secret control rooms of the world and horsewhip sense into them, the way Sissie had done him. Talking, speaking, moving one's mouth, directing the sounds with teeth, tongue, palate or lips no longer seemed the truthful or reliable way to communicate; one found oneself speaking other people's lies and half-truths automatically. Yes, horsewhip the gnomes; horsewhip the crap out of them. There then would be your goddamned deterrent. Or one could eliminate the gnomes the way some peoples eliminated the workers of black magic and people over sixty or people who ate more than their share of kangaroo shit. And not only the gnomes in the attic, no *sir!* The cellars would have to be cleaned out as well; all those sneaky little bastards who felt without a doubt that they possessed as much power as history told them they had, but who had it only by the grace of letting others use it, would have to go. Perhaps sooner than the gnomes. No, at the same damned time. What was needed was an authority such as was never seen upon the earth. One that killed, but killed not with hatred or laughter, but with tears so that the knitty-gritty could swing! an authority kind of insanely holy; a Christ in the temple, not with a whip but with one of those short, wide-bladed Roman swords. Had He stopped them for good in the temple he might not have had to cry on that Friday, *"Eli, Eli, lama sabachthani?"* Perhaps He had been unable to kill out of love.

He had slowed and was on the way home again. Months before, he had not felt the anger; he had not had much to lose, not even *Shadows*. It was as if just that day he had realized an utterly wonderful kind of happiness which had finally come to him was being threatened by things he could not control. He was puzzled as well as angry, for he had once felt that he controlled his own life; he had had to. But by pressing open finger after finger of that tightly closed fist, year after year, the Fates had removed his grip upon himself; they had done it snugly, tauntingly. He had once believed that when the sirens sounded for the denouement he would lie in his bed unmoving, with, if he were lucky, a woman just as fatalistic as himself. But now, *God!* if they gave him five minutes warning, three even, he'd find some way to get Eve and himself out of there. Everything, suddenly, seemed to matter. He wanted to be as happy with Eve as he was capable and to hell with IT and with THEM. In other words, Jack he thought as he entered his building, fuck it, Jack, and forward with the Joplins!

Yes, there had been an unbelievable feel of happiness, one that he accepted suspiciously. He looked out of the window. Clear. Absolutely clear. It'd be as cold as a witch's tit in the morning, early in the morning when they started to the airport.

This, then, is what the Fates would have: Sissie. Ralph fixed himself a drink. Where did the feeling come from, the feeling that everything good was balanced inexorably with something bad? Man, he thought, those goddamn Methodists do a *job* on a cat. Oh, wow! His mordant, humorous thought did not do away with the situation; it remained, and he was glad when he heard them, Eve and Iris, in the hallway, their voices slightly muffled; it was something carpeted hallways always did to people—made them speak softer, as if in a church.

"It's stopped snowing, baby!" Eve said, rushing through the door, her eyes bright with the cold, her cheeks tinted a little darker, her lips sculptured and cold, but warming instantly when she touched them to his.

"We brought champagne!" Iris said, kicking the door closed behind her and Eve. "I loved it, Broth, I loved it!" She hoisted the magnum in one hand. "Bravo!" She threw off her coat, breathless. "I wanted to shout 'Bravo!' but Eve wouldn't let me." She let the coat fall to the floor. "The champagne should be cold already—"

"What's the matter?" Eve asked, noticing Ralph's rather studied smile and a distant sadness.

Iris approached him. "Bro? What is it?"

Eve paused in the process of taking off her coat.

"Nothing," he said. "The reservations are set for eight in

168

the morning. It's the first flight out. We should be there by noon."

"Oh," Iris said, "but no news."

"No."

"I want to talk to Dad before I go to bed."

"Okay." Ralph rose and went to the phone. Iris followed.

12

BIG RALPH JOPLIN shifted from one huge buttock to the other, opened his eyes and stared at the television screen. A cowboy movie; no, it was the telephone. He stared at the instrument. Wearily he pushed aside the small table which contained the remnants of his television dinner. He looked at the clock. It was past his bedtime. He had a long day tomorrow.

He stretched stiffly, picked up the tray, took it to the kitchen and dumped it into the garbage pail. He walked heavily down the creaking cellar stairs to check the furnace. Cold tonight, he thought. Stoke it up good. Once down there, moving in the shadows, he decided that he would call his brother Lewis. The phone call might have been from him. Might be sick or something.

Big Ralph took a long swig of beer and placed the can beside the phone. He paused a moment before dialing to watch the movie.

"Lewis," he said, when he heard his brother's voice. "You call me?"

Lewis hadn't.

"I thought maybe somethin' had come up so we couldn't watch the fight tomorrow. Well, I'm sorry. How inna hell was I supposed to know you was sleepin'?" Big Ralph hung up and turned back to the cowboy movie. He sipped his beer.

The phone rang again. Big Ralph picked up the instrument and said, "Hello?"

"Dad, it's me—Iris."

"Iris? *Iris!*" Beer spurted from the holes Big Ralph had punctured in the container. "Where are you calling from? Europe? What's wrong?"

"I'm at Ralph's, Daddy, in New York. How are you?"

"Oh, pretty good for an old man. Why didn't you write more often?" He laughed nervously.

"You didn't write at all."

"Well, I'm the old man."

"Ralph will talk to you in a moment."

"That rascal. Comes here to see his little girl and never stops by to see me. I hear about it three, four days afterwards."

Iris laughed politely.

"You married again, Iris? Got kids?"

"No, no, I'm not married."

"You ought to, Iris, and you ought to come back to America. Europe, that whole place, nothin' but Communists."

Iris paused a moment.

"Daddy, Mother's very ill."

"Sissie's sick? What's the matter?" Big Ralph took a double swallow of beer.

"Heart. Dad, it's pretty bad, but we're hoping and praying."

"I hope she'll be all right," Big Ralph said.

"We hope so too."

"I'd love to see you when you get back. If you feel up to it."

"Of course, Daddy. Like to talk to Ralph now?"

"Yeah, yeah, lemme talk to ol' Ralph."

After he had finished talking to his son, Big Ralph sat down and watched the cowboy movie again. He imagined himself calling Lewis and saying, "Lewis, Sissie's dyin'." Lewis was sure to answer: "When people get old they die."

PART

III

13

THE PAIN WAS NOT WHAT IT HAD BEEN. Sissie wondered what time it was. Why hadn't Ralph and Iris come? She had to talk to Iris. The years had slipped by so quickly. Ten or twenty times during each of those rushing years she had thought of writing her daughter and telling her, but each time Sissie had decided that Iris would be coming home soon and they could talk then. Sissie had always felt that her daughter should know. She had come to this conclusion time and time again after first considering that the girl might be better off not knowing. But not knowing was a lie and Sissie had long since stopped lying. It was lying that had got her into trouble. Sissie almost chuckled, remembering Arthur.

Now Arthur reminded her of a very pretty dog, a male

dog, that you see loose on the streets, running up to the bitches, teeth showing in a doglike grin, neck erect, tongue lolling. He had been like a favorite hound loping into her life and out of it, returning again and again, forever sure of himself, so sure that he had made her make the mistake of thinking that he could be used. Well, there had been some kind of liking too, a great deal of it. How to make Iris see that? How many times had the scene been set in her mind? Set so often that it seemed to have taken place already.

"Did you see April?" Sissie had planned to begin. Oliver would have gone out somewhere. Iris and she would be alone. "How is April? You know I was always sorry that marriage didn't work; sorry about yours too. What's wrong with my children? Was it the way I raised you all? Honey, you know, I left home when I was a mere child. I was frightened on that train, coming all that way by myself. I met Arthur on the train; he was a waiter, and he was kind to me, and I liked him."

(The long dingy train had had the Jim Crow car fastened to the coal tender. Coal dust had swirled continuously through the car; bags, old papers, chicken bones and crusts of bread had gathered in the corners. The once plush-covered seats had been filthy. It had been stifling, inhumanly hot, but Arthur had come through with sandwiches and coffee and cold water for the old people. She had liked Arthur from the very first. At Cincinnati he had said, "When the train clears the station, you can sit anywhere you want, young lady," though he wasn't much older than she, "and even go to the diner and get yourself some good hot food." He was in college, he told her, sitting down beside her after they left Buffalo; he was working for the summer. The city she was going to, he said, was one of the more progressive ones in the north; it had a tradition, had been one of the main stations along the Underground Railroad. While he spoke, she thought how smart he was, and how much smarter he would be when he finished college. He was from North Carolina. He sometimes stayed two or three days in the city waiting for his train after he had had time off.)

"I got to be pretty crazy about him," she had planned to say to Iris. "And how that man could kiss! You know how it is when you're young and . . . Arthur went away and Big Ralph started to come around. Oh, you know your father. He was a singin' man and kinda big in that raggedy town. Here I was a little ol' country girl with Arthur gone. Big Ralph promised me the moon, and I believed him—tell you I was young! Well, that moon was so far away, girl, and one thing and another. Arthur was back the next summer, coming and going. Me and your father had been done married and had lost Juanita. Your brother? Ralph? Didn't nothin' ever happen to him! Iris, that whole town was poor. We went hungry plenty of times. Juanita started to die when we didn't have money to buy coal to keep the house warm. I got mad, I just got mad. Used to sit home all the time when I was sick; I was sick a lot with all them babies, and if I wasn't sick, I was out there workin' because we had to get some money into that house someway. Me and Little Ralph sittin' home, sick. Girl, I was ma-a-a-d. The only times I wasn't mad were when Arthur was around. I couldn't be mad when he was around." Would Iris smile and understand? "Yes, I slipped out to see him. I'm talkin' woman to woman now. I know you haven't been no virgin since you and Harry broke up, have you?" Here she had planned to reach over and touch her daughter's knee, to give it a conspiratorial push. "I know you understand, don't you, honey? I'm not proud. No, I'm not, and I got to make peace with my God. I'd leave little Ralph with ol' Mis Clark and run to see Arthur. I'd generally get home before Big Ralph got home from the Silver Dollar."

(Arthur. He had not been as dandyish as Ralph. But he had been more certain of himself. And when he had kissed her, he had placed his tongue in her mouth. That had been exciting. Ralph had never done that until, one afternoon, she had kissed him that way. Arthur had come and gone, always talking about college in the fall. She knew that he would wind up with one of those high-yella girls anyway, a teacher like himself. What did he want with a country girl?)

"Hurry!" she heard someone say. A nurse wrapped something around her left arm and pulled it so tight that it almost hurt. Sissie heard a noise, *phiss*, *phiss*, *phiss*, and her arm felt like it was swelling. She heard Dr. Clayton's voice. A sharp, white light bored directly down from above. Sissie wanted to cover her eyes, but couldn't The light shone down like the sun in spring.

It had been in the spring that she had come to the conclusion that she was again pregnant. She must have seemed very abstracted. Arthur was always saying, "A penny for your thoughts." Big Ralph kept eying her with a cold watchfulness. But neither of the men had known the truth about her situation. She had come close to telling Arthur but something had held her back, perhaps fear that she would be unable to trap him. Arthur's plans for the future were so definite. Her idea had been to say that it was his child. She would never have told him it was Ralph's. Arthur said she

178

was unfaithful to him whenever she was pregnant, even though he *knew* she was married and sleeping in the same bed as her husband. She had to keep lying to Arthur and saying that she only did it when Big Ralph made her.

One summer night she stealthily entered the house and reached for the light cord. Suddenly she stiffened and threw both arms across her face. The blow landed, driving her across the room and slamming her into the wall. She collapsed onto the couch, still holding her hands in front of her and kicking furiously. The light went on and Big Ralph stood towering above her. At first Sissie wanted to scream out about the baby but her lips remained doggedly closed. She lowered her hands and caught sight of the knife.

"Oh, God, no," she said softly. She started to scramble to her feet, but Big Ralph thrust his body between her and the door. She noticed that she had a run in her stocking.

"Out with him again," he said. Sissie's eyes widened. Big Ralph knew. "I'll kill you," he said matter-of-factly. He moved closer and looked down at her with disgust. "You gypsy bitch!" Sissie collapsed into a fit of trembling. (Tell him about the baby! The baby! Tell him!) The words wouldn't come out; they were her revenge, and she was withholding them. She tried to think of something to say but couldn't. She sought to escape but each time he interposed his body. "Oh, God, oh, God," she mumbled now. She tasted blood in her mouth and opened her lips to let it drip on her dress, hoping that the sight of blood would bring him to his senses. He looked at her coldly. Sissie darted forward, brushed past him, seized a chair and flung it at him. It hit him and fell to the floor. Sissie stood, her back to the wall, near Little Ralph's bedroom. She breathed heavily and stared at the knife, a bread knife, the lower edge of the blade sweeping up to a point. Big Ralph held it low and stepped toward her. She kicked one of her shoes at him; he merely moved his head to one side the way she had seen him slip punches when he was boxing with his friends. She took a deep breath and shouted:

"*O Jesus, Help me*, HELP ME SOMEBODYYYYYYYYYY!"

His left hand was now around her neck; she couldn't move. He forced her back against the wall and then pushed her down. Then he pulled her toward him and slammed her against the wall so that the wall shook and the dishes in the kitchen rattled. She tried to shake her head. The hand forced her chin up. She wanted to say, Please, no, but her throat seemed like clay in his hand. Then she was looking straight up at the ceiling, unable to move, waiting for the knife.

Footsteps pounded up the stairs. A man's voice: "Ralph, Big Ralph, don't kill her! Open this goddamned door, Ralph. Don't be no fool now."

"Big Ralph!" a woman's voice shouted between the furious knocks, "you let that girl alone, you hear me! *Big Ralph!*"

"Open the door!" the man shouted again.

"Sissie?" The woman.

The door shuddered along its hinges. The sounds grew fainter and fainter to Sissie; she felt the knife blade slip cleanly into her throat, halt gratingly upon the cartilage of the windpipe. A stream of hot liquid flowed along her neck and then she fainted. Big Ralph, a ghostly blur now, stepped away. Sissie slumped forward. Little Ralph, in his sleepers, his shoulders hunched high on either side of his hysterically shaking head, screamed and trembled against the wall.

Bertha Weinstein, the police, the ambulance people and the

neighbors were gathered around when Sissie came to. Her friend Cora Boatwright held Little Ralph, talked soothingly to him. Bertha Weinstein said, "He could have killed you, Sissie. As soon as Cora called I came. You're going to be all right. Get rid of him; put him away," Bertha said fiercely. "And don't worry about anything." She turned to the officer. "She wants to file charges."

"For what?" one of the cops asked with an amused smile.

"For what? Attempted murder."

"Oh, come on, lady. They have cuttings down here every night. Does she work for you?"

"Yes."

"I want to swear out a warrant," Sissie said, looking around. "Where is he?"

The impassive faces of the neighbors stared back.

"Gone," one said.

Another said, "Done gone."

"Long gone," another said, chuckling.

"I'll go with you to the station," Mrs. Weinstein said. "We'll place charges all right."

The cop shrugged. "It's up to you, lady." He went back outside. The doctor said, "Turned out to be just a scratch; not very deep. More blood than damage. Probably didn't want to do it anyway; he could have. Keep that bandage on your throat about a week, then rub vaseline over it." He picked up his bag, closed it with a professional snap and went outside, climbed into the ambulance. The car drove off.

Sissie touched her throat. "He tried to kill me," she said unbelievingly. "He tried to cut my throat." She looked around at the neighbors. They think I deserved it, Sissie thought. "Help me up. We'll go downtown right now."

"You ought to get some rest first, Sissie," Mrs. Weinstein said.

"I want to do it now; I don't want that shiftless man to get away."

The neighbors remained silent, not looking at her when she passed with Mrs. Weinstein helping her. "Cora, stay with Little Ralph?" Sissie asked.

"Sure, don't worry 'bout him," Cora said, avoiding her eyes.

Sissie and Mrs. Weinstein rode down to the police station, placed charges and Sissie returned home. The next morning Cora told her that they'd found Ralph at Lewis' and that he was already in jail.

"Good, goddamn him," Sissie said, thinking that now she could tell Arthur the baby was his baby; he could say that that was why she and Big Ralph had broken up.

Sissie felt warm and pleasantly light-headed. She couldn't hear the voice of Dr. Clayton any longer. It seemed almost like spring to her, but there wasn't any fresh air where she was now nor could she smell the odor of newly blossoming trees. There was an acrid odor in the air. She thought of Big Ralph. The day they had first met. The fascination she had felt seeing him. Had it really been love? Her eyes stayed tightly closed as she remembered. . . .

She had been on her way to church. He had stood, his back to a pole, all slicked and duded up. He had smiled at her. He had been crooning, and as she came abreast of him he broke into a light, suggestive song, louder than before. She struggled hard to keep a straight face and only looked at him once. Cora had told her about him. Big Ralph Joplin, the singer. On the stairs she turned to look at him and saw that he had left his pole and had walked up the street behind her a little ways. He waved. She wished he'd said something so that she could have answered; she felt that an opportunity had been missed. She paused in the lobby, listening to the strains of the *Gloria Patri* and hoping that he would step quietly through the door to join her. Choir and parishioners joined:

"Praise God from whom all blessings flow
Praise him all creatures here below,
Praise him all ye heavenly hosts,
Praise Father, Son and Holy Ghost,
A-a-a-men-n."

His shadow did not fill the doorway behind her and Sissie went quietly into church.

She emerged alone at the conclusion of services, for she was still a stranger there and had been in the city but a month. She wished she didn't have to hurry back to serve dinner. She walked slowly homeward, humming the songs that had been sung in church; she felt as if all her worries had been removed. And then she saw him again. Sissie slowed. He spun around, looked at her. "Hello," he said.

"Hello," Sissie answered. She dropped her eyes and kept walking.

"Walk a ways with you?"

Sissie shrugged. "I don't care."

"Go to church every Sunday?"

"Yes." She glanced at him. "Your name's Ralph, isn't it?"

He nodded proudly. "You heard me sing at the Silver Dollar?"

Sissie laughed. "No, I just heard about you."

When they passed people on the walk, he stepped aside,

tipped his hat, and Sissie found that she liked that; he was polite. They walked up a hill. The lawns were bright green, the trees growing heavy with leaves.

"You work in private family?" he asked.

"Yes."

"What's your name?"

"Sissie Peterson."

"From down South?"

"Mississippi," she said, suddenly missing her family and the farm. "You live here, don't you?" She watched him nod. "Most the colored people live in Bloodfield, don't they?"

Big Ralph shrugged.

"Is that a bad place? I've never been there. They say it's bad, with cuttings going on all the time."

"Just like anyplace else," he said emphatically.

She felt his belligerence and said, "Well, you can't always believe what people say." She stopped; they were in front of the house in which she worked.

"Like to go to the moving pictures?"

Sissie nodded slowly; her eyes danced.

"When?"

"I have Thursdays off."

"What time shall I call for you?"

"Three." She watched his eyes roam over the house; she saw both envy and intimidation. "You'll have to come to the rear door," she said, taking a step in that direction herself.

"Sure," he said, his eyes clouding for a moment. "Good-bye."

Sissie turned and hurried along the rear walk. Wouldn't Cora be surprised when she told her!

She rose earlier than usual the Thursday of their first date.

Her young, farm-toughened body banished sleep at once. She was immediately alert for the sounds of morning: the English sparrows on the elm outside her window, the first robins jerking along on the lawn below, the wagons and horses of the first hucksters heading uphill, the cars.

She pulled her kimono around her and stepped quietly into the kitchen which still lay in darkness. She let up the green shades and sunlight instantly filled the room. Then she went to the sugar bowl and lifted it, saw her money. Sissie counted it with a heavy heart; most of it would have to be sent home. The next payday she would have to buy some things. She wished she could buy another dress-up dress. As it was, when Ralph called that afternoon, she would be wearing the same dress she had worn to church.

She put up the coffee in a big gray-enameled pot and set the flatiron beside it. Later she would press the dress. Returning to her room, the first she'd ever had all to herself—her sisters Louise and Willa Mae had always shared the same room and bed with her at home—she sat down to write a letter and prepare the money for sending. Perhaps before long they could all make their way North and everything would be all right.

Before long she heard the Geigers moving about upstairs. They were good, Christian people, Sissie's father had explained when they sent the money for her fare North.

"Hullo, Sissie," Mr. Geiger said. He always came quietly down the stairs, picked the paper from its door slot and padded into the kitchen. "How're you this morning?" His greetings were unvaried.

"Hello, Mr. Geiger," Sissie said, flipping the toast. "How're *you* this morning?" Her answer was as unvarying as his.

But Mr. Geiger was already halfway through the first page of the *Express*. He looked up suddenly. "Sissie, this oilcloth doesn't smell very good. Can't we do something about it?"

"A good washing doesn't seem to help, Mr. Geiger." Didn't he know that you couldn't keep those things on forever and forever?

"I'll tell Mrs. Geiger to get a new one."

"Yes, sir."

Mrs. Geiger came in, leaned over and kissed her husband's cheek. "Good morning, Harvey, and good morning to you, Sissie."

"Morning, Mis' Geiger." Mrs. Geiger looked pale but she was more spry than usual. "Here're the eggs. Hot now."

"What are you doing with your day off, Sissie?" Mrs. Geiger asked.

"I expect I'll be going to a moving picture this afternoon, ma'am."

"Isn't that nice, Harvey?"

Harvey Geiger grunted. He was to pick up a case of liquor later in the day; it seemed that the longer Prohibition lasted, the higher prices went. He hastened through his breakfast, reading rapidly.

Sissie served them quickly, efficiently, wanting them to finish and leave; Mrs. Geiger went downtown Thursdays to shop and lunch with friends. Mr. Geiger finished first, as usual, and Mrs. Geiger walked him to the door. She returned and finished her breakfast in silence, and left the kitchen to dress, Sissie knew. When she finally closed the door behind Mrs. Geiger, Sissie felt a vast relief. How quickly she had come to feel that the house and all its furnishings were hers and that the Geigers were merely bothersome intruders!

Sissie began to dance through the rooms, then halted before a mirror to primp and pretend that she was a fine lady, finer even than Mrs. Geiger. She would be one day, and she would stand in a beautiful dress and casually remove a cup and saucer—Spode—from the tray of the maid; well-dressed people, all speaking well, like Arthur on the train, would surround her. There would be a Franklin or a Ford or a Chevrolet in the garage. She would be gracious and lovely to Willa Mae and Louise and to her brothers Edward and Agamemnon; they would look up to her. And Ralph would be there, big and stiff in a tuxedo like Mr. Geiger's.

She skipped upstairs, the nearness of the fantasy making her feel effervescent and generous. How could all these things *not* come to her? She entered the Geiger's bedroom and opened the windows. She approached the bed; it smelled like stale bread. With tentative fingers she smoothed around the spots and fluffed the pillows. She could not understand why Mrs. Geiger didn't make the bed herself. Didn't she care if Sissie saw the spots? For a moment Sissie felt uneasy; she was an uncaring machine, a thing without substance, if the Geigers didn't care if she knew; it was as if she didn't exist or as if she were invisible, but able nonetheless to do their bidding. The feeling was one she had had many times before at home. In the bathroom she straightened the towels. Later, when she had pressed her dress, she would return and bathe in the tub; that was another good thing about Thursdays.

Someday, she reflected, she would have all this and more; she would have the best of everything and would not have to take a back seat to the Geigers or anyone else. She didn't know when that day would be, but that it would come, she had no doubt.

Her first doubts came some months later when she was going steady with Ralph. For a long time Sissie had been plaguing Ralph in a quiet way to meet his family; he had seemed ashamed of them. She, on the other hand, talked incessantly of her father and sisters and brothers and had even let Ralph see photographs of them. Finally he had agreed to arrange a meeting. The Joplins sounded to her as if they were very industrious: Lewis worked for the city; Alice had two children and her husband was employed at the depot, as a porter, Sissie guessed; and Emma, who no longer lived regularly at home, worked in a hotel.

Sissie's eyes shone as they walked toward Ralph's house, but when they arrived on the main street of Bloodfield, her pace slowed. The farther they proceeded, the shabbier the houses became. Sissie pressed her lips together; she did not look at Ralph as often now, and he seemed to be avoiding her also. Some of the buildings were worse than the shacks she'd seen at home. She felt out of place here in her white summer dress and bonnet. She walked gingerly, skirting the sections of the walks where concrete had not been laid. When they stood before Ralph's house, Sissie wanted to flee. But it was she who said with false joviality, "Let's go in." The inside resembled the interiors of the shacks you stumbled across deep in the Piney Woods of Mississippi. There had been something hopeful about the people who lived in those places, however.

"Emma," Ralph said disgustedly.

Emma stared at Sissie, grimacing, and then threw her arms around Sissie's neck. Sissie smelled perspiration and gin, baby diapers and food. Emma staggered to a chair.

"You know why I'm drunk? Wanna know why? 'Cause

we just can't do no better than this." She dropped her arms.
"I'm the oldest and I can't do nothin'. Been worried about you
comin', and things bein' the way they is. Know Ralph done
put you off as long as he could." She smiled drunkenly at
Ralph. "You might be good for him, 'cause he done got
ashamed of us and maybe he might do himself some good."
Emma tssskked. "Look't you; you don't b'long here in all
that white, lookin' lovely as a bride. I don't wear white; gets
too damned filthy in Bloodfield. I live with Benny; you know
him; he leads the band at D'Amica's; but I comes by to see
how things is now and again. Had to get outa this damned pigpen myself, but I ain't never told nobody this but you. Just
couldn't stand it. Thing is, we don't know where to turn;
the mens, they works once in a while. Ain't a decent job for a
black man in town." She gestured toward Ralph. "All he
wants to do is sing. Oh, he can sing all right. Benny says he's
a good singer, considerin' what this town ain't got, and that
he could be better if he tried, but goddamn it"—Emma flung
her fists in the air; her arms were taut. "What's the point in
tryin' t' sing for a buncha drunk-ass niggers don't know singin'
from talkin'?"

Behind Sissie, Ralph shuffled his feet. He stared at the floor.
"Emma," he said.

"Hush! I'm talkin'!" she shouted. She turned to Sissie, her
voice still raised. "It's hopeless. All you niggers from down
South comin' up here lookin' for streets made outa gold bricks,
but they ain't none. Not one goddamn gold brick, unless
you-all gonna shit it. We niggers just like you-all. Only
trouble is, we livin' the life you folks was dreamin' about.
This is the way it is. Oh, don't be thinkin' about them niggers
livin' on the side of the hill; they's damned few of them;

189

it's us that counts, 'cause we ain't suckin' nobody's ass to live."

Sissie backed up a couple of steps when Emma bent her head in a coughing jag. In the distance they could hear the rattle of the cans moving on their racks at the can company. Sissie felt Ralph's hand upon her wrist, tugging her gently backward toward the door. "Nice to have met you," Sissie said.

Emma rose unsteadily. "I been to school a little; I ain't nobody's fool." Then angrily she shrieked, "Goddamn it, do you think we'd live like this if we didn't have to?"

Emma gathered her bulk in the door, swelling up to shout at them as they walked rapidly down the street, to the corner, around it in silence.

"She was drunk," Ralph said.

They walked a block in silence before Sissie answered, "Yes."

"I don't know what got into her."

"You always lived there?" Sissie asked. She saw herself again standing in her white clothes in that dreary, stinking room; she knew what had got into Emma.

"We always lived there."

"And never heard from your father?"

"No," Ralph said, surprised. His father's desertion had been accepted as fact the moment he learned of it.

"My father would never do anything like that," Sissie said.

"He sent you up here to work and send money home," Ralph said bitterly.

"To come to this," Sissie said half aloud. She was suddenly frightened. How many Negroes in tattered clothes had she seen along the railroad tracks in the Northern cities, bent against the rays of the morning sun on her way to the city?

She had not seen many Negroes walking big and proud, the way they told of it at home. Maybe Arthur, but on that train he scuffled like a chain-gang nigger.

"Listen," Ralph said, breaking into her thoughts. "I know what you think of my family and where I live. I don't like it anymore than Emma; I want something better for myself—"

They had stopped. Sissie stood watching him.

"I got a good, big feeling for you, Sissie. If we got married, maybe together we can have something better. I love you, Sissie—"

"I couldn't live there," she said in rising horror.

"No!" He said. "We'll find our own place to go into housekeeping. We might even find a nice place in Jewtown. Sissie, I want something better than that!" He pointed back toward the house. "And I'd work hard, for you, Sissie; you'd never have to want for a thing. Before long, we could live as good as the Geigers."

She had loved him from that first Sunday; she even had been unable to lie about Arthur; Arthur had been just another suitor, one she knew she'd never really have.

14

BLOODFIELD, SISSIE THOUGHT, BLOODFIELD. A mask was being
fitted over her face. She could hear the nurses talking. Well,
she and Big Ralph had been sure they'd get out of Bloodfield,
but they hadn't quite made it. The flat they lived in after
they were married was at least out of earshot of the can
company, but the railroad tracks that ran down the main
street of Bloodfield were inevitably there. Their flat was on
the first floor and was approached along an upfaulting side-
walk and across an open wooden porch. The one light that
entered the rooms came from the street-side windows; the
rooms to the rear were oppressively gloomy. The furniture
was maple. Linoleum covered all the floors.

A narrow dirt road ran along the side of the building and

led to a blacksmith's shop. Enough horse dung had gathered to enrich the soil and huge bright sunflowers rose high above the leaning gray fence. The blacksmith was never seen either entering or leaving his shop, was merely heard pounding away; sometimes he would sing out, "Whoa, boy! Whoa, there. . . ." Only two kinds of noises broke the silence enveloping that house, the rumble of the trains passing, the sudden clatter of ironbound wagon wheels and horses' shod hoofs.

The passing trains moved slowly, their bells tolling, a ghostlike mist rising from beneath the engines. The ground shook. Engineers and firemen leaned from the windows of the cab. Negro porters and waiters could be seen lounging on the platforms between the cars. And white faces stared from window after window. When the trains passed, Sissie always felt sad and envious. She thought of home, and of Arthur.

Now, though she continued to work at the Geigers, she slept at home. Ralph rose in the morning and walked her to the Geigers. She gave him toast and coffee if the Geigers had not yet arisen. Sissie knew that after Ralph left her he always went to the Silver Dollar. There he'd talk with the performers or play around with the crystal set that belonged to D'Amica, the cabaret's owner. The discussions in the Silver Dollar were always the same: why Dempsey wasn't fighting Harry Wills, the career of Jack Johnson, the chances of Tiger Flowers, the local Black Hope; Flowers was a frequenter of the Silver Dollar. After hanging around the club for a few hours, Ralph would go home and take a nap. At six he returned to the Geigers' to pick up Sissie. After dinner he returned to the club.

A large cellar had been renovated to create the Silver Dollar. A stamped-tin ceiling had been installed and the walls roughly plastered, covered with red-striped wallpaper. The bar was small and had a radio set on it during the day; at night D'Amica took up his post there. Near the bar was a small platform; it was the bandstand. Red lights were suspended from between the naked rafters; on special occasions such as Christmas and New Year's Eve, D'Amica hung a spinning globe from the ceiling which gave off swift, glittering dimes of light.

Sissie was proud when Ralph performed at the Silver Dollar. He came in on cue and sang a note behind the beat, just as the well-known blues singers did on records he played at home. He held his head erect and looked out secretly from beneath lowered lashes. Sometimes his mouth opened so wide that Sissie could see the roof of it. And all the time he moved his legs restlessly.

"Sing it, Big Ralph," Sissie would hear, and smile.

"Oh, sing it, Ralphie," Cora would shriek, glancing at Sissie. "Oh, *sing* it, man!"

And Sissie would start snapping her fingers and moving restlessly in her seat, wanting Ralph to finish so they could dance and she could be close to him. She enjoyed the nights she was at the club, but they seemed so brief to her.

The letters from Louise and Willa Mae made Sissie think of the farm. But why, she wondered, should she have such thoughts when she was married to so prominent a man, and had started life with so many conveniences. Louise and Willa Mae were amazed that she had a flush toilet and electric lights. Did Big Ralph, they asked, have friends? Sissie basked in their jealousy; they had wished her ill because she was the one who had been chosen to go North. Instead, she had managed to compound her good fortune. Edward was still home, working and chasing girls on Sunday. Agamemnon had run off; perhaps, the sisters said, he would find his way to Sissie's. He did not show up and Sissie was secretly grateful. She went on long walks, attended parties and church functions, saw moving pictures, visited friends on Sundays. Then one day she discovered she was pregnant.

She had believed that, like her mother, she would accept motherhood gracefully. But her condition came as a shock to her. Soon she would not be able to work; they would have difficulty subsisting on what Ralph made. Their life would suddenly be different. Even Ralph was affected by the news but he didn't say much. Sissie faced her coming imprisonment with mounting dread. But there was Arthur and as long as he was in town that summer, she ran about with him.

Ralph Joseph Joplin was born at home. He was pulled from between Sissie's trembling legs and slipped into the hands of the visiting nurse. Although the baby was large, Sissie had not had a hard time of it. She started joking almost immediately. "Now, I'll have to call him Little Ralph, and you Big Ralph."

A week later, despite the payoffs to the police, the Silver Dollar was closed for violating the Volstead Act. "But don't worry," Ralph said, stroking Sissie's back. "We're gonna play house-rent parties and some fraternity dances up on The Hill. Benny's got it all fixed up."

No one ever made much money from house-rent parties. Sissie sensed that Big Ralph was restless and uneasy. He didn't laugh the way he once had and there were moments when she saw fear lurking in his eyes. "How long will it be before D'Amica opens again?" she kept asking. She would watch him shrug—it would be late at night and they would be eating the steak sandwiches Ralph had brought home from a fraternity dance. Big Ralph didn't know when D'Amica would reopen for business.

Then one night Ralph told her what she already suspected: he had been in the Silver Dollar, hanging around, when Benny had come in. Benny had wanted some money from D'Amica, but D'Amica had refused to lend him any. "Things don't look so good, boy," Benny had told Big Ralph. "D'Amica says when he opens up he's got to pay more for the payoff. He just ain't got no money. I got to go along with him; he been awright to me."

It had been hard for Big Ralph to believe that D'Amica was no longer good for a touch.

"Looks like," Benny had said, "all of us better start lookin' around for some work during the day."

"Why?" Ralph had asked, frightened, knowing the answer.

"He say he can't even pay what he *bee*n payin'. And you with that new baby. Goshalmighty, no!" Benny had twirled the way he did when he was angry or disgusted. "Things gettin' tight and gonna get worse. I ain't *never* been in a place where a colored man couldn't do nothin'. They done finished the highway, and all the porterin' jobs 're filled. Goddamn, even down home a nigger could always get some sharecroppin' to feed hisself."

"That's right!" Sissie said, interrupting Ralph's story.

"Benny said," Big Ralph went on, "that we oughta make the move away from here. He's goin' back to Chicago or to New York. He said I could do better there." Ralph remembered Benny's puzzled statement: "Boy, I just don't see what a man can do here to hold hisself together."

"Not with the baby," Sissie said.

"I know," Ralph said. He didn't tell Sissie that he had already been around to see his brother Lewis.

"Hear the Silver Dollar got raided and closed," Lewis had said, rolling a cigarette.

"Yeah," Ralph had answered. Lewis never went anywhere except to the movies. He was called the "tightest nigger in Bloodfield." "But we been playin' fraternity dances up on The Hill and a few house-rent parties. Did all right."

"How's Sissie?"

"She's all right."

"It ain't none of my business, but you got a little gypsy on your hands. Know what I mean?"

"You mean that railroad man she used to walk with? He ain't nothin'; she told me all about that."

"Ain't no woman gonna tell no man all about *every*thing, Ralph. Your wife got some gypsy blood in her and she likes to *run*."

"Ah, shoot, you're talkin' crazy," Ralph had said. "I need me some day work." He had watched Lewis fight a smile. "I thought maybe you'd know of somethin'. Ain't much work to be had around here, you know."

Lewis had shrugged and his eyes had become veiled. "I'll look around."

"I mean, you don't know of anything right off, do you?" Ralph had asked, an urgency in his voice.

"Not right off, but I'll look around." Lewis had glanced quickly at his brother.

Now, almost finished with his sandwich, Ralph watched his wife tend the baby. If she were cheating on him, he thought he would kill her.

The Geigers were unwilling to release the girl they now had and take on Sissie again, but through some of the church members Sissie heard about and secured day work in Jewtown.

For the first few days Ralph walked with her to the new job at the Weinsteins, but stopped when Sissie remarked, "Honey, you could put your time to better use by lookin' for work instead of walkin' me."

The Weinsteins lived in a rambling frame two-story house. The cellars were so large that Mr. Weinstein had let them to a coffin-maker, Moishe Zefner. The acrid scents of Zefner's oils and powders, his woods and varnishes, hung heavily in the air. Zefner moved about his horses and coffins dressed in a white tieless shirt buttoned all the way up, and black pants which were continually open at the fly, and he wore a yarmulke. His full beard sprayed off light as he bent down to hammer in nails which he pulled studiously from his mouth, one by one. Sometimes when he had just finished a coffin, he would take Sissie's hand and glide it over the wood. "How fine? How fine?" he would say, while Sissie, one arm filled with damp clothes about to be hung on the line, fought against the fear the old man produced in her. Sometimes when he was eating the hot soup Sissie brought to him, he would stare at her and smile and patiently nod his head.

Bertha Weinstein gave a robust vigor to the home. She was a fair stocky woman who talked rapidly and moved as quickly. Sissie could not see why this young couple needed help; the home was spotless. Then she realized that Mrs. Weinstein was lonely and really wanted a companion. Mr. Weinstein was in the furniture business. "Anything you need, Sissie, just let me know and we can git it for you

198

from the store," Mrs. Weinstein said over and over in her breathless fashion.

Whenever the offer was made, Sissie would say, "Not right now," thinking of what the people in Bloodfield said about the Jews. "Girl, work you half to death and give you matzoh balls for pay!" Or, "They'll give you things, like they was for free, and come time to get your money and they done took off for what they was supposed to be givin' you for nothin!" Nothing like this happened to Sissie, yet when she was at the hairdresser's she remained silent or nodded diffident acquiescence when such remarks were made, and would feel a twinge of remorse at being disloyal to Mrs. Weinstein. Because she could not buy the things she saw at the Weinsteins, she grew more and more insecure. Now she no longer hurried home to Big Ralph and the baby. Her steps were slow; she would stop off to visit Cora or some other friend. The moment she entered the house she knew whether Big Ralph had had any luck getting work that day. She felt more and more resentment when Mrs. Weinstein gave her dresses and left-over foods to carry home. She didn't have much of a chance to take it out on Big Ralph, for usually by the time she was home he was ready to leave for D'Amica's. It was during one of those periods when she and Ralph were struggling to love each other as they once had that she became pregnant once more. This labor was hard, and Sissie recalled the old saying that a child born in pain leaves home early. The winter Juanita was born the temperature didn't rise above twenty degrees. First the coal gave out, and then the wood. Coke was cheap but gave little heat. Sissie would sometimes get into bed with the baby and Little Ralph while Big Ralph trudged through the snow to Jewtown to buy a sack of hard coal with borrowed money. Juanita died of pneumonia just before Little Ralph turned three.

Sissie and Ralph went to order a coffin from Mr. Thompkins, a porter in a downtown store who doubled as the undertaker for the community.

"How much you gonna put down on it?" Mr. Thompkins wanted to know.

Sissie looked first at the old man and then at her husband.

"Twenty," Ralph said. He'd already told Sissie that D'Amica would certainly advance him that much.

"How about after?"

"Man, I'm gonna pay you!" Ralph shouted. Sissie rose, frightened.

"Ralph, Ralph," Sissie said. "Mr. Thompkins only wants to do proper business, that's all. He knows we're goin' t' pay him."

"Awright, Mis' Joplin," Mr. Thompkins said, with a dry smile, "I'll let you have this pretty seventy-five dollar casket, 'cause I know you work hard and you'll see that it gets paid for."

"Thank you, Mr. Thompkins," Sissie said, not looking at her husband.

"When you gonna gimme that twenty?" the old man asked Ralph. Ralph turned and looked at Mr. Thompkins, who was a trustee in Sissie's church, always asking for just one more collection to calcimine the church ceiling.

"Tomorrow," Ralph said, taking Sissie's arm and guiding her out. The day they gathered in the living room with the mourners was gray and cold. Very little light filtered through the windows. D'Amica came, peered into the casket and shook his head. He touched Sissie on the arm and went out. "It is sad," he whispered. Reverend Polk, young and somber, said the eulogy, ending it with, "Suffer little children to come unto Me, and forbid them not; for of such is the kingdom of heaven."

"Juanita's sleep. Juanita's sleep," said Little Ralph, who sat upon Sissie's lap, poking at Bertha Weinstein, herself now two months pregnant. "Sit still!" Sissie cried to Little Ralph, and hit at him. He drew back, tense and watchful. "Sit still, honey," Sissie said again, as if to mollify the harsh and startled glances which had been turned upon her. She lowered her eyes in shame. Throughout the rest of the services, the long ride to the cemetery morgue where the coffin would lie until the spring thaw, Sissie thought, one less mouth to feed, poor baby, but there's one less. Sissie shuddered and thought of the chilly flat to which they would return.

Sissie went back to work in a frenzy; so much money was needed to be sent home. Money for food and rent. Money for bedding and furniture. Always money. If Big Ralph couldn't make it, she would. She no longer felt for old Zefner, though he remained fond of her; no one else had seemed to care whether he got his soup or not. But now she had fallen silent and introspective. Even she forgot to serve him. When Mrs. Weinstein followed her about, chattering, Sissie pleaded to be left alone. Bertha Weinstein drew back, puzzled and hurt, wondering what was wrong.

The quarrels at home became sudden and violent. If Ralph complained that dinner wasn't ready she shouted, "Look, you, Ralph, I've been workin' all day and I'm tired. Fix yourself somethin'. No point in my workin' so hard to keep us together if you can't pitch in just a little once in a while."

Ralph would shout back, "What the hell you think I'm

tryin' to do? You think I been sittin' on my ass, not lookin'? I don't give a good goddamn how hard you been out workin' —when you get your backside in here, remember you're my wife, and you're supposed to cook my damned dinner and don't ever forget it!"

Sissie's perpetual reply was, "Sure I'm your wife, but I'm not the man in the house; *you're* the man, but you don't act like it. *Some*body's got to be the man here and make some money to bring in here, and it sure ain't you!"

Ralph would stalk out, slamming the door.

Sissie, left in the vacuum of silence which was broken only by the questions put to her by her son, would ask herself, Why couldn't he find work? Why was it that all the men paced the streets mornings, heads bent, steps slow? At what point had she become the man and he less than the man he had seemed to be? Sissie stroked the head of her son without looking at him. How long would this go on? The women could always find work in some kitchen someplace. She remembered what Emma had said: looking for bricks made of gold. That *was* the way they'd told it at home. Freedom up there; do what you want, go where you pleased, speak what you chose. Freedom. But some of what was down there seemed to be up *here*. Different, but the same: keep you raggedy and nervous. If you had the money you could do all the things they said you could do in the North, but if you didn't have the money...?

Always after the arguments she felt contrition. Ralph wasn't there, and so she would embrace Little Ralph, and talk to him. He would smile gratefully and Sissie would know that she was away too much. She would get him ready for bed, as the trains passed. The trains would remind her of

Arthur. She needed someone who had been untouched by this decay, this hopelessness, this chaos—someone who would make her feel like a woman instead of a drayhorse.

Whenever her husband returned, she was grateful. Even if he had been drinking, she was grateful.

After they had had one particularly violent argument, he returned, drunk and remorseful. They made love with reckless desperation. When spring came she could not accept the possibility of her third pregnancy, and again she fled wildly through the soft nights to Arthur. The summer that followed was the summer Big Ralph had tried to kill her.

15

BIG RALPH KNEW that he hadn't wanted to kill Sissie. He stood in the warm office looking into the garage where his truck was being fueled. Impatiently he pounded his feet against the floor. Standing and waiting there brought back the old jail-house fever. No one had come to visit him in prison but Lewis.

"You doin' all right?" Lewis had asked, studying Ralph, who was seated behind the wire. "I guess so," Ralph had answered, pulling a hangnail. "You don't look so good." Somehow or other Lewis always said the wrong thing.

"I brought you some Duke's Mixture. Had to leave it with the guard. He'll give it to you later."

Ralph had nodded and had studied his fingernails. Ralph

sensed that Lewis was enjoying seeing him in jail. It was as if they had been returned to childhood; Lewis was once more the superior. He had never been in jail.

"They got a band here so you can keep in practice?" Lewis asked.

"No, there's no band here."

Lewis hesitated. "Maybe it's a good thing; maybe you should go into something else when you get out. You're getting time off for good behavior if you don't mess up. And the connections I made. . . . Besides, it was only your wife, or leastways, that's how they look at it. If it'd been a white man —" Lewis smiled. "Listen, they started takin' colored on some of the trash crews. I think I can get you a job hauling ashes."

"How's Sissie?"

"What?"

Ralph looked directly into his brother's eyes for the first time. "I said, how's Sissie?"

"She's gone," Lewis said bleakly.

Ralph's fingers shot through the wire. "Gone? Gone where?"

"Goddamn it, sit down." Lewis looked hastily at the guard. "I don't know. Someone told me last month. Saw her gettin' on the bus."

"For where?"

"Dammit, I told you I didn't know. Besides, what the hell you want to worry about her for?" Lewis said quickly, drawing back from the wire. "I hear she's pregnant."

Big Ralph sagged. "I told you so," Lewis mumbled. Ralph stared at him with dull eyes and then went back to pulling at the hangnail. In a hoarse voice he said, "Where's the boy?"

"She put him in the City Home."

"She just went off and left him?"

"I guess so," Lewis said impatiently. "You got enough to worry about. I'll look after the boy, me and Emma and Alice. We'll see to him."

A relieved smile started across Ralph's face. "Thank God, yes. Take him outa there—"

Lewis moved quickly in his seat. "I didn't mean—hell, I'm working all the time, and with that small room—Emma with her drinking—"

Ralph said grimly, "And Alice with her own kids. . . ."

"I meant we'd send things and maybe go by and see him," Lewis said angrily. "What did you want us to do, anyway?" He paused. "Now you stop worryin'. That boy's gonna be all right. He's tough, like you."

Lewis had left and had returned ten months later on the day that Ralph was freed. The world lay just outside Auburn prison which hugged close to U.S. Highway 20. Ralph and Lewis had walked from the prison to the bus station without once looking back. It was turning spring and, as they moved past the gently rolling fields, Big Ralph said tonelessly, "It's good to be out." The fields were heavy with the odor of horse manure, and the first shoots of green hung like mist around them.

"Yes, yes, it must be," Lewis said. "Well, you look in good shape. You ought to be able to haul trash and ashes all right."

"It's all fixed, then?"

"I told you not to worry about it," Lewis said. Lewis laughed. He elbowed Ralph and winked, passing him the sack of Duke's Mixture. "It pays to have a politician in the family, hey boy?"

Ralph poured the tobacco without stopping and rolled a cigarette. He ran the stick match along his behind without breaking stride and applied the flame to the cigarette. He handed the sack back to Lewis. "No word from Benny?"

"No, Silver Dollar's the same, though; that wop D'Amica is still rakin' in the money. I don't know what's worse, Jews or wops."

Big Ralph was silent.

"That music. It had to end sometime. Maybe other places it goes good, but not here. Besides, you got that boy to look after now."

Ralph nodded, but he was still thinking about not being able to sing anymore. Ralph lapsed into silence. Sissie gone, Benny gone, old Mis' Clark dead. A different world.

There were only twenty some odd miles from Auburn to the city. The road ran along flat terrain which gave way in the east to a series of green gullies and one large hill. The trip seemed only to have begun when it was at an end.

They got out of the bus near the square where the soldiers and sailors monument stood, and began walking briskly out along the broad thoroughfare where mansions stood surrounded by deep green lawns. They puffed up a hill, turned and panted up another, steeper hill. Across the street were the untended playgrounds of the City Home. The swing racks were still empty, the teeter-totter supports bare, the struts for the shoot-the-chutes, naked. Ralph felt an unrest in his stomach as they crossed the street and entered the wide, low building that reeked of urine.

It took them only fifteen minutes to find Little Ralph. Something went out of Big Ralph when he saw his son. The child stepped forward and said softly, accusingly, "Daddy?"

Big Ralph picked the boy up and busied himself buttoning the boy's clothing. He put him on his back and carried him down the hills, across the city and home. They sat in the dark flat with its Salvation Army furniture that Lewis had rented for them, looking at one another. Lewis had gone, leaving five dollars behind.

"You want some ice cream, son?" Big Ralph asked, wishing the boy would smile.

"Yes."

Ralph held out his hand and felt an undefined elation when the boy took it without hesitation. They went down the stairs to the corner store, passing the Fro-Joy ice-cream sign fastened on the door. Afterward they walked around the corner to Cora's.

Cora Boatwright embraced them both. "Big Ralph," she sighed. "Sure is good seeing you again." She looked down at the boy, watched him with ice-cream cone for a moment. "And this is Little Ralph, growin' like a weed. Well, well, well." She led them into the kitchen. "You folks have got to eat, I know."

"We were goin' to the restaurant," Ralph said.

"That ain't no place for a child. Least of all the first day out for you an' for him. Sit down there and hush."

The meal did not take long to prepare. Cora kept up a running conversation. "You start workin' tomorrow, don't you, Ralph?"

"Yeah, on the trash and ash trucks."

"You all through singin'?"

"All through, Cora."

"Ain't been the same at the Silver Dollar with you and Benny gone."

Big Ralph looked at his son. "I guess it's all over, Cora."

"It's a shame. You sure could sing!"

Ralph laughed. He looked at her. The impact of being away ten months struck softly home. She saw his staring and said, "Your place's all fixed up, Lewis tells me, but maybe I'd better step over there later and take a look. I know how Lewis is with a dollar. Cheap. Tight. He'd make the Indian on a nickel straddle the buffalo." She looked straight at him. "All right?"

"All right, Cora." The thought was full upon him now, warm and all out of proportion.

"Better put the boy to bed early," she said gently. "I 'spect he's had a full day."

"Sure, he's been a busy little somethin'."

"Heard from Sissie?"

The question startled him. "No," he mumbled.

"If you want, I'll bring her address with me." She stopped serving and gave him that bold open look. "You want it?"

He mumbled again with head bent, "Yes, please."

Black Tiger Flowers was Ralph's throwing partner. They went ahead of the big awkward White trash truck, on foot, bursting the still mornings with cries of "Whoap!" or "Okay, hold it!" The dumper was a small man; he rode in the van and steadied the containers as they came flying up. He up-ended them, dragged them empty and kicked them down again to Ralph or Black Tiger Flowers. The driver was an Italian, a politician two rungs above the lowest on the patronage ladder. He left his cab only to eat, submit to the evacuatory demands of his body, and to quit at the end of the day.

Nearly every morning Tiger was still drunk from the night

before or nursing a hangover. Tiger was a half-head taller than Ralph and broader. He was built and looked not unlike a gorilla. He walked sometimes with a half-stride and a half-shuffle, moving along sideways like a crab. At his peak in the ring Tiger wore specially made white gloves and shoes which contrasted sharply with his indigo skin. Ralph remembered him from those days; they had been good days for Tiger, who appeared after every victory in the Silver Dollar clad sportily in plus fours and wide plaid cap. He bought drinks; he had women. And then he began losing fights. Lack of training, the *Express* said. Tiger was losing so often that the time had come when the fans had bellowed unashamedly in the Arena, "Kill the niggeh! Kill the niggeh!" Week after week it was the same story: Tiger backpedaling, his skinny shanks like brittle sticks, his bulgeless rump shivering beneath the silk pants, sliding on his big feet and flailing with his now comical white gloves, more to cut the smoke than to strike his opponent. The night he appeared low on the card in black shoes and wine-colored gloves the fans stopped yelling; Black Tiger Flowers had himself acknowledged that he was through.

Now Tiger danced, when he and Ralph began throwing together from trash can to trash can, snuffling, hooking and crossing his great fists. "Keeping in shape, Ralph," he explained. "Go with me." Ralph would block and weave until Tiger, recapturing the instant of past glory, would slip an open hand up against Ralph's face—a mock knockout blow, and cry, "Uh-*huh!*" and freeze there smiling toughly as if waiting for the photographers. If the photographers did come again, Ralph reflected, it would be for murder; now Tiger roamed the streets on fight nights, his white gloves on, beating up visiting white sports and blacks he didn't know.

Little Ralph was sitting on the stoop, Sissie remembered, watching the white boys play steps with a dirty tennis ball. Sissie held the baby in one arm, with her other hand she gripped her bag. She wondered if the child ever played with the other boys. He looked lonely seated there. She was here, finally, after coming all that way by bus; after dingy Southside rooms in Chicago and the old down-home sisters who had looked at her as if she were a whore because she had had a baby; Sissie had wanted to shout that she was an honest woman who, like any other, had made a mistake. She had longed for the sanctity of home and husband, had cried many nights thinking about Little Ralph. She wished she had taken him with her. But drying her tears, she would realize that had she brought him they would surely have starved. It had been bad enough leaving the baby with strangers while she walked to Drexel Boulevard and back to do the day's work. It had been the graciousness of God that had directed Big Ralph back to her.

Now Sissie was closer to her son. He had that look of being angry and melancholy at the same time, the look Agamemnon had had. Sissie put her bag down. The boy looked just like his father. He was so intent watching the game that he didn't notice her. Sometimes his pink tongue flicked out to wet his dry, dark lips; sometimes he kicked his legs in joy, pleased by the progress of the game.

"Little Ralph?" Sissie said, smiling nervously.

The child turned, irritated at the interruption, then his face went blank.

"What?" he asked defiantly, suspiciously.

"You know who I am?"

211

He pressed his lips together. He rolled his eyes at her, at the bag, at the baby.

Sissie hissed, "I'm your mother, boy!"

Little Ralph smiled uncertainly. "My mother?" he asked tentatively. "My mother?" and he broke into a sudden grin, as if he'd just caught on to a joke.

The baby whimpered. "Hush, baby," Sissie crooned. She struggled up the stairs, fretting at the darkness and at the unsteady railing. She breathed heavily when she got to the top. The door to the flat was half-open. She pushed against it with her bag. Big Ralph wasn't there. He couldn't be far off, she thought, not with Little Ralph downstairs on the stoop. And it was Sunday, the day she had agreed to return so that he would be home from work. Sissie put the bag on the floor; settled the baby on the bed, and changed its diaper. She looked around the flat; it was pleasant enough; the odor of fresh paint was there, and the furniture was new and substantial. The furniture made her think of the Weinstein's. The flat would be a little crowded with four people living in it, but Iris wasn't grown (neither was Little Ralph, really; he wasn't even in school yet), and they'd be in another place —a little farther from Bloodfield—by the time she got up to some size.

Little Ralph's voice wavered up the stairs: "Daddy, some woman's upstairs. She got a baby. Daddy—is she my mother?" The last word was pitched low, in almost a whisper.

Sissie didn't hear Big Ralph's reply. Instead there was a crashing up, up, and up the stairs. He burst through the door and came to a stop in the bedroom.

"Hello, Ralph," Sissie said. She looked up from the edge of the bed where she sat, studying her husband.

212

Ralph's eyes wandered from Sissie to the baby and back. "Are you all right?" he asked. His eyes dropped to her throat and then he looked quickly away.

"Uh-huh," she answered. "I'm all right."

Big Ralph took a deep breath. "The baby all right?"

"She's fine."

"What's her name again?" He moved forward and crouched down to see the baby.

"Iris."

"That's pretty. She looks like you," he said. Sissie detected the relief in his voice; no matter how hard he looked he would not have found any resemblance to Arthur.

"Do you like the name?" she said.

"I like it."

"If you want to change it—"

"No, I like it. Are you tired?"

"It was a long trip. I am, kind of. You know how those buses are."

"Yeah. Why don't you get some rest?"

"Maybe I'd better fix something for Little Ralph; it's close to dinnertime."

"He just ate a little while ago. That's why he's downstairs; likes to go play after he eats."

"He didn't know me," Sissie said. "I didn't want to leave him with those rowdy folks we knew. That's why I left him at the City Home." Her eyes were averted. "Besides, it was awful in Chicago. I don't know what would've happened to us if there'd been another mouth to feed. Imagine, in this day and age and in this country, worryin' about another mouth to feed."

"That's all right about the City Home," Ralph said, and he

was not looking at her either. "He knew you. He was just playing," he said. "He's a playful little cuss sometimes and with a straight face. If you don't understand—"

"No, he didn't know me, but I'll make him love me again."

"Sure you will."

In the silence which came then, Sissie toyed with the baby. Ralph lit a cigarette and watched them; his smile was stiff. "How'd you like that Lindy?" he said, to break the awkwardness of the silence.

Sissie brightened at once. "Wasn't that good? Now you know God had to be with that boy. All that way alone over all that ocean. That was good," she said, shaking her head.

"Yeah. Hear about those two Italians who got executed last month?"

"Them Reds? Oh yes, I heard about them." Sissie breathed deeply; it hadn't been so bad. She looked at her husband, then lowered her eyes, waiting.

Big Ralph said, "Get some rest, girl. I know you got to do for the baby and all. I'll take the boy for some ice cream. He's crazy about ice cream. What shall I bring back for you?"

Sissie pretended to think, then said, "Oh, nothin' right now, thanks."

Ralph looked at the baby again. "Iris?"

Sissie said, "Iris."

16

TWO YEARS LATER Sissie and Ralph moved to Jewtown. Jewtown lay but a few blocks south of Bloodfield. Trees were plentiful in this area which was only a mile or two square and had acquired its name because Polish and Russian Jews lived there. Jewtown, however, was not predominantly Jewish; the Jews were most heavily concentrated on the streets in the Joplins' immediate neighborhood. Two frame synagogues stood within a block of each other; on Saturdays the sidewalks in front of the building were crowded with worshipers; on weekdays one saw reluctant schoolboys entering the basements on their way to *cheder*.

The street on which the Joplins lived was entirely lacking in racial homogeneity. At one end of the block stood an

Italian restaurant and beside it a *bocci* court, for the Italians had not as yet settled in their corner of the city. Facing the Italian establishment was an Irish diner from which emanated the odors of stew and corned beef and cabbage. Ransom's adjoined the diner. Ransom sold hair pomades for both sexes, cheap perfumes, and penny candies and cigarettes. There was always a stale smell in this small gloomy shop. At Ransom's one could also pick up the Chicago *Defender* and the *Vigilante*. The latter was a Negro sheet, four pages long, dedicated to the promulgation of protest and gossip; Ransom, an irritable twig of a man, considered himself a militant. But this did not prevent him from being in the policy racket. In addition to taking numbers and acting as the Jewtown drop, he took care of the weekly payoff to the occupants of Police Car 26.

Across the street from Ransom's was the only Negro barbershop on that side of town. Whenever Sissie passed by, Gideon and his customers waved. Gideon had moved from Bloodfield, his instinct having told him that the swelling population there, continually augmented by the influx of Southerners, would overflow into Jewtown. And he knew that his clientele would follow him wherever he went. Since Gideon cut white as well as Negro hair, he reasoned that he could pick up additional business in Jewtown. Gideon was a true democrat, a veteran of the war; he knew every liberal cliché.

Alpert's was lit by neon and crammed with barrels of dill pickles and herring, and every variety of delicatessen. The lush scents of this market mingled on the street with the odors from Saslow's Fish Market. Volinsky and Bloom, bakers, competed with one another, filling their windows with popovers, half-moon cookies, cakes and tarts; Guido's sat between them—his shop had the sharp scent of Italian sausage and cigars. Schor's was the kosher butcher shop; Ayling the nonkosher. Ayling was bitter because Schor's business was so heavy. Two more fish markets and an ice and coal house completed the commercial aspect of the neighborhood.

High above on a hill stood the university. A clumsy shaft of sandstone, one of its sooty Gothic towers was visible from Jewtown. From that tower came the majestic sound of the chimes played by the Delta Kappa Epsilon boys. Perhaps the chimes were responsible for the odd bond that joined the university and Jewtown. Generally the chimes were played twice a day, at eight in the morning and at noon, but during the football season they were also used to announce victories with a medley of fight songs. Because Mr. Weinstein had attended the university, Sissie and her family felt even closer than most to the school. The Weinsteins never missed a game, would go off leaving their son with Sissie. Invariably they returned bringing pennants and celluloid football dolls for the Ralphs, Big and Little.

It was with the commoners' amused tolerance that the residents of Jewtown lined the streets to watch the students snake-dance down from the hill in their annual "Beat Colgate" parade, Torches flared, the streets abounded with clean-looking, block-lettered youth. The people of Jewtown dimly hoped that their children someday would be students, snake-dancing down the hill in one of those torchlight parades.

Warily, sometimes, Sissie rummaged through her dreams and thought what all the other Jewtowners were thinking. One day, perhaps, that rare black face in the crowd of students might be her daughter or son. And Big Ralph himself, carried away by bathtub beer, often haltingly voiced the possibility that his son would become a football star. "A natural little atha-lete," he would say proudly, and Sissie, pleased, would snort and smile.

The municipal garage cut its trash crews, but Big Ralph promptly got a job with an asphalt contractor. Sometimes on her way to work, Sissie passed the asphalt gang. It was composed entirely of Negroes and reminded her of the chain gangs she had seen at home. With their shoes wrapped in tattered and tarred burlap, the men raked and shoveled the steaming asphalt. When the asphalt was in place, they took the thumpers and patiently pounded the tar, and then stood back to let the steamroller finish the job. But it was work, Ralph said, as Sissie and he lay side by side in bed. It was work a man could put his back and shoulders to; he felt good at the end of the day. In the darkness Sissie smiled.

Sissie had not seen her father for years, and then he came to visit. His hands were gnarled and he had very little hair. Joseph Peterson—Sissie's father—was as large as Big Ralph, and with or without his spectacles on, his eyes were keen, as if he had spent a long time looking at great distances. He still had that manner of speaking rapidly, clipping his words. He brought with him the odor of open windswept places and of sun and slow-moving water. Sissie even imagined one time that the smell of Sephora the mule had come with him as well. The smells were enough to set her thinking again of the land he was trying to keep. He had not discussed the farm with her, but she knew that he had come to see if there was some way in which they could help. How bad was it? Would the white folks really be able to take the land away? He kept saying things were going all right, and this only made Sissie feel worse. It was as though she were no longer a part of the family. But suppose she and Ralph took the kids South to help out? Ralph would more than make up for the loss of Agamemnon. And he'd scare those crackers into some sense. She would be there to help Willa Mae and Louise. The kids would enjoy being out of doors. These thoughts were pure fantasy, Sissie knew. Big Ralph would never go South, and neither, she reflected, would she, except to visit. That was all behind her. Bad though it was up here, it was better than the South. Here, at least, you could delude yourself. Poor Poppa. Agamemnon gone, to God knew where, and soon Edward, his loyalty exhausted, would leave. Eventually Louise and Willa Mae would also journey North.

"Sissie?"

"Poppa?" Sissie was playing with Iris. It was a Sunday afternoon and Ralph and the boy had gone to a baseball game. Sissie watched him place his thumb in the Bible he was reading. He peered over the tops of his glasses, an indication that a serious discussion was about to break.

"You sure acts funny about that little girl of yours. Like you scared to be decent to her when your husband's around."

"Oh, Poppa," she said.

"Don't turn away when I'm speaking, girl. Is everything all right? Is there somethin' you haven't told me that you should have?"

"No, Poppa."

"Sissie?" His voice was a warning that she shouldn't lie to him.

"Sir?"

"You sure?"

"Yes, Poppa."

"He's a good boy," Joseph Peterson said, reopening his Bible. "A good ol' nigger. Be good for farm work. Man ain't got no business up here in these dirty cities. People livin' so close together. Can't even see the sky half the time. Don't know what's goin' t' happen. All the young folks leavin' home to come up North as fast as they can save bus fare."

"Yes, Poppa."

Long after her father had gone Sissie pondered over that afternoon. Surely she was as devoted to Iris as she was to the boy? Why had her father said that she wasn't? And Big Ralph liked the girl; he had been stiff with her at first, but that had passed. Sissie chuckled. No use telling Ralph now and raking up the past. Some day, she thought, she would tell him, but things were going along so good. Even the bad luck (Sissie paused to rap on wood), seemed to be staying away.

Big Ralph entered singing one of his old favorites.

> *"Down the street come Sat'dy night*
> *Head held high and walkin light*
> *Come Big Stingaree! Big Stingaree!*
> *Mens cut they eyes and walks away*
> *But girls is glad when he say:*
> *It's Big Stingaree! Whee! Stingaree!*
> *Stings sweet all night 'n' works all day*
> *Fells them logs 'n' sleeps in th' hay*
> *Ol' Stingaree! Big Stingaree...!"*

He winked at Sissie and said, "Watch out for the stinger, Sissie." She knew that they would make love that night.

They did not know where Wall Street was or precisely how, if at all, they were related to it and the collapse of the stock market. But the next night when Ralph came home he called to Sissie in a loud cheerful voice from the cellar, "Honey, I'm gonna take as much of this stuff off my clothes as I can. You go ahead and wash 'em; can't tell when they'll call me back."

Sissie paused in her work; for a moment she wanted to cry because the tone of his voice had been confident. Lately, it seemed, she was always wanting to cry when he said or did something that made her feel good. When he came up into the kitchen he said, "Ol' Wiggins tells me he's goin' to work the State Fair, in the toilets. Gonna go upstairs to talk to him about helpin' out."

"Oh," she said impulsively, "I was just thinkin' that I could go the full week at the Weinsteins'." That too was something she had been feeling lately, the wish to give him something tangible; something that would tell him that she loved him.

"Let's see how this goes," he said, laughing deep in his throat. "Can't be as bad as they say it is. Besides, you got the kids here to look after." He patted her on the buttocks and went upstairs to see Wiggins. The kids, Sissie thought when he had gone, the kids. How they circumscribed your life. Instead of a new chair, you bought a mattress for the crib; instead of a dress you got shoes for them. . . . She tried not to think about it anymore, and she worked briskly until Ralph returned, smiling.

He went cheerfully the first morning, garbed in Wiggins' extra white jacket. He said nothing about the job when he returned home late that night. Something was wrong, Sissie

221

knew; she had wanted to talk and laugh with him. In the morning when she rose, she saw that he hadn't touched the supper she'd left him. She was unable to really approach him during the time he worked at the State Fair. Perhaps he would tell her what was bothering him when the job was all over.

They had been in charge of a toilet in the cattle building, Ralph finally told her. They had set up a shoeshine stand and bought paper and cloth towels. When the farmers had come in, smelling of home brew and cow dung, Wiggins and he had stepped forward to brush them off, chanting as they did:

> "Shake it high, shake it dry,
> And tip ol' Sam when you pass by."

"One farted in my face," Ralph said quietly, "and I could've killed him."

Sissie remained silent.

"Them peckerwoods," he said bitterly. "So goddamn big 'cause they give you a lousy nickel or a dime. Damned few of them had dimes. It must make them happy to be able to give you things instead of getting the hell outa the way and lettin' you get them yourself."

"I'm glad you didn't fight," Sissie said. "I wouldn't want anything to happen to you."

"Ol' Wiggins," Ralph said with a morose smile. "He was pretty good at suckholin' around. 'Yassuh, boss. Yassuh, cap'n.' You know what I found out, Sissie?"

"What?"

"I couldn't make a nickel until I acted just the way he did. I didn't feel like a man; I felt like an ape, grinning all the time, hand out, talkin' that Sambo talk."

Quietly, Sissie said, "But honey, we had to have money."

222

"Why else," he said in abrupt harshness, "did you think I did it?"

"We're too poor to be proud," she said, quietly again.

"Nobody's that poor. That's all a poor man has, his damned pride, which he can't give his family to eat."

"No."

"Stopped by to see Lewis today."

Sissie waited; if anybody knew of a job it was Lewis.

"He's got an eye out."

"That's nice. A little rest'll be good for you."

"We all paid up at Guido's and Ayling's?"

"Except for the Wings you got yesterday." Sissie thought of old man Guido with his little account book in which he recorded the items they bought on credit; and she thought of Ayling who she was sure added fifty or seventy-five cents to the bill each week.

"That's good," Ralph said, wearily. "Goin' out on the porch for a while."

Sissie nodded. What did he think of as he stood on the porch night after night, smoking cigarette after cigarette? From the bedroom she could watch the red dot of his cigarette glowing and fading. Once she had known almost everything about him, now she knew nothing. She stayed awake that night, waiting for him to come to bed. She was alive with love; she had almost made up her mind to tell him about Iris. She watched his cigarette glow in the dark. He kept smoking one cigarette, then another. She finally fell asleep.

From Wings cigarettes he switched to Bull Durham roll-your-owns; thirteen cents was too much to pay for a whole pack when you could roll a mess of good cigarettes for a nickel. Mornings, Sissie watched him go out in search of work, his face expressionless. He would be home by noon, before Little Ralph came back from school for lunch. He kept pacing the porch, or went down to the cellar and sifted the precious, half-burned pieces of anthracite from the ash, sprinkling them with water. Every day he visited D'Amica's. "Maybe I'll hear of something there," he said. He got two or three houses to paint, some flats to wallpaper, some trash to carry out. But such work was irregular.

"I'm going to go full time at the Weinsteins," Sissie announced. "She's been wantin' me more."

"Who's going to look after Iris?" Ralph asked; his voice was low and menacing. Sissie knew that Ralph knew the answer.

"On the days when you go out," Sissie said, watching him carefully, "you can leave her with Mis' Wiggins. She'll fix lunch for Little Ralph too."

"You talked to her already," he said. His voice was an accusation.

"It's only until you start some steady work, Ralph."

"We'll cut some more corners," he shouted, slamming the wall.

"Ain't no more corners to cut," Sissie said, suddenly unafraid. "Guido's lookin' at me fish-eyed. The kids got to have more than neckbones and rice or hoppin'-john all the time. Cornbread and hoecake bread. . . ." her voice drifted wearily. She watched him go to the porch. A clamor arose in the street. She saw him look up as an airship passed overhead; a soft, distant look came into his eyes. Sissie backed away from the

224

window so that he could not see her. When he came in she said, "I don't see why you have to be mad."

He shrugged.

"It's only for a little while," she repeated.

"If it's only for a minute," he said, brushing past her, "it makes me feel as useless as a ball of cowshit."

"Ralph—"

"Go ahead," he said. "Go ahead, I don't care."

"But what else can we do?" she pleaded.

He shook his head. "What else?" He shook his head again. "Nothing."

Two weeks later, she approached him as he sat in the kitchen reading the sports page of the *Express*. She held a pencil and paper in her hand.

"Honey?" she said, sitting down.

"What?"

"Listen. There's an upstairs flat around the corner. Ten dollars a month cheaper than this. Same number of rooms. . . ." She watched him deliberately lay the paper aside. He fixed her with a cold stare. "Honey, please listen," Sissie said. "We got to figure out how to stay *alive*. No furnace, so we can get a couple of pot-bellied coal stoves. Cheaper." His eyelids flickered. "Just for now, Ralph. We're scratchin' and scratchin' and don't seem to be able to get ahead at all." Why did he take it so hard? she wondered. There was many a man out there in the street who'd be happy to have the use of her brains. She went on more firmly. "Mrs. Weinstein can get me some washing to do at home." She shoved the paper at him and pointed with the pencil to some figures. "Bring in eight dollars, and saving ten on the move, that's eighteen dollars, honey."

He nodded. His eyes passed over the table, lingered a moment on the paper then drifted back to hers.

"Okay?" she asked.

"Sure," he said, closing his lips tightly.

"You'll have to pick up the laundry for me—"

The noise of his fist hitting the table startled her. "I'm a fuckin' *man*," he said rising. "Why in the hell can't I *be* one? What's makin' it so that I *can't* be one?"

Sissie lowered her head. She stared at the paper on which she had written her figures. Would he hit her? She closed her eyes and waited. A second or two passed. She opened her eyes. He was still standing motionless. "Okay," he said, waving his hands. "Okay, okay, okay."

They were only a single block away from the old flat, but it seemed miles. They could not see the university, and though they heard the chimes, the bells no longer held any special meaning for them. The street they were on was cobbled. Trolley tracks no longer in use glinted malignantly in the sun. Devoid of trees, the block seemed a desert, the community a ghost town: there were almost no customers in the Greek store at the corner, a weariness hung in the show window of the pawnshop, and there was the dingy gloom of the ice-cream parlor with its marble-topped counter and three-cent phosphates. From the pretzel bakery next door to the new flat came the perpetual odor of baking; roaches and rats also came from the bakery. The rat traps that Ralph and Sissie set were always filled in the morning. Ralph was constantly covering rat holes with the tops of cans, but the rats always found new entrances.

A year, two years passed—each day sullen and precarious. But at night they sought each other, as if this were the last escape left to them. Sissie felt that each time they made love, Ralph sought to reassert himself. But when it was over Sissie could only think of rising in the morning and going out to earn their bread. She wanted him to be a man but knew he couldn't; vaguely she perceived that the fault was not his, yet she couldn't find out whose fault it was. When she found him struggling with the wash or trying to iron she became frenzied. Soon he gave up helping at all. Nights he sat silently in the kitchen while she ironed. She was quiet, knowing that too much anger was dangerous, but the thought of working day after day kept plaguing her. Something had to happen, she told herself, to make everything all right.

When she discovered that she was once more pregnant, she obtained some quinine; taking quinine, she had heard, would bring on an abortion. At the Weinsteins' she tried jumping from the top of the stairs. Finally she stopped doing anything about it and spent night after night crying in Ralph's arms. Why hadn't they been more careful? What would they do with another child? How could you raise a family in the place in which they lived?

Ralph said he was going to try harder than ever to find work. Sissie lay in his arms, her face wet with tears, and knew he had lost hope. She had seen the long lines of desperate men; she had passed Gideon's where the job seekers congregated in the afternoons. Like them, Ralph was beaten. She knew he would find nothing and that they would have to go on relief. As if the new pregnancy were not enough, Little Ralph had taken to running away. Sometimes he would be gone a whole night.

"You beat that boy too much," Ralph commented one evening when the boy was gone.

"Well you don't hardly at all," Sissie snapped back. He's got to be disciplined."

"No cause to tear the skin off his back."

"I never, but he'll get it when he gets back here."

Ralph said, "He don't never leave unless you been beatin' on him. I don't know where he can be; looked every place I could think of. What'd he do, Sissie?"

"Lost some money in the snow."

"Kids always lose money."

"We can't afford to, we're poor."

"Never mind. He'll be back."

He always did return, and would patiently receive his beating. There was a sullen rebelliousness within him. Once, when Little Ralph had forgotten what he was to get at the store and returned with the wrong thing, Sissie snatched up the leather belt. As she whipped him, she lost all sense of time and of reality; the strap snarled through the air again and again. "Cry, damn you," Sissie hissed, her breath growing short. When she saw the hatred in his eyes she beat harder. It didn't seem as if she could ever stop. Suddenly she was jerked upright. She whirled and saw the angry face of her husband. He tore the belt from her hand and hit her across the buttocks with it, once, twice, three times, deliberately and with all his strength. He looked her in the eyes and then threw the belt on the floor and walked out. Sissie touched her hips and felt the three welts there. She looked unbelievingly at the boy and knew the extent of her blind rage, the infiniteness of his hatred for her. Her legs felt rubbery, her knees sagged and she found herself crouching on the floor, like an animal, crying and sobbing. "I didn't mean it," she repeated over and over. Iris, frightened, stood behind the crib. "No, honey, Mother didn't mean it. I'm sorry. Did Mother hurt you? Mother's sorry. Mother's sorry. Come, let Mother hold you?" Sissie lifted her head and waited. "Come," she said, frightened, "let Mother hold you." Moving stiffly, Little Ralph sidled slowly around her out of the bedroom. He picked up his lumber jacket and cap which were on the chair beside the door, bent to see if his jackknife was still in the little pocket on the side of his high-topped boots, then, like his father, he walked out. Slowly, Sissie rose to her feet when she heard the downstairs door slam. She washed her face and picked up the baby. She hugged Iris to her bosom.

Now Sissie attended church more frequently than ever before; Ralph and Iris were sent to Sunday school. But Mr. Thompkins was always asking for another collection to repair the parsonage in which Reverend Polk lived: there were also extra collections to calcimine the church ceilings. Sissie grew bored and angry with all of this begging; none of the people in the congregation had money. Various groups organized church dinners and those who could afford to attend retired to the basement after the service for the meals. Some of the parishioners invited their employers to these dinners. Reverend Polk always introduced the guests, their names having been slipped to him before church. The strangers sat in the last pew during the service and ate at the special table set aside for that purpose. There was something so pretentious and false about those dinners that Sissie never invited the Weinsteins.

The rats and roaches came day and night that summer. Soap and water and scrubbing didn't help. One morning, preparing to go to work, Sissie looked into the childrens' room. Something gray streaked across the floor. Sissie stared, then screamed. Iris' face was trickling blood. Little Ralph had his hands raised in horror. Sissie heard Big Ralph running toward the room. She herself stood as if hypnotized. Then she pointed. The rat, its snakelike tail curled, crouched, frozen. Big Ralph reached for the rolling pin and ran into the room with a shout. The rat ran madly across the room. Big Ralph lunged, scattering the children, and the rat tumbled gray and hideous upon the floor under the crib. Big Ralph kept clubbing it, shouting as he did, "Goddamn you! Goddamn you!" The room was filled with the stench of the creature. Ralph wiped up the mess of blood and fur with some newspaper. Sissie dressed the wound on Iris' face. When she returned home from work that evening, Big Ralph said, "We're moving tomorrow."

"But Ralph—" she began.

"Goddamn it, we're moving!" he said sharply.

Then she saw the bare cupboards, the pans out on the table, the boxes already packed. "Where? We don't even have money to pay the moving man."

"Son," he called to Little Ralph, "bring me some of those pans. C'mon now, step on it."

Sissie looked at the boy; he was smiling at his father.

"Hello," Sissie said.

"Hello, Mother."

"Attaboy," Big Ralph said, taking some pans from Little Ralph. "More now. Hurry."

"Where we movin'?" Sissie asked, sitting down.

"One seventy-nine Horn Street. Near Asher's ice and coal house."

"You mean that big upstairs flat with the screens all around the porch?"

"Yep."

"But that's expensive."

"I jewed the landlord down. Three dollars more than this place. Got some money from Lewis," Ralph said proudly. "We can't stay here no more, honey. It's too awful. You rest awhile. We ate already, so don't worry about it. I'll get the kids off to school in the morning and then see about the moving. I'll have everything there when you're through work. Just don't forget and come back here. I'll leave all the furniture for you to arrange, if you want."

Almost as soon as they moved, their luck improved. Offered a part-time cooking job in a fraternity house, Sissie went back to working half-days at the Weinsteins'. Big Ralph was signed for one of the WPA crews and suddenly again there was singing.

Willa Mae was the first to come North and then Louise followed. Big, rawboned young women, stiff and polite in the manner of Southern maidens, they immediately secured jobs with private families. How long, Sissie wondered, would it take for them to lose all their brightness? Only Joseph Peterson remained on the farm now. Edward had gone up river to Chicago, anxious to get into the insurance or undertaking business. Poppa, the girls said, would give in finally; there was nothing left on the farm. He just stayed there out of habit. Agamemnon? Nothing. Not a word. Whenever a family started to break up there was one member who vanished, remembered only from old photographs. But maybe he wasn't dead, maybe he would appear unexpectedly, learned and wealthy, a fairy godbrother.

Anyway, things weren't so bad, what with Ralph and

Sissie both working. They even accepted the advent of another pregnancy, for they had managed to save a little money. She was getting along in years, Sissie reflected, but a soft squeeze of her breasts, a stroke upon the buttocks, a lingering kiss, and she forgot about caution. In bed, in the darkness, Ralph was a man.

They should have expected bad luck, they were used to its presence; but when it came again, as always, it shocked them into silence. One day the news came about Agamemnon. He had been found dead, shot, in Oklahoma. Joseph Peterson urgently needed money for his burial. How could you refuse money for a burial? How could you only send part of it? And because so many men needed work, Ralph was placed on rotation; he would not work steadily, only one week out of every four.

Mary Ellen was born that winter. From the beginning Little Ralph was her favorite, and she was his. He lingered to play with her in the morning; he rushed in at lunchtime and after school so he could be with her. It almost hurt to watch the two of them, they were so close. Mary Ellen learned to recognize Little Ralph's step on the stairs. When she heard him coming she would laugh and jostle in her high chair. With the coming of spring she walked for Little Ralph, she seemed to trust no one else. Then Mary Ellen caught pneumonia the first cold day of autumn and died two days later. Sissie didn't know who her tears were for; herself, the baby, or the other children. Big Ralph cried at the wake as though he were bone-weary. Little Ralph hung onto the casket and kissed over and over again that cold, firm cheek. A few months later Sissie came home to discover that Big Ralph had gone. There was no note, nothing.

First she threw out his work clothes; rotation had been a farce. Then she arranged for the woman next door to watch out for the kids while she was at work. Late at night sometimes, she sat at the kitchen table slowly drinking from a half-pint bottle of whiskey. Ralph was having trouble in school. Iris was wetting the bed. Only Robbie was good. The other two made her feel like a jailer. Garlic! What in the *hell* could that boy be doing sitting in school chewing *garlic?* And Iris, pissing on one mattress after another. If only she were free. Free of them, the kids. Or if they were grown and on their own. Was this the meaning of her life, to have kids who didn't obey her, to work her fingers to the bone just to keep crumbs in their mouths and rags on their backs? Big Ralph was free now, no good, shiftless. Didn't want the responsibility of a family. *She* had come back.

Now a watchful silence prevailed among the children when Sissie came home. They spoke in low voices, traversed wide circles around where she sat. She had begun to lose herself in a succession of lovers who tiptoed up the stairs late at night and left early.

One day Ralph arrived home from school late; he had been kept in and hadn't put out the trash at the Weinsteins'. Sissie's voice rose in anger, beginning with recriminations and ending in curses. Ralph started to walk out of the room as if disdaining to have anything further to do with her. She picked up the broom. She swung it with all her strength, but his hands shot out and grabbed it in midair. He held the broom motionless between them. Sissie pulled and she panted. "Goddamn you," she said through her teeth, "let go, goddamn you." The boy held on, patiently. He finally let go when he knew she would do nothing. Slowly, Sissie lowered

233

the broom, and dragging it on the floor behind her: She went into her bedroom and cried. He was no longer a boy.

She got up without wiping her face. The children were sitting silently in the living room; they looked up when she entered. Sissie smiled sadly. "Well, I guess you think you're a man now, don't you?"

Ralph did not answer.

Sissie crossed the room and stood looking down at him. Grown at fourteen, she thought, with anger, pride and sorrow. Perhaps that was what her life was all about, bringing them up to be men and women. "Ralph," she said, "I don't want to fight with you anymore. It's not good for us. Fightin' like cats and dogs around here; it's awful. We got to love one another more. Okay? Okay?" she repeated, and not waiting for an answer, bent to kiss Ralph's cheek. As she did, his eyes stared into hers with hatred.

PART

IV

17

OLIVER HURRIED INTO THE ROOM and approached the bed. Sissie lay still, but smiled at him. "Hello, old woman," Oliver said, taking her hand. Her graying hair lay wild and scattered on the pillow. Oliver patted her wrist and lowered it carefully to the bed.

"The kids," Sissie said slowly. "They coming?"

"Mrs. Duncan, please," the nurse said, rising from her chair.

Sissie closed her eyes and then opened them disdainfully.

"You rest like she says," Oliver said. "They're on the way; should be here about noon. Jones went to pick them up."

Sissie nodded slowly.

Oliver sat down. The nurse walked over to the bed and tucked in the blankets.

Dr. Clayton entered, glanced at Sissie who lay with closed eyes. "Your children are on the way, Mr. Duncan?" he asked Oliver.

" 'Bout noon," Oliver answered laconically. "You said she was rallying."

"She's strong and she has rallied. A powerful woman. If she doesn't exert herself. . . ."

"Sure," Oliver said.

"How long's it been?" Dr. Clayton asked.

"You mean the kids?"

Dr. Clayton nodded.

"Oh, 'bout thirteen years for the girl, about six for the boy."

"That long?"

"Lost one in Korea. And two others, babies."

"She's sure proud of those children," Dr. Clayton said.

"I was hopin' she'd get to see her granddaughter. You know, Ralph's little girl."

Dr. Clayton nodded gravely. He remembered the hard days after Meharry, the pneumonia cases, the tubercular cases which had been so rampant in Harlem. Always the babies. If they got up to four or five, they lived. He had never rid himself of the feeling of sadness when the babies died never having lived; he could not accept the idea that they were better off dead.

"Mr. Duncan," the nurse said, "why don't you step outside and smoke? I'll keep the watch." From where he sat, Oliver could see Sissie's eyes opening.

"Pay them twenty dollars a day," Sissie croaked, "and all

238

they can do is keep you awake, these nurses. And the colored ones're just as bad as the white ones. Worse sometimes."

"Hush, Mrs. Duncan," Dr. Clayton said. Sissie closed her eyes, and once more slept. Oliver took out his pipe and walked into the corridor.

As he stood in the corridor smoking, Oliver's mind returned to that first day he had met Sissie. He had just finished his basic Army training and had gotten his first weekend pass and taken the bus to town. He found himself in a square, almost exactly like a hundred others he'd seen, with an immense soldiers and sailors monument in the center. The first thing he did was ask the way to the colored section. It didn't take him long to locate a blackjack game and he spent the night gambling. He ended up a big winner. Then after breakfast the next day Oliver headed for the church. A man his age didn't hang around looking for women. At church he could find a lot of good sisters.

A woman and two children sat in the same pew with Oliver and after the service the woman remarked to him as they moved toward the door, "Aren't you a little old to be a soldier boy?" Oliver smiled and said that it wasn't his fault he had got caught. At the door the minister said to the woman, "Always nice to see you and your family, sister Joplin. Heard from Ralph this week?"

"Got a V-letter yesterday, reverend."

"Praise the Lord he's alive and well."

"Amen," Sissie said.

"Take one of these fine soldiers home for some of your cooking, sister, and He will see that your son, in return, never knows hunger out there in the Pacific."

Outside, Oliver paused to put his cap on his head.

"Mr. Soldier," the woman said, laughing, "Why don't you join me and my children for dinner?"

"It'd be my pleasure, ma'am."

"You from Kentucky?"

"Yes'm."

"I thought so. They raise some mighty polite people there. What's your name? Can't call you Mr. Soldier."

"Oliver Duncan."

"Mine's Mrs. Joplin, and this's my daughter, Iris, and this is Robbie. Ralph, my other son, he's in the Navy overseas."

Ralph, Oliver thought. He recalled the winter evening Ralph had returned home. Ralph had walked in, seabag slung over his shoulder, carrying a ditty bag and a Japanese .29-caliber rifle. Iris had shrieked and Sissie and Robbie had risen from the table. Oliver had stood, accepting Ralph's cold appraisal. The two men had shaken hands warmly but nevertheless Oliver had sensed Ralph's hostility.

"Your mother and me, Ralph. We're goin' to get married later this year," Oliver had said.

"Oh, yeah?" Ralph had said, and became silent. The silence had lasted until the break-up of Ralph's own marriage. After that somehow or other they became friends.

Oliver did not like to think of those days, for his marriage to Sissie had had nothing romantic about it. They had worked like dogs, living in as maid and butler in Beverly Hills while Robbie had been taken care of by a friend. But they had saved. They had bought themselves a used Ford with a worn-out clutch. They had stopped living in and had rented their own house. Robbie had worked after school. They had kept on saving, denying themselves almost everything until the

240

first trip to Yellowstone. The Ford had given out on the freeway and they had bought a Chevrolet. Oliver had taken a part time job, compelled to earn more than his wife, forever battling to stay the head of the family. The years, it seemed, had been spent speeding back and forth on the freeway. Then Robbie had gone into the Army and was seen only briefly on hectic furloughs. Oliver knew that this youngest child had been most free of whatever had tainted the other children's spirits. Robbie who, if he were tough, didn't reveal it, was the happiest of them all. He left for the Korean War just when the family moved into a larger house.

Professional servants now, a part of that vast, knowing underground of American life, Sissie and Oliver had worked their way up to the new Pontiac that was the car they had driven to Union Station to meet Robbie's remains. It had taken Sissie a long time to get over Robbie's death, but they had continued to prosper materially. Now they were able to purchase their own house; Sissie walked into the new home, carrying, as she always did on such occasions, a box of salt, a cake of soap, a loaf of bread and the Bible.

Only then did she feel secure; there was land beneath her feet again; she had come full circle. Oliver also had that itch for land, that desire to own a piece of earth. Now they began to grow fat California peonies and brilliantly colored roses; they sheared the two banana trees regularly. Tucked behind the garage was the vegetable patch which Sissie spoke of fervently and attended with her usual energy, grunting as she pulled, raked and hoed. Out of the patch came collards, peas and beets. "Fresh from the garden," she said proudly when there was company for dinner.

Now the furniture belonged together; the bad pieces had

been discarded—the taste was sure. In the driveway the car stood, sleek, black, big and new; it was replaced every two years. But though the accoutrements of middle-class life had been obtained they still felt cheated—old age was upon them. They kept addressing themselves affectionately as "old man" and "old woman," aware of how far they had come together. They had earned the right to live. . . .

Oliver looked at his watch and walked back into the sickroom. The nurse sat with a magazine open. She pulled her sweater about her shoulders. Dr. Clayton returned, bringing another doctor. Oliver leaned forward, studying the faces of the two doctors.

18

"TO THE RIGHT," the captain of the plane was saying over the intercom, "you can just see Cleveland—"

Ralph smiled at the too casual way Iris turned to look out the window.

"—and in approximately—uh—a few minutes, you'll be able to see Chicago—"

The name of the city was like a trigger; Ralph thought of those days at Great Lakes:

Boot camp. Camp Robert Smalls. New boots and old boots. Cascara sagrada and mineral oil: black and white. The Hospital Corps School, first class of Negroes (the Japanese snipers, they said, were wreaking havoc on Corpsmen). Main side, all snap and dash, crisp salutes. Sissie there for graduation. Proud and clinging. Watch as a gift (broken, salted over, rusted, useless in the Russell Islands). And Liberty (how accurate a phrase) and fleeing into Chi on the North Shore line, neat, dapper in razor-sharp whites to land at Fifty-fifth Street on the South Side, to break for the Parkway Ballroom by jitney or to the Pershing, the Rhumboogie; Joe Louis introduced at the boxing matches behind the Regal Theatre. Negro USO at Forty-ninth and Wabash. (It swung.) Street fights, pickups, fornicating in rented jitneys, and finally the long drunken ride back to the Lakes, creeping past the guards to keep the liquor in the sock from sloshing so much; and up early. (God, the body could take it then!)

Thoughts of the Navy, still triggered by *Chicago*, thrust his memory back to the six months of island-hopping without mail. He remembered his desperate and angry letter:

"*Mother, are you writing? Is anybody writing?*"

He had been in a malaria ward on Bougainville when the mail clerk had come in, dragging a half sack of mail. Ralph had gone through it eagerly, noticing the lip prints, the SWAKs, the perfumed envelopes, Big Ralph's crude writing, Sissie's bold scrawl until, near the top of one of the letters:

"*Dear Mr. Censor. My boy has not got any mail now for six months. Please see that my boy gets his mail. We are all worried. Thank you.*

> *His mother,*
> *Mrs. Sissie Joplin*

It had been one of the things that had made him know that love still existed.

244

"My birthplace," Iris said, nodding her head in a cocky gesture toward Chicago.

"What?" Ralph asked.

"Chicago—"

"Oh!" he said. "Yeah, yeah." Chicago and Uncle Edward now grown fat and pompous in the insurance business. "Gramps died there," Ralph said, and they looked at one another thinking of the end and the beginning of things.

The Navy, Ralph thought again. Chicago was already far behind them. The Navy, the goddamned cracker-assed Navy. It might have been the Navy that had saved him. What would have happened if he had not gone away? He thought, nodding sagely, he might have turned into a rip-roaring faggot because Sissie had been that strong. But there had also been the hatred awakened by her beatings. . . . *Skibbidum!* he thought, romanticizing himself into a classic situation. Why, there had been Peggy, dirty Peggy, and Lulu downstairs where the old man coming home had almost caught them one day. Naw! I was screwing like a jackrabbit, he thought, as soon as I was able. Mostly when we lived in One Seventy-Nine.

One seventy-nine. Suddenly the flat had seemed too large with Big Ralph gone, his blues no longer filling the rooms. There had been only Iris' voice, thin and reedy. Sissie would leave the house before they went to school and would return home long after they did. She talked to them rarely, mainly to ask if they'd been all right while she had been away.

Iris had fallen asleep and snored softly. Ralph looked at her with tenderness and thought again of Sissie's comings and goings. Year in and year out she had trudged out to save carfare, carrying in her arms bags of half-eaten food, clothes

245

too large or too worn for others but good enough for the Joplins. And the tarnished, bent silver which had to be straightened and cleaned so that it would look somehow as though it had always been at One Seventy-Nine. . . .

"Out scuffling to get those crumbs to put into our mouths and shoes for our feet and praying for something to happen so that all the space in between would somehow get taken care of."

"What'd you say?" Iris woke up.

"Talking to myself."

"Watch it."

" 'Kay, baby."

When the Depression had finally overtaken the Weinsteins Sissie had gone to cook at the sorority and fraternity houses.

And he remembered Sissie laughingly telling Miss Cora how, when she was at the ZBT house, one after the other the boys had propositioned her. Even now the thought infuriated Ralph. But the unsuccessful ZBT boys had not been the only ones. The years had been filled with "misters" who had come to sit in the kitchen, laughing loudly, rattling beer glasses.

Ralph's head nodded and his mind went off on another tangent. He thought of the Jehovah's Witnesses patiently climbing the stairs on Saturday afternoons carrying their copies of *Awake!*, Sissie listening impatiently to their talk. On Saturday the Watkins man came too; old, wretched, his face seamed with dirt, he would drag himself up the stairs. Sissie abused him but he returned again and again until she gave in and purchased something, a liniment or a lemon extract. Finally death relieved him of his weary plodding through Jewtown. Old Chernik, the secondhand furniture

246

man, came on Thursday nights to collect the fifty-cent payment. Sissie kept complaining that the furniture she'd bought had been misrepresented. She'd mutter, "Dirty old Jew-kike," when she put on the hall light so he could find his way down the steps, and then, "I hope he breaks his neck," when she put the light out a second later. But old Chernik was a wise and patient man, and when the light went out he merely sighed and waited until his eyes became accustomed to the dark. And then there was the insurance man and the milkman and the breadman, each demanding his ounce of flesh.

"Don't do that," Iris said.

"What'd I do?"

"You hit the seat. Scared me. I thought the damned plane was coming apart."

Ralph said, "Give it time. Sorry. Go back to sleep." He had begun to think of Ayling, standing behind his stinking chopping block, wearing his black-rimmed glasses, and that stupid straw hat and butcher's coat. Filthy. Passing out his spoiled meat, leaning his heavy red thumbs on the goddamned scale until Sissie got hold of him one day and almost killed that peckerwood. "Do you remember—" he started to say, but Iris had begun to snore again, and he chuckled to himself, recalling how Sissie had kicked Ayling's straw hat through the sawdust and then with a more powerful kick up toward the ceiling. Then she had snatched up Ayling's cleaver and had chased him behind the freezer. Oh, *go*, Sissie! Oh, *go*, Mother! Got the best meat in town after that.

Iris' head leaned gently against Ralph's arm, interrupting his reverie. She hadn't talked much about the play. He had thought she might mention the scene when the mother comes home and the children gather around her, waiting for her to shake the snow off her coat. The mother is tired and irritable. She notices a bandage on her daughter's leg. The mother asks: "What's that?" The daughter laughs and says, "I hurt it at school today." The mother suddenly takes hold of the leg and rips off the bandage. Silence. At the spot upon the leg where the bandage was the tape has left a neat square, and nothing more. The mother throws the bandage to the floor. The other children avert their eyes. The mother asks the daughter: "What did you do that for?" and shouts, "*Don't beg!*"—thrusting the child from her. Did Iris know *now* what it was that she wanted *then?* Or had she blocked it out, as he had done with so many things—he noticed he was using Bluman's term. God, he had wanted to smash Sissie down then. Smash Mother down. Instead he had retreated, had crept slowly upstairs to the attic.

To Ralph the attic and its summered corners were Thermopylae (he had studied the Greeks that spring), the fortress at Nicaea (there was an old steel engraving of a Crusade battle in the living room), Le Bourget Field and the elephant's graveyard (he never identified with the African natives; he was always Tarzan). He prowled aimlessly. There was an old trunk in one corner of the attic. Each summer he squatted before the trunk and emptied its contents. When he was weary of examining each trinket and piece of paper, he went to the roof and climbed the main gable. Sometimes in the dead of winter when one of the coal stoves went out, Ralph would go to a corner of the attic and pry up pieces of flooring which he used as kindling. He didn't have the nickel for a bundle of wood and knew that Sissie would be furious if she entered a cold house. He ripped out the floorboards, not only for fires but in search of a treasure. Often in the summer he pried up boards and pounded them in again with the concentration of an archeologist. His treasure trove had included a half dollar, an old newspaper, a rat's nest, and innumerable buttons. Only a few boards remained untouched.

One afternoon Ralph, "digging" in the attic, had come across his greatest find: some letters hidden under a board. The letters had been carefully stacked and tied. But now the string was loose, and dust covered them. He reached down and lifted up the bundle of dried paper and read:

"Dear Hon, . . ."

Then another:

"Dear Hon, . . ."

And:

"Dear Hon: please, please come back. I missed you so much while I was away and after I came home again. I do not care about the baby, and I'm sorry for what I tried to do to you. I'll just make believe the baby's mine. You can't stay there all alone and work and take care of the baby too. Please come back. I love you. . . ."

It was signed thickly, *"Ralph."*

The next letter was written in a sweeping, curlicued style. Ralph read; *"I'll come home next month."* The letter was signed *"Sissie."* The third letter Ralph read was in a still different hand. It said:

"Darling, I wish you wouldn't go back, not with our child. Soon, if you have patience I will take care of you and we will be very happy. First, of course, I have to finish school and then we'll be all set. If I could spare some money I'd send it, but I can't right now."

This was signed "*Arthur.*" Ralph frowned.

The next letter had no stamp, but it was sealed. Ralph debated but a second, then ripped it open.

"*Dear Arthur. I am going back to Ralph. I want to make a clean brest of everything. Iris is not your girl. She's his. I was mad with him and wanted to get back. I didn't tell you right away because I hoped you'd come and get us. I don't believe you loved me at all. You just wanted to get what you could. It's too late to tell Ralph the truth. He won't believe me now, and maybe I won't tell him at all because this is not the kind of living I thought was here when I left home and I guess I'm still mad, but I was raised to do the right thing and my place is with my husband and my boy. Anyway, you don't really care about me.*"

This letter was signed "*Sissie.*"

There were more letters and Ralph read them slowly. When he was finished, he returned the letters and the boards to their places, and climbed through the rear window to the roof and straddle-walked the gable to the chimney. For hours he sat hunched against the column of brick, thinking. . . .

"Coffee, sir?"

Ralph looked up at the stewardess.

"With," he said.

"And your wife?"

"My grandmother," he said. "Black, I think. Hey," he said to Iris, "wake up. Coffee coming."

"Umm, it's so good to sleep," Iris said, snuggling closer to the seat. "Did the captain say Grand Canyon?"

"Yes."

"I missed it."

The coffee came. Iris glanced at the stewardess.

"She thought we were married," Ralph said.

"An honest mistake."

"Benefit of the doubt?"

"Yes."

"All right. Forget it."

"I have."

"Lousy coffee."

"No, it's not bad."

"Okay."

After a while he asked, "Did you get your nap out?"

"I guess. Hard to sleep. My mind's on so many things." She sipped her coffee. "First time I've ever been across country. See America last."

"You ought to see it," Ralph said. He was thinking of that network of highways moving back and forth across the nation. Where were the futuristic cars of the lightest metal and Plexiglass driven by turbines that the manufacturers had promised in his youth? The psychogeographic Americans—Conestoga wagons gone, the old railways of the West, lined by the graves of Chinese, Irish and Negroes—still roared at the highest possible speeds from one ocean to the other, often just to be able to say that they had.

"I'd like to drive across America just once more," Ralph said.

"South too?"

"No, of course not. I went once."

"What happened?"

"What I expected. But I didn't do what I thought I'd do. I tucked my tail between my legs and drove twenty-five miles an hour until it was safe to blast, and blast I did."

"Coward."

"A bloody one and no shuck. Living there must be like living in a concentration camp or occupied territory. People have guts; the spooks I mean."

"I know what you mean."

"Baby, you know, if those spooks with their paper bags and cardboard suitcases hadn't come North looking for all that gold that the Irish and the Italians and all the others had come for, the North would have been hopeless for Negroes. Those people really wanted things. I hate to think of what it would've been like if they hadn't come."

Iris turned from Ralph frowning disturbed by the sudden thought of her mother. It was as if she was once again in the flat upstairs over the A&Z Market. Iris seemed to hear the sound of Sissie's stiff, outspread finger tips thrumming against the wall. There had also been the rhythmic creak of the bedsprings, and the muffled voice of a man. Iris remembered how she had perspired as she lay listening to the bodies thudding against the wall. She had wanted, whoever he was, to come to her too. Was it the same man each time? When, Iris wondered, had she stopped caring and listening. . . ?

"May I have your cups, please?"

Iris passed her cup and cushion.

"What're you looking so evil about?" Ralph asked.

Iris smiled. "Was I?"

"Man, were you."

"Thinking."

"Sissie?"

Iris nodded. She'd never told Ralph, who had shared the rear room with Robbie what had gone on. He might have suspected, but he never knew. Nor would she tell him. "I was

252

thinking," Iris lied, "about the Elks Mother's Day thing she took us to."

Ralph began laughing quietly. "It was a gas, even then, I remember."

Iris started to laugh as well, thinking back to the Elks Home where the performance had taken place.

" 'Who ran to help me when I fell?' " Ralph said, waiting for Iris to pick up the cue.

" 'And who would some pretty story tell?' " she said smiling.

" 'Or kiss the place to make it well?' "

" 'My mother,' " they said together, and fell to giggling in their seats.

Ralph remembered how the women had looked in their white dresses and purple sashes, and the men in their best suits and fezzes, all going through the program with genteel desperation until at last it was time for the cake and punch.

"She really dug those Elks meetings," Ralph said. "Guess there wasn't much else except church."

"Are we close?" Iris asked suddenly.

"I think so. I think so. But the sign isn't on. Relax."

"Suddenly I can't."

"Try, for Christ's sake."

"All right." Lord, don't let her die, Iris thought.

A room. She lies still, too still. Curtains at the windows. How many windows? The curtains, criss-cross or straight? With blinds too, lavender? Furniture: bed—naturally. Beds very big things in the family. Dressing table? Chest? Stool or chair? No. Only the room in the flat above the A&Z Market. On a corner. That room thirteen years ago. Not in that one

253

now. Another. Three thousand miles away. No. Almost there. Anyway, transpose the past upon the present. Yes. The room is dark. It is clean and casually feminine. There are the odors of perfume and powder and fresh bed linens. Additional odors: pipe smoke. Oliver is a part of the present with his pipe. He looks sad when he smokes or maybe it is just that the pipe makes him look wise. Same thing. He is as he was. But in the room, a hospital room into which she materializes and walks to Sissie and peers down, telling her with her eyes alone that she knows.

The church. Calcimined walls yellowing, stained-glass windows. An eye opened, unblinking, red. ("Crispus Attucks.") Three chairs on the dais; the bishop in the center one and a deacon on the left. Reverend Polk sits on the right. Three. Three wise men watching the procession with eyes that know the cue for grief. Below, the parishioners moving down the outside aisles to the ragged singing "Nearer My God to Thee." The heavy musk of gardenias. The restless black line, passing in its millenium-old rhythm on the worn wooden floors, scraping, irritating. The puzzled children, frightened more by the living than the dead. She rests peacefully, fingers laced calmly through fingers. Lips rouged (not her color), face powdered (not her shade), hair neatly combed. The neat Elks Women's Auxiliary uniform, all white, unwrinkled, the purple and gold running from hip to shoulder. Background of satin, unbelievably pure white satin.

> "Nearer my God to Thee,
> Nearer to Thee—e-e-e...."

Herself singing.

> "... till my restless soul
> shall find-d-d-d
> > Rest!
> beyond the river-r-r-r-r. . . ."

Unobtrusively, at the end of the line, the undertakers step up, heads lowered, pull up their white gloves and close the coffin. Softly. They clamp down the lid, obscuring their movements with their bodies. Apologetically. The pallbearers materialize. Elks. With their silly fezzes, tassels swinging. The Auxiliary is behind them, smoothing white dresses. The pallbearers start out of the church, go down the steps, bumping the walls lightly, and into the street. A pause while the head undertaker opens the doors of his Cadillac hearse. The coffin is placed gently inside. The sleek doors are closed. And locked. The caravan winds slowly through familiar streets, passes a boy and girl roller-skating along the same route. The caravan treads softly on its rubber. Up the hill over the plateau, out along the edges of the city. Prowling, demanding of passersby the recognition of the inevitable. Ahead, the motorcycle policeman. Mason. Bored. Amused. Confident. Proper and dutiful. Outside, the green mounds drifting slowly to the rear. Suddenly neat groves of trees, elm, maple, chestnut, poplars, and then an ugly space of sky. Signals, winking blinkers: *tink, tink, tink.* . . . Juanita. And Mary Ellen. And Robbie traveling dead and perhaps in pieces ten thousand miles to lie beside them, and now Mother, Sissie. . . . *tink, tink, tin*—! Beneath them now, gravel and dirt. A pebble pressing from beneath a tire: *thung!* The metal troupe comes on, glistening. Up front, Mason has concluded his briefing with the caretaker, who waves. On each side of the road, bumps, green bumps, longer than wide. Markers: Juanita Mae, Mary Ellen, Robert Joseph, small, sad, inexpensive. Great headstones, obelisks, praying angels. Vaults. Fresh flowers. Dead flowers. Filthy American flags listless in the wind of the dead. Rolling. Gravel endlessly underneath. There on the slight rise, where the earth is freshly turned and the men stand near it smoking, retreating now at the sight of the caravan, then pausing to lean on their shovels. The procession stops. The handles of the doors open in a series of clunks and clacks. People climb slowly out of the cars, into the hot sun. They move toward the new earth. Brown earth, rich, dark. Its smell is good; its smell is definite, final. She glances at the men with the shovels. The people gather around. The casket comes. It is placed on the boards and straps. The people move nearer; they peer into the hole. Reverend Polk steps up, blots out the sun. He speaks. People cry. Reverend Polk reaches into the mound of earth. His fingers press absently against the clod he has taken. A slow, theatrical movement. The earth returns home, spraying from the side of the coffin. The men with shovels come up. The people move back. The straps are lowered. The casket rocks down into its place. The men with the shovels hesitate. Their hesitation is rehearsed. The first shovel slides neatly into the mound of soft earth. A curve of earth arches over and into the hole. It lands solidly upon the casket. Where the face would be.

"Baby, you got to relax," Ralph said to her, looking worried.

"I'm sorry," she said quickly, tensely. Then, "We're slowing down!"

Ralph turned his head. The warning sign was not yet on. "For Christ's sake, Iris, will you relax!"

She sighed and touched a hand to her forehead. "Yes, yes, of course. I'm sorry again."

She eased herself back against the seat, trying to force herself to relax. She relaxed when she thought of Time. I will write and ask him to meet me; I'll go back to Paris and I'll ask him to take me back. I'll beg him, if I have to. She stared below into the creases of the mountains. Cold, she thought. It would be cold in Paris now. Time would be cold. He never quite got used to the chill of European houses. How silly, she thought. My sadness only makes me think of how happy I might be. She seemed to hear a mocking echo of Sissie's voice crying out, "You'll never amount to anything!" How many other things had Sissie screamed in her frustration, determined to make them somehow *show her?* Well, they had shown her. Only she hadn't been there to see. If only she'd been present at Berns that night. . . . Well. She hadn't even come to New York for Ralph's opening. Sissie hadn't even given them the pleasure of being present; it was as if none of it had counted for anything. In spite of all that she had said. Iris turned again to the window, the view of the brown, cold mountains. She thought of what her return to Barcelona would be like. Emptiness. After Barcelona, what? Paris? London? Rome? Stockholm? Estoril? Amsterdam? Bonn? The thought of all those cities, with their airfields, train depots, and hotels made her wince. All the countless men; she didn't want them. She wanted one man—she wanted Time. But it was as if he were dead, as if she had killed him. Sissie had killed her man also and perhaps more than one. She thought of Time with a cable in his hand. "*Mother dead. Must see you. Iris.*" Ah, a cheap thought. Sissie wasn't dead yet, and what if she shouldn't die? Iris daydreamed again: Time arriving in New

257

York to begin a new life with her. Suddenly she said to Ralph: "What do you think it'd be like if I came back here, Bro?"

Ralph looked at her guardedly. "What it would be like if you came back?"

She nodded. They exchanged weak smiles; she watched him close his eyes.

"The truth?" he asked.

"Yes."

He smiled again. "Okay."

He closed his eyes again and she turned to the window, waiting.

Ralph heard her stifle a sigh. He listened for a moment as the giant craft hissed through the air. How to tell her? He closed his eyes again. What right had she to ask? Had they not come from the same place, along the same way? Looking for roots. Gone, baby. Grown quickly and dried up; the family tree leans in sand, sister. No earth to hold it now. Listen, you've left behind your cold, pissy bed—for how many years, poor sis, did you wet the bed? Wet it because of your fear of Sissie. Took me a long time to understand that, baby. Maybe you understand too now. White folks' books, Iris. Give you *beaucoup* answers. In only three decades you've gone from pissy beds to perfumed satin ones; from one pair of runover, paper-padded shoes to a closetful of hundred-dollar shoes; from rat-ridden rooms to penthouses and the modern castles of the Riviera; from roller skates to Citroëns. From wanting to being wanted—and being bored with it, I imagine. In only thirty years. And don't you think, even in your most depressed moments—do they come often now, Sis, like mine?

258

—how lucky you are that you were not one of those five or six earlier generations. Aye, there's the rub, Olivier would say. There's the paradox, baby, for it is the where we are now as against where we came from so quickly, thrust forward by all those other restless generations, poor, poor bastards we'll never know, that has indeed destroyed this weak tree of ours. Perhaps, of all, Robbie might have best bridged the gap, for she loved him. She knew he was the last. Some of her love for him was for us, too, Iris; I've thought about that a long, long time and I'm sure of it. He could've done it, too; he was a wise, jolly little bastard. He could've touched you, baby. But he came back in that box. That box, Iris, with the flag. God, can you see yourself explaining your life and work to Sissie? Can you think about being back home with all the broads you grew up with and not feel goddamned guilty about having made it? It makes me feel bad; it makes me feel as though they hate the hell out of me. You can feel it: a word here, a look there, like you were—not a criminal—oh, I don't know. Like a white folks' nigger. To a Negro, you know, that's worse than being a criminal. You'd come back and that's a part of the way it'd be. Unless you brought your own old man with you, there'd be a line of jive-assed niggers from New York to San Francisco waiting to put you on their arms, willing to grace the pages, the society and gossip pages of *our* own press. Not because of love, but prestige. That's a big thing with us now, baby, a horrible and painful thing. You'd knock 'em out with your Citroën. Also you dig good books, theatre, painting—you know, all that shit. You'd find us a little light; most of us fake it around the edges 'cause you're supposed to have a little layer of it, you dig? Why we

259

don't have more than a little layer is because we're still concerned with: who in the hell are we and just where do we belong. Maybe we wouldn't try so hard if we could see a reflection of ourselves outside *our* press; in the movies or on television or theatre. Theatre. That's supposed to be my business now, Iris. Ain't *that* a gas! What a business, but this end's better than being a Negro actor, I'll tell yuh! A star in one production and a walk-on for the next five hundred. Whew. And still they keep coming. Broad said to me once. 'How in the hell can they make so many movies in New York or about New York and not have a black man, woman or child in a single scene'. . . . Are you following me, Iris? It's not an accident. We have to try, I guess, to be like the white folks who're all around us. But goddammit, when we get dap in our four-button suits and make it down the avenues with attaché cases, people look at us the way they look at those monkeys on the T.V. shows. Lousy shows too, honey; if you came back, you could probably get a few shots on them. They like certain kinds of colored talent. Come to think of it, you wouldn't fit the format.

"The bulkheads're pretty wet, are they?"

"What?"

"The bulkheads," Iris said, frowning and smiling at the same time to make him remember what he'd said in Barcelona. "They're—"

"Yeah," he said remembering and cutting in. "Oh, *yeah.* I was just thinking about that." He fell silent a moment, then said without looking at her, "Eve and I had it in the back of our minds to visit you soon. She'd like Europe. It'd be good for her and I want her to see it."

"Oh," Iris said, thinking idly that he didn't want her to come back. She wasn't angry and not even curious, really. As if to confirm her thought, he said, "There's something so enormously free about you, Iris."

He deciphered her look as meaning, Man, if you really knew! and said, "I don't know about the personal bit. I do know that when you speak, you have to hesitate to get the French or the Spanish accents out of the way; you've trilled a few r's and caught yourself. You're not in the groove we're in here; you're that much free at least. You look at me and at other Negroes as if we could give you a clue to yourself. I look at you and I think, 'She doesn't know who she is.' To live here is not only to know who you are but what you are. Sound like shit to you?"

Iris shrugged and wrinkled here forehead. "What do I know?"

"What do you remember?"

She turned her smile full upon him. "Being hungry; not for food. Something that wasn't there." She chuckled. "And being wet!"

After a long silence she said, "What if we'd been the Weinsteins?" She remembered Hope Weinstein, remembered wanting to be like her when they were in high school. Once she had run away when she had seen Hope coming down the street because she had on a sweater Hope had given her. She now recalled the afternoons she had worked at the Weinsteins' in Sissie's place. Mrs. Weinstein had given her money for her lessons, cautioning her not to say anything to her mother. She remembered old Mr. Zefner in the cellar, rubbing his coffins, pausing for breath, slurping his cold soup. "Would it have been different?"

"Different, yes," he said, "but still it always costs, you know, whatever you are, to do what you've done."

NO SMOKING

FASTEN SEAT BELTS

There was the murmur of voices and the click of seat belts being fastened. Iris looked out the window. The view almost reminded her of the Mediterranean, with its white, amarillo, pink and brown houses clustered on the sides of the mountains. Now, sweeping below them was a plain where there stood neatly laid out, streets, walks, lawns, back yards. The plane moved, slowly, majestically over the Santa Maria Mountains and southward past International Airport. Then the ocean, fiercely reflecting the sun, slid beneath them. Iris thought: Time, oh, Time.

"You'll do what you want," Ralph said, "but if I were you, I wouldn't come back."

"Funniest thing," she said as if she hadn't been listening. "What?"

"I've been thinking that I didn't want Mother to die, but when I imagine her, seeing her, she's already dead."

"She might be."

Iris nodded but did not speak. She turned again to the window as the plane came out of its circle and started to float downward in a long, graceful line. Here we are, Iris was thinking. So here we are full circle. She watched as the ground rose imperceptibly. The roads widened; the rooftops spread out. It was silent in the plane.

Abruptly the power roared back on. The plane shuddered. The wing near Iris shivered convulsively. The ground fell away from them. The plane nosed upward, struggling in the

262

buffeting wind. The movement had been so unexpected that Iris and her brother were slammed backward into their seats, heads burrowing into the soft upholstery. Iris heard Ralph swallow hard. She did not look at him. A click which announced the opening of the intercom sounded sharply.

"This is the captain, ladies and gentlemen. Don't be alarmed. An unauthorized aircraft slipped in on the landing field just ahead of us. It's all right now. We'll be down in another five minutes." The intercom snapped off.

Ralph said, "I expected to find the pilot of another 707 right in my goddamned lap." Almost, Doughnut, he thought soberly.

Iris giggled nervously. When the power had gone on again and the plane had nosed frantically upwards, her first thought had been that here was the solution: no sleeping pills, no growing old, no dull, harsh mornings. Just a plane crash. But when the plane had regained altitude she knew that she wanted to live. She giggled again.

"That would've been a bitch," Ralph murmured, staring past her. "And when these things hit," he said, "forget it. Do a hundred people make a community? A whole community wiped out then, that is, if they all lived in one place."

"He's got it made," Iris said quietly. She also was watching.

Inside the plane the whistling air outside sounded unnaturally loud. "There," Iris said when they were down. She looked at herself. "I'm trembling like a leaf," she said in surprise.

"The plane. You'll be all right," Ralph said drawing a deep breath himself.

"No!" Iris said. "I mean no, I don't think it was."

"What then."

"Something else, I don't know."

As they passed down the aisle to the ramp, Ralph bent down and looked out. He could see Century Boulevard, with its few isolated dust-covered palm trees. He grimaced; he hated Los Angeles. He paused on the ramp and looked back at the silver hulk of the plane. The sun glistened on its fuselage. He had never been sure that he liked such swift traveling. He distrusted placing himself in the hands of some faceless being; it gave him a helpless feeling as though he had stumbled into the midst of a crowd and was unable to get out. Until he died, he thought soberly, he was committed, like everyone else, to getting to wherever he wanted to go as fast as he could.

19

SISSIE'S STUPOR HAD BEEN A COTTONY GRAY and she had drifted through its layers, some of them comfortable and warm so that she had wanted to pause in them, and others bitterly cold, so frigid that she had not been able to move away from them quickly enough. She had seemed to spread her arms, like a bird, to control her downward spin from the zenith of gray, and in so doing had passed many familiar places.

Sephora on a hot Mississippi day, slopping down the sides of sun-heated furrows, stinking, her ears long, dark, foreboding, like the points of spears, while the heat rose in twigged waves from the tin roof of the barn; standing lightly in the still, blistering air, the dry, sharp smell of the chickens and their grain fermenting in sun and dew. And always unavoidable, the heavy reek of the pigpen. Cutting across the smell, the whinny of the horses. Down, way down beyond, the creek, shallow, the bedstones white with heat, splashing weakly along its route. The fine green line of pines in the distance sharp against the reddish brown, worn earth.

Her fingers briefly upon a hot damper when it has been turned just enough to trap the heat and allow in a little air. Inside the stove, glowing coals and licking blue flame. The drafts steady and sure through the emptied ashpan; the skillets heating on the opened lids.

A June Sunday in church. The choir singing a hymn in ragged *a cappella*, the rhythm coming in the pauses, emphasis, phrasing. Through the opened window, the smell of sunscorched grass.

The train rumbling by, its wheels mechanical, moving, rhythmic; its great tubular body throwing off heat, water hissing into steam upon it.

The odor of the pretzel bakery on a hot day, bringing the rats and the roaches, the rats sinuous and gray, the roaches' feet moving frantically, rhythm and nonrhythm horribly joined.

The sound of her own feet crunching in the freezing snow, the snow slipping down into her boots to melt and soak the paper covering the hole in the sole of her shoe. And then across the cold face of morning, the lilt of the tags jingling upon the neck of a skinny dog skittering from garbage can to garbage can.

The silent cacophony of a room in which there is no heat. Kids huddling in sweaters and jackets, not looking at her, not talking, noses running, sniffling and hawking the mucous. The masculine cadence of hard coal tumbling upon wood and paper flashing flame in the belly of a stove, cracking and popping.

The way home through the crowds of kids on The Hill with the chimes sounding high above, deep-lunged, pulsating. Well-clothed white kids with their loose steps and naked voices and unveiled eyes; wearing good boots in which to run and walk; red-cheeked, merry in the cold.

The fan belt of Car 26 running, whishing lightly around and around, the pulsating motor and the officer leaning out: "Cold, baby? Get in. Take you to a real hot place."

Mr. Moyshe beating nails into the coffin, making sounds like the blacksmith. Mr. Moyshe taking her hand, making her stroke the coffin. "How fine? How fine?" and then loudly, out of the gray, the rhythm of his sanding block upon the coffin.

She was screaming and Mrs. Weinstein suddenly appeared; pale, blonde and pregnant. Standing proudly beside her is Joseph Peterson, stern, and proud. He vanishes. Mrs. Weinstein is also gone; Little Ralph and Iris stand in their places. At first both stare accusingly at her, then Little Ralph swells until he explodes, but there is no sound. Iris is now distant and small; she hums and dances and eludes Sissie's outstretched hands, a secretive smile on her face. The voice of Big Ralph comes, bellowing to the rhythm of the guitar and bass drum, "Do the breakaway! Do the breakaway!"

Sissie's eyes opened. The sudden movement of white seems like snow sliding from the gable of a roof. The nurse. She turned her glance in the other direction. Oliver. Where were the kids? she wondered. They should be here. Thank God she was still alive. With great effort she raised her hand; the nurse moved.

267

"What is she doing?" Dr. Clayton asked, crowding close to the bed. Behind him stood the other doctor.

"She just raised her hand," the nurse said.

"When your children come don't talk, just listen, Mrs. Duncan," Dr. Clayton said, "you mustn't excite yourself."

"I will talk."

"Sissie," Oliver said in soft remonstrance.

Dr. Clayton leaned on the bed. "Mrs. Duncan," he said patiently. "Please try to understand. You're seriously ill. A woman like you who was always on the go might not understand that. But you are sick." He paused to exchange glances with the other doctor, who said, "Go ahead."

Dr. Clayton patted Oliver's arm then turned again to Sissie. "Yesterday we took a carotid arteriogram; it told us about blood clots. A small one passed through the brain without damaging it. We're now giving you anticoagulants to prevent formation of clots large enough to injure you."

Sissie blinked. "Yes."

Dr. Clayton went on, touching his hand to his heart. "Now those clots come from your heart; your heart is throwing off tissue which blocks up the arteries. The more you move, the more you excite yourself, the harder the heart pumps and the harder it works right now, the more tissue it tears off and throws." He paused. The sudden, powerful roar of a jet plane, a different sound than that of jets whose passings he had become used to, filled the room suddenly and ominously for a second, making the window panes rattle. Dr. Clayton removed his hands from the bed. "When those clots get stuck, Mrs. Duncan, there's trouble. Now you've got to remain still."

"Now tell me this," Sissie said in a low, blurred voice.

"Could I die just lying here not talking and not moving?"
Dr. Clayton lowered his head as if in deep thought. "Yes."
Another silence.

"But," Dr. Clayton said, "Your chances are one hundred per cent improved if you don't upset yourself."

"But I could die anyway, doin' nothin'?"

"Yes."

"Then I'll see my kids when they come."

"Sissie," Oliver said. "Sure wish you'd listen to the doctor. The kids'll understand."

In the same tone of voice Sissie said again, "But I could die anyway."

Jones didn't talk much and Ralph was glad. Jones was an old friend of Oliver's and Ralph remembered him. Now they sped along the broad streets. Ralph stared coldly at the neat homes, the palm trees, trying to convey to his sister without speech that he disliked the city, disliked it intensely. But Sissie had liked it. And Oliver. Country-assed town, Ralph thought. Filled with crackers who had brought everything with them. And the cops—oh, wow, the cops. Beat your black ass just as soon as look at you. Tell me nothing about Los Angeles cops. . . .

Right there, Iris was thinking, turning her head to see, looks like the formal gardens at Estoril. Nice weather here. Kind of weather I'd like if I lived here in America. Snow's nice too, I guess.

Jones braked suddenly and eased the car through a dip. Ralph grinned. "Forgot all about those things," he said to Jones.

Jones nodded.

He's nervous, Iris thought, watching her brother who at the moment she made the observation, slapped her knee lightly and asked, "You making it okay?" She nodded.

She's nervous, Ralph thought, picturing them walking into the room and Sissie starting to recover right away, like in the movies.

Traffic rushed by. Warm air drifted in. Jones took off his cap and wiped the sweat from his forehead. "Hot one today," he said without looking at them.

"Yeah," Ralph said, watching the women in front of their homes. They were wearing shorts or slacks or brief summer dresses. He preferred the gloves and sometime hats of late afternoon New York to Los Angeles' casualness.

Beside him his sister lit a cigarette and he took one out himself and lit it. His throat felt constricted and he loosened his tie, muttering, "Hot," to Iris who had looked at the movement.

Another red light. Jones leaned forward, the emergency weighing heavily on his mind. Oliver had charged him to get them there as quickly as possible. When the light changed Jones mashed his foot on the accelerator; the wheels shrieked and the car shot away. The wind rushed in through the windows again.

Ralph did not know when it was that he'd found Iris' hand in his or his in hers. It made him remember a reception he and Robbie had gone to for the son of one of the native and therefore, to their minds, prominent, Los Angeles Negro families. It had been a savagely formal affair; the Negroes coldly correct; the conversations precise, the glances shrewd and measuring. And at one point, passing through a narrow hall, Ralph had found that he and his younger brother were tightly holding hands. Ralph patted Iris' hand. They were racing along again, caught up in the rhythm of the city's traffic.

Jones slowed with a sigh into a quiet street. The hospital stood square and brutal among the stucco and frame houses. The palms surrounding the building had been carefully trimmed and now only the tufts stood sprayed at the top. "I'll put your bags in Oliver's car," Jones said. "I'll be out here somewhere. You kids hurry on in now."

Clutching hands, the brother and sister leaped into the street, raced across it and up the steps into the waxed reception lobby.

"Mrs. Duncan," Ralph said breathlessly.

The woman at the desk looked up, signaled a nurses' aide and said, "Follow her, please."

They passed rapidly through the halls. There had not been a single colored nurse at the hospital when Raffy was born, Ralph thought. Now he could see Negro nurses and aides all around him.

Ralph pushed open the door of Sissie's room; Oliver, gray and lean, his clothes seemingly too large for him, was seated in a chair. Oliver rose, put his finger to his lips.

"Five minutes," he whispered. "She's been talkin' too much."

Ralph, followed by Iris, approached the bed.

Fatter now, Iris thought, recalling the old cast of Sissie's face. She seemed to hear her mother's voice echoing shrilly again. She closed her eyes. There were thick wrinkles around Sissie's neck. Iris imagined the lumpy body hidden beneath the blankets. But no, this was not her mother—this was only an old colored woman who called herself her mother. No mother would have behaved the way Sissie had. Ralph noticed

271

that Iris stood stiff as a statue. He turned his eyes away quickly and once more studied the face of his mother. What strength there was in the features. Yes, and still that slight pugnaciousness in the lips.

Suddenly Sissie opened her eyes. Her gaze circled the room and finally fixed itself on Ralph and Iris.

"Hello, Mother," Ralph said. He smiled.

Iris bent and kissed her mother. But her hand eluded Sissie's.

"So glad," the sick woman said in a whisper. She smiled and looked wonderingly at Iris. "Lookin' like five million dollars, Iris. Came all that way to see your old mother." Slowly, she turned her eyes back to Ralph. "Both look good. Grown. Ralph, where's your wife? She here? Let her come in?"

"I didn't bring her, Mother."

"Oh, shoots. Man go runnin' around without his wife? Shoots." Hurt, Sissie said, "you was just 'shamed to bring her to see me."

"No, I wasn't, Mother," Ralph said in a voice as soft as hers. He was just beginning to understand why he hadn't wanted Eve to come. No, shame had not been involved; he had wanted his wife and his mother to be kept forever separate. Sissie altered in some way everything she touched. He had freed himself from Sissie and guessed that she understood this. Through Eve he had found his way to his own life.

Sissie opened her hand and looked at Iris. Iris hesitated and Sissie's eyes clouded. Iris limply placed her hand in her mother's. "It's good to see you all," Sissie said. She tried to smile. "Honey, don't be so stiff. Say something. Ain't said a word."

"I'm glad you're doing better, Mother."

"Woman now," Sissie said. "A woman." She sighed and turned her head away.

"Maybe we'd better not stay too long, Mother," Ralph said.

"Shoots, I don't care what that ol' doctor said. I got to talk. Oliver?"

Oliver approached the bed apprehensively.

"You can stay if you want, but this is for the kids." Her breath was coming faster.

"Don't talk anymore, Mother," Ralph said. "Oliver, where's the doctor? Get the doctor."

"The nurse—" Oliver started to say.

"Please, Oliver."

Ralph turned back to the bed as Oliver hustled through the door. Disengaging Iris' hand from his mother's, he said, "Be still, now, Mother."

"Oh, shoots," Sissie said, trying to fling one of her hands in a gesture of dismissal at Ralph. "I got somethin' to say, now, I keep tellin' you, an' I better say it."

"It'll keep, Mother, now—"

"Iris, you're your father's child," Sissie said as loudly as she could.

Ralph stopped tucking in the blankets; Iris recoiled a step. Brother and sister exchanged glances.

"I know you'd understand, honey," Sissie said, weariness blunting the desperation in her voice. "You're a woman. Not married. You know what it's like, playin' around?" Her voice faded.

"We already—" Iris said sharply before Ralph cut her off with:

"Mother you got to hush!"

"You tell your father," Sissie panted, "you tell him what I said. You wasn't none o' Arthur's baby, you was his! His an' mine and I lied to him." Her chest was rising and falling convulsively. "I didn't mean it. It was just like the devil was ridin' me." Now she was looking at the ceiling. "An' Ralph, me an' you had some battles, didn't we? Oh, shoots, we had some battles." The smile flitted over her face again.

"It's all right, Mother, what the heck."

"Shoots, you was a hard-headed little nigger boy, Ralph. Whew! Head like a lead pipe." She slowly placed her arms to her chest and pressed. "Old woman was doin' the best she could. Tryin' to get you all grown and learn you how to mind—"

"It was hard, but it was fair," Ralph said hurriedly. "It's okay, baby. We understand. We don't hold it against you. Now, stop talking."

For a moment, Sissie was silent and then she said in a ragged voice, "Iris? Iris? I didn't hear anything from you."

Iris stood motionless, staring.

"Iris!" Sissie's voice had risen.

Iris turned from the bed and almost tripped. Ralph looked at Sissie. "Didn't you hear her, what she said, Mother? She said she loves you."

"Shoots, Ralph, I didn't hear nothing. You always takin' up for everybody."

"No! No! She said it." Ralph placed his hands upon Sissie's shoulders.

With great effort, Sissie forced herself to an upright position. "Iris, ain't you got a heart? Don't you know what those years were like for me? When you had shoes to wear, I didn't.

When you had school paper, I didn't have lunch. I couldn't have a single dream so you could have a little teeny one. Iris, honey," Sissie's pain-filled voice went on, "look at you. It's been a long time since you were married; you ain't been no virgin since then. You probably done the same things I done; I ain't askin' for much. Just say somethin'!" Spent, Sissie leaned back toward her bed, and, as her body sought its place there, it seemed to halt momentarily in mid-air. Then and only then did it fall to the bed. Her body remained still.

"Mrs. Duncan," Dr. Clayton said, entering the room and rushing to the bed. His stethoscope clicked as he placed it to Sissie's heart. Ralph glimpsed his mother's breasts, dark and wrinkled. "She's gone," Dr. Clayton said.

"No," Oliver said. He had come in behind the doctor. "She was just talkin' a minute ago. He moved close to the bed and peered down. "Sissie?" he whispered. He shrugged off Dr. Clayton's hand and said it again. "Sissie?"

She's dead, Ralph thought. She's dead. Soon they'd roll her out of the room and down the neat halls to the morgue. They'd put a tag on her toe and push her into one of the refrigerated compartments. Suddenly he looked around for Iris, brushed past the nurse who had just entered and walked into the hall. He caught sight of his sister. As he started toward her he felt like a lover who has grown weary after a long weekend.

"You okay?" he asked.

For a moment Iris said nothing. She stared into her hand mirror and carefully powdered around her eyes. "Go ahead, say it."

"Do you want me to?"

"Yes."

"Poor Iris."

The powder puff trembled in her hand. She looked up from her mirror. "Ralph, it was the only thing she ever gave me besides clothes and food—the right to refuse. God, I wanted to say 'Okay, it's all over, I forgive you,' but ever since you told me in Barcelona, I've lived for the day she would say it. Three years almost I waited, longer than you waited for Doughnut. I heard her say it and it suddenly was not all right."

She dabbed her eyes. Then she lowered the mirror. "I don't know which is me, the broad who was in there or the one out here who keeps wanting to cry."

"Anyway we're through with the lies; she told the truth, and you told the truth."

"And you, Ralph?"

"Yes, I did too."

Iris turned from him. "Why the hell can't I stop crying? I've done it, so why can't I stop?"

"C'mon. Let's go back in for a minute."

In the room Ralph went close to the bed. Sissie was dead. Dead, yet she was alive through himself, himself and Eve. If they had not wasted too many years there would be children. And there was Raffy whom she'd never seen. Poor Raffy. As Ralph had been touched, so had she. Iris? Perhaps her refusal to lie would bring other truths.

He moved away from the bed. Ah, Sissie, he thought. It cost too much—pain, guilt, hate, rage and much too little love. It was almost too much to demand for the dubious privilege of living.

"We haven't had a chance to really say hello," Ralph said, turning to Oliver.

Oliver kept staring past Ralph and Iris to Sissie. "She'll be wanting to go back home with the others," he said.

"She say that?" Ralph asked.

"No, but I know," Oliver said.

Maybe the train ride with Robbie had only been practice for this, Ralph thought. She'd know every step of the way. He thought of the trip, could almost hear the rhythm of the train, rapid across the lowlands, sluggish and straining over the mountains. Overhead the sky would be that dry western blue. Iris and Oliver and he would accompany the body. The train would crawl along the rim of the snow-collared Rockies, and then glide past the Great Salt Lake. Finally the long trip would end at that wide, slow curve, thousands of miles distant, where the underpass stood which he had played under as a child, watching the "crack streamliners" roll by. The station would be almost empty when Sissie's train got there, for the "streamliners" were themselves now nearly obsolete.

"Yes," Ralph said to Oliver, "I suppose she'd want to go back."

ABOUT THE AUTHOR

John A. Williams is author of eighteen books including *The Man Who Cried I Am* and *!Click Song*. He has been a foreign correspondent for *Newsweek* as well as Professor of English at Rutgers University where he is currently employed. He is the recipient of the American Book Award, The Richard Wright-Jacques Roumain Award, The Centennial Medal for Outstanding Achievement, and the National Institute of Arts and Letters Award, among others. Two of his novels have been adapted for film and television. He was born in 1925 in Jackson, Mississippi, and currently lives in Teaneck, New Jersey.